GRAVELBELLY

GEORGE REARDON

Copyright Notice
©(2021) All rights reserved worldwide. No part of this book may be reproduced or copied without the expressed written permission of the author.

This book is a work of fiction. Characters and events in this novel are the product of the author's imagination. Any similarity to persons living or dead is purely coincidental.

DEDICATED TO:

SALLY

Loyalty is thicker than blood.

PROLOGUE

There is no more pure form of military service than that of an infantryman. No frills, no armoured vehicles or fancy equipment. Just you, on your belt-buckle in the dirt engaged in a firefight with the enemy.

It shapes who you are, and it stays with you forever.

That's what a Gravelbelly is - more than a person, more than a phrase or predefined label.

It is a way of life.

CHAPTER 1

A UK politician dying was always going to be the headline story on the Ten O'Clock News. 'A terrible loss to his family, to politics and to the country, 'the news reporter said. Thomas Compton, the Secretary of State for Transport, died of a heart attack, 'whilst out walking his dog, 'the reporter continued.

Thomas Compton was a political force of nature. A bright sharp-witted character amongst the dry personalities of Conservative and Labour MP's. He would grip a debate in the House of Commons with both hands and look the 'Right Honourable 'debating against him in the eye, as he bellowed out his case. He compelled support and commanded respect. He wasn't even halfway through his political career, and he was set for greater things yet. He was also the political sponsor and main lobbyist for High Speed Two (HS2), a rail link between London and The Midlands, most notably Birmingham. Being from that area himself, he was always outwardly supportive of investment in the Midlands and wanted to draw some of the UK's power out of London to the regional cities. This made him highly controversial, especially amongst his Peers, who, being landowners of the Great British countryside, were seeing their constituents 'landscape be carved up for the construction of the track.

Compton's heart attack in isolation was one thing. But less than two weeks earlier, there was a major incident along the route of the track. At a construction site north of Banbury, a small town in the West Midlands, there was a subterranean explosion. One of the construction dig holes had been filled with propane gas, and when an electrical socket sparked, the subsequent explosion shook the ground like an earthquake. It was only through the integrity of the engineering involved that the dig hole didn't collapse inwards and bury several construction workers alive.

At the time, all the theories were running wild. Was it an accident? Was it Eco-Warriors who wanted to preserve the countryside? Could it have been Local Farmers? Some put it down to an act of God. It was a major setback, both commercially and politically. However, the great Thomas Compton was there to absorb the drama, to make the decisions needed to keep the project going. He supported the workers and their families and funded PTSD therapy where needed. He kept industry calm, he kept the international press and their bated breath at bay. With Thomas Compton leading the disaster recovery aspect of this incident, HS2 was going to survive.

Now less than two weeks later, Thomas Compton was dead. And this threw doubt into the air around HS2. Was it now a viable project? Who will channel the extra funding into the shocked and jilted workforce? Was the link to the Midlands needed? Who was going to support HS2 the way Compton did? Were there any takers? Already, the nay-sayers and the conspiracy theorists were sounding off all over the internet, social media, and the press: 'The tragedy.' 'The irony.' 'Serves him right.' 'Save the countryside.'

Mitchell switched off his TV from his sofa and dropped the remote onto the coffee table in front of him. He leaned back and stared at nothing for a while. He pondered. The way he does when he starts his thought process. He didn't see it coming.

Should he have seen it coming? Are they connected? Should they be connected? Was he, along with everyone else reading too much into two tragic things and linking them for no good reason? Pondering moved to frustration. He should have seen it coming. He was one of MI5's top analysts. He looks at incidents affecting National Security and then makes up his own theories, interrogating those theories to come up with causes, justification, accountability and more importantly, what might come next.

If there is a link, then who? Who has the resources to stage an explosion on a government-funded industrial project such as HS2? And could they then also fix it, so a politician has a heart attack whilst out walking his dog? If they were connected, there's a lot to work out. A real-time attack on the UK? Mitchell's first task was to work out if there was anything to work out in the first place. If they were genuine non-connected incidents of bad luck and misfortune, so be it. But Mitchell knew better. It will be put on him by his director that they are connected and therefore he will be asked by whom and why and what will happen next? Tomorrow was going to be a hard day at the office. His boss, his colleagues and his team will all be looking at him to have the answers. He is the problem solver, after all.

Jim stood up when he judged the surf was thigh-high. He, plus his three teammates all standing up together, out the sea in full combat dive equipment was a fearsome sight. Staying submerged for so long, to get as shallow as possible, gave them the intimidating presence they wanted when they did show themselves. And now if they had to, they could shift on foot. The water is not too deep, slowing their legs down. Weapons raised, masks and breathing apparatus still in place, they moved into what is known as the littoral battle-space, they had come from the sea to land, ready for a fight. They patrolled up the beach a good 50 meters before the Officer in Command called EndEx.

All four men lowered their weapons, took off their masks and rebreather and gave each other an acknowledging nod and smile. They all made their way to the team vans which were parked facing sideways onto the sea at the top of the beach before they started to unzip their drysuits and de-service their equipment. Jim was panting. As they all were. It was a hard swim in. But for Jim, who had been away from anything conventional or maritime for years, this was a good reminder of his roots. This was the bread and butter of the SBS. He appreciated being part of the training exercise. Not the dive per se, but the planning of the whole drill. Three days earlier, the four of them had parachuted into the Bay of Biscay and met a small boat. On that boat, there was a full briefing room setup. There, they planned the dive to shore. The boat travelled towards the UK while the team prepared their equipment and covered all Actions-On: Action-on the undercurrent being too strong, Action-on someone struggling to breathe, Action-on spotting the enemy. The list of Actions-on was substantial but necessary. Every man on that dive needed to know and understand what to do, and when. The boat stopped over the horizon from the UK coast. Onboard was the SDV. The Swimmer Delivery Vessel. A six-man submarine, though technically not a submarine at all. More a huge torpedo-shaped pod with a motor and lots of air tanks. The team, in full dive kit and weapons, crammed into the back of the SDV, whilst the two-man pilot team got into the front. It was the job of the pilots to navigate the SDV towards the Dorset coastline. The four men in the back had to simply sit and wait. Plugged into the vessel's air supply to save their own equipment, there was nothing to do but wait in the dark. Jim felt the electric motor of the SDV hum away through the shell, as it propelled them forward. Once as close as tactically possible, via their radio comms, the pilots gave the team the 'dive 'command. The team disconnected from the SDV bit down on their own rebreather mouthpiece and exited. Their surroundings went from pitch black to murky blue. The team commander got his bearings and led the fin to shore.

That was exactly what Jim needed. A refresh on this aspect of the job. It was mentally taxing, as well as physically exhausting. They'd not slept for more than an hour or two since the whole exercise had started. That was part of it, planning and operating whilst deprived of sleep, physically draining, and constantly thinking.

At the vans, Jim had pulled the top part of his drysuit over his head. His clothing underneath was wringing wet. Not from the sea, but from his own sweat. It gave off steam as it evaporated into the cool air. The Officer in Command of the exercise hung up his phone and looked at Jim for a moment before calling him over.

'How was that then, Jim? Was it how you remember?'

'Well, it certainly doesn't get any easier, does it? But yeah, it was good. Glad to be going over the orders and planning stage of it all again.'

'Good, I'm glad you got value out of it. You've been doing surveillance work for so long now, it's easy to get skill-fade on this sort of stuff.'

'I agree.'

The Officer changed the subject, 'I just got off the phone to the CO.'

'Oh OK. The CO, I remember when he first joined the Service. 'Jim said, more by point of fact than a reminisce.

'Well, quite. So, listen, there's been a request for you to go to London.'

'London?'

'UKSF Headquarters, no less. DSF himself has requested it.'

'The Director? The Brigadier has asked for me? That's a wind-up. Surely?'

'No wind-up Jim. Don't ask me what it's about, I wasn't told. To be honest, I don't think the CO was told either. Not pissed anyone off in Africa recently, have you?'

'Always! But even that doesn't sound right. I left the country and debriefed off that job weeks ago. When am I due in London, then?'

'Thursday.'

'This Thursday?'

'This Thursday, Jim.'

The Officer gave Jim a wry smile. A smile Jim knew too well. They all had it. It was the smile of 'Life in a green suit 'or 'The joys of being in the Service. 'There was no need for the conversation to continue. Jim had been given his detail and there was nothing more to be said about it.

Jim continued to de-service his equipment. He rinsed off the saltwater from his drysuit and equipment with fresh water. He disposed of the lime salts in his rebreather apparatus. He cleaned and oiled his Diemaco assault rifle. His head was racing. But he eventually resigned to the fact he couldn't second guess this one. He had to wait until Thursday to find out exactly what was going on.

Millbrook was riding shotgun in the last vehicle. He needed to see everything that the other three vans and more specifically, the men inside were doing. The vans were moving, at speed along a single-track road. Fast, close together and in low gears, to get as much torque as possible, so the driver of each van could bully it around the windy track of the training area. As they came to the end of one track, a large house appeared from out of the trees. It was a triple-story building, with pebble-dashed exterior walls and shutters over the windows. This house was the Killing House. The SAS's training facility for all things hostage related.

The team was practicing a hostage rescue. Everyone else on the team was in place. The snipers from afar were watching each aspect of the building. There was a helicopter up for overhead visibility. The medics were in place. This was a big training drill; the whole Squadron was involved. All that was left was for Millbrook and his team to turn up, smash their way into the building and rescue the hostage. Easy-peasy. Millbrook needed it to go well. It was the final exercise of this training package. The training package he'd been running for the last six months.

As they closed in on the Killing House, the lead van shot round to the left and then to the rear aspect of the building. The second van, to the right covering that side, and the third to the left again but stopping short of following the first van to the rear, and it covered the left side. Millbrook ordered his driver to get as close as he could to the front of the building. The stop came hard and fast and as soon as it did, Millbrook was out, along with the team in the back. A total of 24 men were now out of the vans and surrounding the house. All in black counter-terrorist Nomex suits and wearing S10 respirators and carrying Heckler and Koch Semi-automatic weapons. If this was a real operation and there really were bad guys inside holding someone hostage, they would shit themselves. Fact.

Once the rear and side aspects were secure and Millbrook got confirmation from the snipers that they had control of the windows, all the men moved to the front of the building. C4 explosives were already being placed on the door hinges and as soon as the door was breached, the operators piled in. Thunder flashes led the way into each room and hallway. Shouts of 'Clear! 'echoed through the building. Red lasers indicated where the rounds from each weapon would land if the triggers were pulled. As expected, there were enemy soldiers, and with the sound of blank fire, they fell to the ground. Millbrook shouted on the radio as he moved up and through the building, ensuring each team was covering their Area of Responsibility. As he made his way into what we can assume would have been the master bedroom, there, sat zip-tied to a chair, was the course Officer. Millbrook's Boss. Millbrook called EndEx over the radio and took off his respirator.

'Well well, Mills. Not bad. Not bad at all.'

'Thank you, Boss. '

'You can start by cutting these off my wrists, and then we can get on with a hot debrief.'

'Absolutely.'

The men walked out of the dark smoky building to the fresh air of the Welsh countryside. All the other men stood, waiting to see what came next. Waiting to be given the nod to de-service kit and hear the outcome from the hot debrief. The nod came, and they got on with their own business.

The message came to Millbrook in almost the same manner as it did Jim. A message passed down the chain of command. Ordering Millbrook to be in London to meet DFS on Thursday.

'....and they didn't say why Boss?'

'No, nothing. I did ask for you.'

'It can't be about my posting back to the Royal Protection Team, can it?'

'Mills, I don't know. I can't see it being that, to be honest. Why would it be?'

'I don't know. I don't get it. So, when am I due to be there?'

'0900 this Thursday.'

'Brilliant.'

CHAPTER 2

Jim got the train up to London early that Thursday morning. But even by 0700, Waterloo station was a hive of activity. Rush hour trains delivering hordes of commuters to the city. All moving with the intent of an army of ants towards the exits and off to their offices. It was moments like this that Jim was grateful for the fact that he served and did not make a living like this. That said, a living it was. Or more specifically, a well-drilled lifestyle. He instantly dropped into surveillance mode, watching everyone. Sizing them up. Even for fun, in his head, everyone was a potential target. He character-profiled everyone. Snap decisions on who they are and what they are up to, based on what they were wearing, what they were carrying, their gait, the focus of their eyes. It was more passing judgement based on his own experiences than the science-based profiling like a criminologist would do. But over the years, he'd become pretty good at it.

He made his way down the escalators to the Underground. He got on a train on the Northern Line, which ran north to south down the centre of the city. He stood with his back to the side of the packed train. He got off the train at Camden and instead of getting a taxi, decided to walk to the Barracks. Though a country boy at heart, Jim felt at home in London. He'd done some work here in the past when he was called in to support the surveillance team that was dedicated to London. They needed another car on the road, to cover all the road access and egress options around

Wembley and the roads surrounding the area. It was a good week's work, and the team got the result they were after - a confirmed bomb-maker. They imposed surveillance on a member of his faction, and he led the team straight to their guy. After that, the Special Branch took over and arrested him.

Jim walked through the streets towards Regents Park. UKSF HQ, also known as DSF - the place as well as the person - was nestled inside a multi-service Military building, Regents Park Barracks. As he walked, he continued to profile people. A bit out of habit, a bit for practice and a bit for fun. Some people he gave ridiculous characters, with ridiculous reasons they were out on the road at this time. He saw an ageing punk and decided he'd been in a coma for the last 35 years and had just woken up, wondering what the hell was going on. He saw a mother and child on their way to the underground station. Jim guessed the kids' school was on the same line as her work, maybe even the same stop and this was their morning routine. The mum would be doing all she can to hold her own in some cut-throat corporate role. But whenever they were running late, because the kid had lost his PE trainers, she would have to walk into the board meeting and make some excuse about why she wasn't there at the start. Something about the Doctors or an accident always works best in those situations, rather than the unglamorous truth.

Jim turned left onto the road the Barracks was on. As he walked down the road, he had Regents Park on the right and residential homes on the left. Soon, the homes turned into a looming brown brick wall. 30 meters high, or more. It didn't look like a Military base, but it did look like an old Government facility. It could have been a prison or a boarding school as much as it could have been a barracks. The only real tell at this stage was all the CCTV cameras surrounding the entrance and the gatehouse that was set just back off the pavement. Even when you are close to the entrance, you must be square on to the building and look up to see a faded sign indicating that you were indeed at Regents Park Barracks.

As Jim got close, a black cab pulled up on the opposite side of the road. A man got out. Instinct took over again, and Jim profiled him. 40-45, 6 foot, 15 stone, dark hair, moves with intent, dressed in chino trousers and a shirt and tie. Much like himself. Jim looked again. He knew this guy. It was Millbrook or Mills he likes to be known. Jim wasn't the only one meeting the Brigadier today, after all.

Mills crossed the road and spotted Jim approaching the entrance to the Barracks. They briefly paused on the pavement before heading to the gatehouse. They didn't shake hands. Not on the street. Instinct said not to.

'Hello, Jim, long time. Did you get a cryptic message about coming here as well, then?'

'Mills 'Jim said with a smile, 'I did, yeah. I was hoping I was the only one. It might have been a bit more meaningful then!'

'Yeah, I've been wondering about it too. Just us two, do you reckon?'

'No idea. Let's get in and find out, shall we?'

'Let's do it mate. '

The men walked to the gatehouse and showed their Military ID from their wallets. The security officer checked their names, confirmed they were there for DSF and confirmed with the men that they knew where they were going. They did. Both had been here before. Both had been involved in missions that needed briefing from the highest level. The highest level of briefing you get is from the Chief of Staff, not the Brigadier. The fact the Brigadier had, by all accounts requested them personally, was the bit that didn't sit too well with either of the men. Though neither said it. Right now, this could be as bad as it could be good.

DSF was a couple of minutes 'walk from the gatehouse. They walked in silence. Mills was sizing up why Jim was there. Jim was of equal rank to himself, a Warrant Officer. Spent a similar amount of time in UKSF, too. Around fifteen years. Similar age. Jim was a well-respected surveillance operator, Mills knew that. Jim had done some great work over the years in The Republic of Ireland, Africa, Balkan States, you name it. He was also known as a Judo guy. Representing GB at some European events while he was in the Marines, but before he went SF. He still looked the part. He looked bulky like he was keen on lifting weights.

The pair got to the DSF office block. The front door was a large wooden door, with well-polished brass fixings. To the side, was an electronic buzzer and intercom. Mills pressed the buzzer. A voice came out of the intercom:

'Hello?'

'Hello, it's WO2 Millbrook and WO2 Davidson. We are here to see the Brigadier?'

'Come in, please. '

The magnetic lock clicked, they pushed the door open, walked into the lobby and waited. Mitchell came to meet them in the lobby. He extended his hand to both.

'Good morning gentlemen. Sorry to keep you waiting. I'm James Mitchell. '

'WO2 Millbrook. Everyone calls me Mills. '

'WO2 Davidson. Called Jim…'

'Like the comedian. '

'Exactly that. Still, it could be worse. Could be Harris, eh?'

Mitchell didn't quite know how to take the comment. But it was obvious to him that WO2 Davidson has had people stating the obvious about his name his whole life. Or during his Military career at the least. Sometimes you don't need to state the obvious. Mitchell should have known better.

The two men followed Mitchell through the building. It was a typical MOD building. Magnolia walls are scattered with old Military photos. Mostly black and white, of some detachment in someplace around the world. Normally the jungle. The team of four or six would have khaki shorts on, no top, lightweight boots, and a cap or bandanna on their head. Some would be standing, and there was always at least one in the picture squatting down next to a machine gun or a mortar tube.

The corridor led deeper into the centre of the building. Jim followed behind Mills, who was behind Mitchell. Jim and Mills' careers had crossed over a few times over the years. Mills was a fearsome character in the SAS. Known as Milly when he joined the Parachute Regiment at 16, he had to fight for the respect he now commanded. Milly became Mills the day he passed Selection for the SAS. Jim knew that Mills ran a tight smash & grab team over in the Provinces of Northern Ireland. Dealing with extremists on both sides of the Religious and Political divide over there. He was also a keen Close Protection Operator. Supporting the Foreign Secretary on international state visits, as well as being on the Royal Protection Team. The last time they crossed paths was in Farah, Afghanistan several years back. Jim was on the streets imposing surveillance on an Al Qaeda cell out there. Jim's job was to report when the cell members were housed in a certain building and then Mills and his team would walk through the front door and 'lift 'the individuals. Mills would then deliver them to the Defence Human Intelligence Corps for questioning.

Working Mitchell out was Jim's ponder. He didn't come across as Military. Or not Military on his and Mills 'level, that's for sure. Army Intelligence? RAF Intelligence, more likely. What Service he was in didn't really matter, it mattered that he was here. If he was an Intelligence guy, then certain niceties were taken out of this meeting. The Brigadier didn't invite them here to thank them for their years of sacrifice to the cause.

They continued walking, though not the biggest building in the world, they seemed to walk for a while and the narrow corridors and thick oak doors gave it a claustrophobic feel. They headed downstairs. Jim had been to DSF before, and he was sure Mills would have been here before too. But he'd never been downstairs before. And catching Mills 'eye as they turned the corner, he knew he'd not been down here before, either. As they turned the corner, they were met by a large safe door. The kind you'd imagine on a bank vault. Over eight feet high, made of iron and painted red. With a Manifoil safe lock and key to secure it closed.

Mitchell paused before entering the room.

'Gents, I'm sure you already have done so, but if not, please can you turn off your phones. And leave them out here for the duration of this meeting?'

Neither of them had turned their phones off. But they complied. There was a small wheelie-trolly outside the door, they left their phones on it. Jim also took his smartwatch off and tapped on the screen a couple of times to turn that off, too.

Both had notepads and pens with them. Just habit through the years of meetings and briefs. If you're the guy without a notepad, you're the clown who gets singled out for not being on top of their admin. Mitchell shook his head and said they were not needed. The men entered the room.

The room felt more claustrophobic than the corridors. Underground and behind a thick safe door, the only air came through a ventilation duct in the ceiling. There was an Oak table in the centre of the room and only enough room around it to walk or sit. If you wanted to get past someone sitting at the table, you had to ask them to tuck in a bit and turn sideways to squeeze past. There was a projector in the middle of the table and at the far end of the room, was a drop-down projector screen. Nothing was coming out of the projector. It wasn't even plugged in.

At the same end of the room as the projector screen, was the Brigadier. He was sitting next to one other person, unknown to Mills and Jim. There was a spare seat on the other side of the Brigadier. Mitchell invited the men to sit down and walked to the empty chair next to the Brigadier. Though he did not sit. Jim sat himself down to the right of the room and Mills took a seat two to the left.

The Brigadier stood up, made the introductions, and started the meeting.

'Jim, Mills, thank you for being here today. I appreciate you didn't get much notice, and you don't know what is going on. On my left, is Superintendent Steve Phillips, of the Special Branch. And on my right, who you've just met, is James Mitchell, of MI5.'

The pair of them just sat there. Cold realities were starting to hit home.

'The reason you are here today 'The Brigadier continued, 'is that we have a very specific mission for you. It comes from the Prime Minister himself and carries a great weight of responsibility. That is why I've chosen you two. I've worked with you both over the years. Mills, when you were a young trooper straight from selection, and Jim, when we were hunting war criminals in the Balkans. The reason you both are here is that I selected you. Because I trust you and I know your capabilities. I'm going to hand it over to Mitchell now. This Operation is led by him and for all intents and purposes, you take direction from him.'

The Brigadier sat down, and Mitchell took a step forward.

'Gents, the brief you are about to get is classified as Diplomatic Top Secret. The information you are about to receive is sensitive in many countries and directly affects National Security. Do you both understand?'

Both nodded. Both felt a bit insulted they had to be asked that question in that manner. But let it go. There are more important things in life to get excited about.

'You must be aware of the gas explosion along the HS2 route two weeks ago? The formal investigation is still ongoing. The result of that investigation will put the cause of the explosion down to a damaged gas cylinder that leaked, filled a ventricle and caused a chain of explosions that led to the compromised integrity of the walls and some severe casualties, though no fatalities. But I can tell you now, there was no damaged cylinder. The volume of gas needed to make such an explosion would be ten-fold that of what was down there. I can tell you now, categorically, the explosion was intentional. And more to the point, it was done by a government agency. '

Jim breathed in. He knew where this was going. Or at least he thought he knew where this was going. Mitchell continued.

'We have an agent in Moscow who is part of the Ambassadors support team. He has been working there for two years and has built up a trusted network. He had it disclosed to him that the explosion was caused by a Russian Agent.... As was the death of Thomas Compton. Thomas Compton MP was the

Transport Secretary and biggest political backer for HS2. With him out of the picture, there is doubt over the survival of that project.'

'Why would the Russians care about a train line? 'asked Mills.

'They don't. Not at all. But what I'm saying, is Russia is back in the 'fucking with us 'game. Big time. It's no secret that they have receiving ships sitting in international waters, listening in to our radio transmissions. And you are aware that several times a year, we have to scramble our jets to escort a Russian spy plane out of our airspace?'

Both men nodded.

'This is the same thing. But escalated to a much greater level. Russia is back in the superpower struggle. But this time, it's not against America, it's against China. It is full-on bravado. Both countries have formidable Armies and Military might. Both have a cyber reach that far surpasses ours. They are neck-to-neck in ability. Hence the point now is to prove who is the better. Scoring diplomatic wins against each other. The Russian's approach is to knacker us. To weaken our economy, our stock market, our politics. Because the weaker we are, by default the stronger they are.'

Jim piped up. 'Ego? Compton and the explosion, was Russia impressing China?'

'Not quite. I believe we are the testing ground for much worse. Either using a similar approach in America, or in China itself. Quite literally to muster up another global-scale ground war. Russia wants China's minerals and China needs Russia's land. I do believe it is that crude. You have seen how Russian interfered in the US Presidential elections? That was not for the benefit of any candidate running for the Oval Office. That was to show the Chinese authority how advanced their cyber-espionage programme was. And now that point has been proved, they have moved on to infrastructure.'

'Infrastructure? Are you sure? 'Jim wasn't buying it.

'Yes. We believe they are reviving their Cold War tactics. The Soviets had agents trained in all sorts of engineering trades. Part of the former Soviets plan, if they needed it, was to close off an entire country by attacking gas, water, and electricity stations. If a country has no utilities, it can't function, never mind fight.'

'And you think this is what has happened on the railway. ' asked Mills.

'I am certain of it. Time moves forward. Power stations are just one option now. Transport links, data centres, commerce, are all possible targets. And their attitude is more advanced too. Why hit just the physical aspect of any given target, when they can hit the political or financial aspect too?'

'So, HS2, it got hit physically with the explosion, and it got hit politically when Compton *got hit...?* 'Jim confirmed.

'Exactly that. How strong is that picture on the International Stage? Not only can they get to us physically, but politically at the same time. If they just did the explosion on the line, it would be a terrible incident. If just Compton died, it would have been a shame. One can survive without the other. But both? It showcases how good they are.'

Mills wasn't impressed. 'What about China then? Are they

up to this as well?'

'So far, we think not. Russia has the one-up on this right now. And I believe that China will use another platform to showcase its reach and abilities. '

'So, what do we do about it? I mean, Mills and me?'

'You're going to be hunting them for us. Or more specifically, when we find out what they are up to, we will send you after them.'

'To stop them? 'Mills asked.

'Yes.'

'To kill them?'

'Yes.'

Jim scratched his head. 'You want us to assassinate Russian KGB agents, undertaking sabotage missions, on UK soil?'

'Well, technically they're not KGB anymore…'

Both men just looked at Mitchell with deadpan expressions. 'But… yes.'

The Brigadier got to his feet and walked to take over the brief. Little room for emotion and even less room for wasting time. When The Brigadier spoke, you listened.

'Thank you, James. Men, to be clear, your mission is to protect UK interests, both physical and human, from the very real threat of Russian agents. I will say that again: Your mission is to protect UK interests, both physical and human, from the very real threat of Russian agents.'

Both men nodded. They knew this routine from day 1 in training. The Officer in Command, giving the battle orders, gave them twice. So, there was no mistaking what the point of them being there was. Once the mission was stated, nothing else mattered. After two decades each in the Military, and three decades of Special Forces service between them, this moment suddenly became very real. An inner conviction took over them. Duty. Pride. Obligation. Call it what you will. Both men were now tuned in to what was happening and what was going to happen. The Brigadier knew it. He sat down.

Phillips got up.

'Gents, it's only fair I give you my part of the deal right now. I've been in the Police for over twenty years and in the Special Branch for twelve of them. I'm here because as James alluded to, this is technically a Military operation. But because it will be happening on UK soil, probably on the streets, or in the case of the late Mr Compton, in a field, you need the Police involved to keep the public and press at bay. When James gets the intelligence brief that there will be an attack of sorts, we hope he will get areas or personalities that will be targeted. It's my intent to have a team in the area, ready to respond to 'an incident.' Now to be clear, because of the political sensitivity of this, we will be responding post-incident. Meaning, you do what you need to do. And if you make a mess, my officers will be close to taking control of the area. Keep the regular bobby away. So, if there is a Russian agent in a bad way, we can deal with it. We can keep reporters away, or even kids with their phones out of the area. We are the clean-up crew if you like?'

Jim was not too convinced at first. 'So, you'd just sit around, listen for when the fun stops and then come waltzing in with a mop and bucket?'

'Jim! 'The Brigadier stopped the sarcasm dead in its tracks.

'Sir. Sorry, I mean if you're there…'

'But we might not be. That's the point…'

Mitchell offered Phillips support. 'If I may? Let's say we get a lead that an agent - or we expect two to be taking on a task each, one infrastructure, one Politician linked to that infrastructure - we would send one of you to each of the areas that intelligence leads us to. Steve and his team would also be in that 'area', but as I'm sure you can imagine, would need to be a tactical bound away. Yes, they are all plain-clothed officers, but that's not what I mean. The agents will be looking out for that sort of activity. Half a dozen new faces showing up near their target will alert them. So, you as individuals go in. You do what you need to do and if say, there is a report of a gunshot, then that call will be diverted to Steve's team, and they will close in to take over an incident. At which point you will be long gone.'

'This is getting heavy. 'Mills offered up.

'It is. I can't stress the magnitude of this mission.'

'And then what? Job done? 'asked Jim.

'Well, so far I don't know how long this game will continue. They have had success with the HS2 site and Compton. But the success was dampened because they were not close together, nearly two weeks apart. The impact was not as great as they would have hoped.'

'You know this for a fact? I mean, the link has been made…' Asked Mills.

'It's my view that they want maximum impact. I think they will try both simultaneously next time.'

'So, you know there is more than one of them? 'Pressed Jim.

'I don't know. But I can pretty much guarantee it, based on everything I know about how their system works.'

'So, no telling when this might end?'

'No, but I'd say when we have won the political battle.'

'Which will be?'

'I don't know.'

Both men glared at Mitchell. Committed, because they have their mission. Pissed off at not knowing all the factors in that mission.

Mills was the one who broke the silence. 'I'm not being funny here, but I have a posting to go to in a few weeks.'

'Mills, they will keep your posting open for you. 'Said The Brigadier.

'Sir. OK, but what is in it for us? I mean, we are on a kill or be killed mission, by the sounds of it?'

'OK, fair question. The risk is high. No doubt about it. So let me tell you what is in it for you. When this is over, you will receive The George Cross for your valour outside of a War zone. You will get an OBE commendation. You will get a Brigadier's pension and five hundred thousand pounds of Government Bonds. That's the deal. Take it, because if you don't, you'll be doing this job anyway, with nothing to show for it.'

Mills didn't say a word. It was a good deal. But closer to home, he had just pushed the Brigadier and the Brigadier had laid down the law. Voice legitimate concerns, yes. But don't be a little bitch about things.

Mitchell cleared the air. 'The final factor I need you to understand, gents, is about Operational Security.'

'We live by OpSec, mate. 'Jim Stated, a bit indignant at the comment.

'Not like this, you don't. You've noticed we are in a safe room. A Tempest controlled room. Meaning no signals of any sort can get in or out, and still, I made you switch your phones off and leave them outside?'

Both sat there. Nothing showing on their faces.

'Russia is world-leading in Cyber-Espionage, Mobile Phone Tracking, CCTV hacking, you name it. Gents, we know full well that when we put our heads above the parapet on this one, meaning when we intervene in their next mission, they will do all they can to find out who we are, who you are, and do something about it. To survive this one gents, you really are going to be playing Cold War tactics. You are going to be completely off the grid. No phones, no internet, no radio comms, nothing. You will pay for everything with cash, you will live under an alias, you will have no contact with family, friends, other operators or your home unit. You will be undetectable and uncontactable by every modern means. '

'And so…? 'Pressed Jim.

'And so, you will receive your briefs and orders the old school way. Via the letterbox system. When we go live on this, you will be given the location of your first dead letterbox - a hidden note that you collect and read in secret. You then destroy the message and carry out that order. If we need to meet you face to face, you will get notification of that in your dead letterbox, that your next letterbox will be a live one.'

'And how often do you send these letterboxes out? 'Asked Mills.

'There's no set pattern, and you will be working independently. You won't know each other's details.'

'So, we are working together on this, but completely isolated?'

'Completely. For your own safety.'

'It's really that serious?'

'Yes.'

'But, what about an emergency?'

Mitchell offered this over to Phillips 'Steve?'

'At your next brief with us, before this job goes live, we will put you in touch with someone who can rent you a flat. All paid for by us, of course. But, when you get that flat, write down the address and put it and the spare key in a sealed envelope. When you come here for your final brief, give me that envelope. If we need to come and find you, I will come and if appropriate bring some of my team, so we can flood the area with cops and get you out of there. Make it look like an arrest, or something similar.'

Jim and Mills looked at each other. Mills wasn't too

impressed. 'Off the grid. Only Comms is via a hidden note. The only link to us is in a sealed envelope. Hunting Russians and no end date? This is the most fucked up job I've ever had.'

Jim agreed. 'Um-hm. We've got more briefs?'

'Yes. You need to come back Monday, to start collecting cars, money, weapons and so on. 'Said Mitchell. 'Then you will have all next week to settle into your accommodation and have a soak period. I will keep my link with our man in Moscow going. Then next Friday, we have one final face to face like this, so I can give you all the intelligence I have, and then we will be fully operational. '

'Until it's over.'

'Until it's over.'

The Brigadier stood up again. 'So men, that is it for now. Nothing more to say at this stage. You heard what James said. Monday is an update and the logistics part of your brief. Then back here next Friday for the final intelligence picture. Clearly, I don't expect you to go back to your units now. There is not a single thing you can do regarding all this between now and Monday. So go home and relax. '

The men left the briefing room and collected their belongings and followed Mitchell upstairs. No one spoke. There is a difference between not talking and being silent. They were all silent. When they got to the lobby, Jim piped up first.

'So, that's us until Monday?'

'Yes.'

'Long weekend… what will I do with myself?'

Mitchell said nothing.

Mills pressed Mitchell. 'And there really is nothing else you can tell us?'

'Not now. I hope to have more on Monday for you.'

'This all seems a bit far-fetched to me.'

'I know. And you know we can't talk about it now. Not here.'

'OK.'

'You don't fancy breaking this one to my wife for me, do you?' Jim asked.

'No, but good luck. I don't envy the conversations you guys must have to have with your families, sometimes.'

'Yeah.'

Mills said nothing.

'Until Monday.'

'See you then.'

'See you then.' Said Mills with a sigh.

The two men walked back across the courtyard towards the gatehouse. They stopped a few feet short.

'So, from Monday, we are off the grid, hunting down Russian spies, or assassins, or whatever they are, and killing them stone dead. On the streets of London, or wherever, and Phillips and his crew mop up our mess? 'Summarised Mills.

'That seems to be the long and short of it, mate.'

'It does seem far-fetched, doesn't it?'

'Yeah. This is real Cold War stuff going on.'

'I can't get my head around it. And I'm pissed off they are delaying my posting.'

'I gathered that. I'm pissed off, too. I was meant to be on the run-down to going outside.'

'I extended for two years to lead the Royal Protection Team. '

'You'd think they'd find someone younger…'

Both men had a low chuckle at the absurdness of it all. But both could see it for what it was. As mildly flattering as it was that they were 'hand-picked 'to take on this task, they were Servicemen and if they get told by the Brigadier, they are going off the grid and hunting Russian spies, that is exactly what they are doing. If he said they were going to strip naked and do the Can-Can through Soho, they would strip naked and do the Can-Can through Soho. Life in a green suit.

They made their way out the gatehouse. Mills went first. As he hit the street and turned left, he gave a glance over his right shoulder. A counter-surveillance drill. Drilled to the point of being instinctive. Cover your arcs. He took off down the road. Jim walked out onto the street. He gave a look over his left shoulder as he turned right. He clocked Mills, he had his phone to his ear. He was walking, not getting in a taxi. Jim instinctively put his surveillance head-on. Jim mapped Mills 'route in his head - 'Walk to Great Portland Street Tube Station, cut across to Marylebone Station and get the Western train to Hereford. Jim smiled to himself. If he was on a surveillance job now, he'd get in a taxi and get to Marylebone Station before Mills. Watch what train he got on and get on the same one. He'd call ahead and get someone from the team to drive at speed up a similar route to the train. That way, if Mills did get off at any point along that route, the team would have some sort of presence in the area to support Jim. When it's going well, surveillance work is great fun. The ultimate high-stakes game cat and mouse. As Jim walked back towards Camden Tube Station, he got his phone out of his pocket, looked at it, and put it away again without turning it on. His watch was off too. He kept it that way. Even though the job wasn't starting for over a week, it felt weird. Better to be paranoid on this one. It felt like the game of cat and mouse had already started, but he was the mouse.

CHAPTER 3

The Russian sat in his safe house festering. The mission was a success, finally. But he had not made the political impact he should have. His detail was to create the biggest possible disruption and make the biggest political stir possible. Clear directive. One that should have been achievable. The plan was always to take out a section of the railway construction and its political sponsor within days, if not hours of each other. These were meant to be seen as related incidents. Not for the tabloid press to speculate over. He was directed to present a show of force to the Chinese. Now it was looking laughable. The Russians couldn't make that link. They couldn't cripple a soft target. They could not bring infrastructure to its knees by sabotaging it and taking out its political sponsor.

For the last twenty years, the world has been focussing on cyber security, with billions of rubles invested into encryption, cyber-espionage, malware, trojans and all the other new names those in that world had given to what they do. Real espionage, real sabotage, real action on the ground had fallen out of favour. Agents like Vladislav were a thing of the past. A memory. A chapter in an old book was pushed to the back of a shelf in an old library, in a town no one could remember the name of. And to make it worse, the Chinese were winning the cyber game. By a long shot. Their data and communication physical infrastructure had a global reach. Their advances in Artificial Intelligence were beyond impressive. Scarily impressive. And the man-hours they could throw at developing what they had and creating more, was uncapped.

To re-establish themselves, what Russia had to do was to scare the Chinese by showing them how efficient they were at the dirty work. Make an example of someone. A showcase. Russia, or at least the Soviet Union was the best at the dirty work. Back in Vladislav's day, a Soviet agent was the most feared and respected of all the undercover agents. Mossad, MI6, CIA. They all had nothing on what the Soviets had. And they all knew it. Back in the day, Vladislav was one of the best. And still is. But times change and focus shifts. Every now and then an opportunity arises. Litvinenko. Skripal. A chance for the world to see what was possible. But somehow, even that gets put down to Domestic Politics. And written-off by the press. Written-off by the Politicians and Ambassadors. What was needed was to attack them directly. Make them see. Make them fear. And so, like the mythical beauty Phoenix herself, the order was resurrected. Make an example. Showcase the ability. Restore Russia's place at the top of the table. And who was hand-picked for the task? Picked by his former comrade and now President? Vladislav.

No greater honour. No greater accolade. And now, because it had not gone the way he wanted, no greater pressure.

The construction site was a perfect target. Vladislav had been given a blank canvas on what he could do. He could attack any infrastructure, building or service if the political head of that division was also targeted. The point was to completely neutralise that sector, hit the government, embarrass the UK and showcase Russia's ability. Having been an agent in the UK for too many years to remember, Vladislav knew everything about HS2. He knew its political implications; he knew how emotive the line was. He knew how it would be viewed as an engineering and commercial success when it opened. And he knew how much of an influence and character Thomas Compton was.

The particular construction site he chose, was chosen because it was where a large Signals junction was along the line. And also, too close to London, could have got the attention of National Security. Something at this stage, Vladislav did not want. Plus, on these projects, 'out in the sticks 'as the British referred to the countryside as had a large contingent of Eastern European workers on site. Agency workers. General construction and labour. Doing all the lifting and shifting while the lazy British Foreman and Clerk of Works (Called COW, which always made Vladislav smile when he heard it) sat in the Portacabin with their feet up, eating fried food.

Easy target. Vladislav found accommodation with some other economic migrants and registered with the agency utilising the false documents he made himself. After a couple of days, he was called up to cover some hours. Despite being older than the average labourer, he had assured the young girl in the recruitment agency of his ability to do the job by offering to do some push-ups for her. He knew she wouldn't have taken him up on the offer and to be truthful, he had no intention of doing them, though he could. The point was to get him on site. And it worked. At 0530 on a Monday morning, Vladislav stood outside the agency, along with the Polish and the Romanians, and was collected by the recruitment agency's minibus driver and taken to the site. He clocked into work just before 0600 along with everyone else and sat down to receive a patronising instructional video on Health and Safety, site policy and the rules around breaks. Then, they got to work. Being a construction site, general labour was needed as well as tradespeople. So general labour it was. Moving soil. Digging. Collecting bricks. Watching security. Learning routes in and out. Understanding where exposed areas of utility services were. Good old-school sabotaging had fallen out of fashion. But it was Vladislav's bread and butter. He felt twenty-three again. When he had just been selected from the Infantry to train for 'Specific Duties', as they were called then. He had worked as an agent for fifteen years before the internet came to fashion. And before he had a chance to even offer to re-trade as a cyber-spy, he found himself running the desk. An administration officer. A role he did well at, of course. But it didn't give him the buzz he got from being on the ground. From making a real difference. From being a real agent.

There was a team of welders working on the line, inside the site. Deep enough inside that, the impact of his efforts would be effective. Close enough to the perimeter that he could get out and run if he had to. Though when his plan was executed, his intent was to act like a lost sheep, like everyone else. Get ferried back onto the minibus and driven back to the recruitment agency office. There, he could slip away and never be seen again.

He already had his method of operation planned. And more to the point, he could not go a second full day on this site, being spoken at by the British like he was stupid. 'Fucking foreigner, ' he may be. But being ordered about like he was a dog, no. They needed to be taught a lesson. Day two, they would receive exactly that.

Vladislav didn't sleep that night. His head was full of thoughts. The need for success. To restore pride. To make an example. The process. The routine. The equipment. The excitement was overwhelming. As was his sense of duty. As was his honour in being selected for this task. He got out of bed too early. But that didn't matter. He quietly moved to the kitchen, being mindful not to wake any of the other workers, who would sleep until as late as possible, before rushing out the door to make it to the minibus in time.

His incendiary was makeshift. Homemade. He already had the thermos flask full of petrol. He also had a condom full of fertiliser, and a 9-volt battery in another condom, tied up. The plan was a simple one, but effective. On-site, he would drop the condoms into the thermos flask and walk away. The petrol would erode the condoms over the course of a few hours and when the batteries 'poles arced and the fertiliser, which was to act as an oxidising agent mixed with the petrol, the thermos would become a mini highly flammable bomb. If placed near the welder's cylinders, with any luck - not that Vladislav relied on luck - there will be a significant explosion. And it had to be significant.

At the site, time was a precious commodity. He wanted to be off-site early. He didn't want to be seen too much. Didn't want to be caught up in the numbers after the event. 'Are we still looking for survivors?' 'Where's that old Russian guy?'. After the morning induction and safety brief, off to work they went. Personal belongings were kept in the mess area, including lunch. So, his thermos flask and condoms had to be hidden underneath his clothing. But with a Hi-Vis jacket over the top to break up any shape, he was fine.

Taking a wheelbarrow as some sort of cover, he made his

way towards the welders area. When he was sure no one was watching him, and he was sure, as he was watching everyone, he took out his thermos flask and gently dropped in the condoms. He only had a couple of hours maximum, before the petrol ate through the condoms, mixed with the fertiliser and ignited. The welder's line was quiet. And so, the flask was placed as innocently as possible, next to the cylinders.

He walked away from the area, just as the welding team were turning up to work. They passed each other. Vladislav avoided any eye contact.

What happened next changed the course of everything for Vladislav. One of the welders was vocal about some 'lazy bastard 'and as Vladislav turned to see what was going on, the welder picked up the thermos flask and threw it away from his workstation. When the flask hit the floor, it exploded. Burning fuel, over-oxidised, meaning burning faster and hotter than it should, covered the welder's work area. It covered the welders who were now screaming in pain and fear. And it was on Vladislav's jacket. It was burning through to his skin. He ripped off the jacket and started to run. The emergency alarm sounded and there was chaos on the whole site. Vladislav's back and right arm were blistering. The pain was unbearable. The burning fuel was heating up the cylinders. Though not right now - Vladislav needed those cylinders to explode. He had made it outside the perimeter wire just before they did. The ground shook and the noise was deafening. Equipment fell to the floor. Men fell to the floor. Everything around them that was not over a tonne in weight, bounced four feet off the ground. It was like living in a TV show. Nothing was real. The noise, the fear, the disbelief. All Vladislav knew was that he was hurt. He needed to get away from the scene. He had only just got away with this. With his life and with the mission.

The directive was that Compton - the political minister linked to HS2, was to die within a couple of days of the explosion. Infrastructure and political damage at the same time. That is how the point was going to be made. That is how the Russians would showcase their ability to disrupt a foreign country. And now, nearly two weeks later, Vladislav had already failed. Compton was still alive. And the construction site explosion was old news. Vladislav had taken communication from Moscow and they were waiting on a result.

Vladislav had escaped the explosion and over the course of that day and night, made his way back to his safe house and had spent the following ten days nursing his burns and blisters. He suffered from fever because of his exposed wounds and was still severely dehydrated. But he had to redeem himself. He had his mission. Though not a cyber expert, Vladislav knew his skillset. And it didn't take him long to use the Dark Web to lock onto Compton's internet account. And because he used a Smartphone, actually tracked his location. Vladislav got a map image of where he was. Live, all the time. An absolute gift. The weekend was close. Vladislav waited to see if he left London.

Thomas Compton, despite being at his family home for the weekend, had already done a radio interview and a 'chat 'on breakfast TV via the internet by the time he got round to having some breakfast. Afterwards, despite Compton's pleas, his kids decided they didn't want to go for a walk through the woods to 'start the day. 'It seemed that YouTube and Xbox won again.

Compton and Maggie, his Spaniel walked out the village via a public footpath and made their way onto the rolling countryside. He was no more than a mile from home when Maggie stopped in her tracks. Not unusual for a Spaniel, she may have spotted something worth a stalk. But not this time, Maggie was not in a good place. She could sense something was wrong. Compton didn't pay too much attention. He wasn't a hunting man. He didn't have Maggie to be a working dog. She just looked the part. She was appropriate. A Tory MP can't have a Rottweiler or a Staffordshire Bull Terrier. It's just not the look. What Compton did pay attention to, was the cold that hit him in the back of the neck. Like a frozen dart. He stopped and felt his neck. When he inspected his fingers, he saw his own blood on them. And they were wet like ice had just melted onto his fingertips. His chest tightened. Nausea overcame him. Compton heard something move in the bushes. A man circled round from his right and stood in front of him. Maggie was shaking. Possibly wanting to attack or issue a warning bark, but she was struck with fear. Dogs instinctively know what is happening. Even if they can't articulate it. She crept to Compton's heels and wouldn't look at the man.

Compton couldn't move. His joints felt like they were locked in place. He felt like all blood had drained from his face. He could not talk. He could not blink. He could only just breathe. His heart was beating so hard his chest hurt on the inside. The man stood in front of him. He just looked. Watched. Observed. Compton's mouth was filled with saliva, and he started to feel weak. He was panicking and he felt every pulse beat harder and harder. And then the pain came. Every muscle in his body spasmed. His back muscles contracted, and his torso arched back like an invisible string had got hold of his sternum and pulled him up towards the sky. He fell back, almost completely rigid and hit the floor like a falling ladder. Fingers curled and stretched, his legs contorted, and his head snapped back as Compton drew a desperate breath.

Maggie hid in the bushes. Compton's final image was of the man standing over him, intently watching. Maybe he was even smiling.

Vladislav was proud of his work with Compton. But his elation was short-lived. He was still hurting. And hurting bad. Blisters on his back and arm either stretched his skin until he wanted to rip it off or had burst and was a seeping open wound. Cold baths offered only temporary relief from the agony. His only communication from Moscow was to question the delay in timings between the explosion and the assassination. His tact had to change. If this operation was to succeed, if Russia was to move on from the pitiful UK to America, so it could truly showcase its ability, for Vladislav to showcase his ability, he needed to up the stakes. He was one of the last agents from the old ways. He pulled rank. He commanded respect. He should not be doing the donkey work now. He should be running the mission. He needed a team. He should be the operations director and he needed operators to work for him. Then he could time everything correctly. He could have the impact Moscow demanded.

His communication went out. Not via the internet. No incognito IP address. No VPN. No Dark Web. All too predictable and still traceable, despite what Hollywood fantasists might like to tell you. Vladislav had a SatCom radio, with an antenna attached that looked like a hand-sized fan; a centre cone with four metal fins. When folded up, it could fit in your trouser pocket. Connected to his radio was his issued laptop. Simple and normal in design, but Vladislav could access the hard drive. He could hide messages in the binary coding and when he pressed send, the digital message was encrypted in the radio, and it was burst-transmitted to the satellite and received less than a second later at the receiving station in Moscow. All communication was sent blind. No conversation. No chance to appeal. When he received the message questioning timings, and then no message to congratulate him on Compton. Vladislav understood that he was on his back foot. There was no discussion. Just orders. Statements or nothing. So, Vladislav sent his communication in the same vein. He commanded a team to assist him. Two men. Of his discipline. To take his orders. To sabotage and assassinate. Vladislav was to orchestrate. As an Agent of his status should do.

He closed his laptop. He dismantled his equipment and stowed it away. His shirt that he was wearing had ointment on it, to try and help with his burns. It was soaked through from the pus and the open wounds. He replaced it with another dry shirt. He picked up his bottle of whiskey. His second of the night and took a long hard mouthful. He fell back onto his bed. He was asleep before the bottle fell from his hand onto the floor.

CHAPTER 4

Monday morning came round far too fast for Jim's liking. Despite getting an even earlier train than on Thursday before, and then getting to Regents Park Barracks well before 0900, he was mildly pissed off to see Mills sat in the lobby waiting for him. Mills even had a takeaway coffee in hand. Jim decided that Mills had come up to London the night before.

Mitchell met them and pleasantries were made. Then, as before, they all made their way through the corridors, down the stairs and sat in the briefing room. This time, only Mitchell was briefing them.

'Right Gents, thanks for coming up today. I hope you had some time to relax over the weekend.'

Jim sighed inwardly. Though he's had the 'I'm off on a job ' conversation with his wife many times before - too many to remember - this time it was very strained. He was supposed to be on a run-down from operational duties. And to make it even harder, he had to let her assume the worst. He couldn't tell her he was going to be 30 miles away, driving the streets of London. He gave a sideways glance at Mills, who only starred forwards.

'Today 'Mitchell continued, 'is all about logistics and the practical aspects of the job. Accommodation, cars, weapons, money, that sort of thing. Hence the Brigadier and the Sup not being here. They will be here on Friday for the last Intelligence brief before we go live on this one.'

'No Int today? 'Mills asked.

'Not really. I can confirm there has been some sort of communication between London and Moscow via satellite transmission. GCHQ noticed a burst transmission leaving London a few days ago. They recognised there was encryption that would be indicative of the type we expect Moscow to use. But of course, we can't decrypt that. Even if we could, the transmission was practically over before we picked up on it. So, no. It's the same style of transmissions we'd have our agents using in the field. So, my theory is they are planning their next round of attacks. I'm expecting confirmation of this from my guy before the end of the week.'

'So, what's the plan for today? 'asked Jim.

'The plan for today is to set you up with all you need. We have a week to get you established, let you do what you need to do by way of preparation and have a soak period. When we meet again on Friday, we will be crossing the proverbial start line. It doesn't mean action first thing Saturday morning, but it does mean we will all be ready. Waiting.'

'We are going to be doing a lot of waiting, aren't we?'

'Hard to say right now. But my guess is yes. And when we, you, are called upon, it's going to be full-on.'

'OK, so what now? 'Mills piped up, sounding as impressed as Jim felt.

'Now, I'm going to send you over to see the storeman, Knocker. He will issue you money, weapons, cars, and sort you out with accommodation. His store is across the courtyard. The door you are after is metal and painted white. It has an old-style bell on the outside. The type on a coiled spring and a rope you must pull to ring it. He loves that bell. Use the bell, don't knock on the door. He says that echoes inside his store. I don't know, it's a Knocker thing.'

The walk across the courtyard, which in reality was just a big car park inside the barrack walls, took only a minute or so. They soon got to the door mentioned by Mitchell. It was next to an up-and-over style double-garage door. Jim rang the bell. A few moments later, the door opened. Behind it was an older gent. Rough looking, like he'd lived a bit. Grey hair, beard, carrying a bit of weight around his waist and dressed in work pants and a scruffy polo t-shirt. 'Knocker. 'Jim thought he fitted the name perfectly.

'Alright lads, follow me. 'Was all Knocker offered up by way of greeting and introduction. He had a strong Geordie accent and when he turned to walk into his store, Mills and Jim noticed his gait immediately. Subtle, but it was there. They'd seen it before. It was the gait of a guy with bad knees. Infantry knees. Knocker wasn't another Mitchell. He was or had been in the past, one of them.

Again, heading down narrow corridors, Knocker led the men to his store. It was through an arched doorway and the desk on the far side of the arch had been built to fit the shape and width of the uneven room. As Knocker made his way into the store and to the far side of the desk by lifting the hatch on the left, he finally started to engage with them.

'Right fellas, I'm Knocker 'which sounded more like Knokka in his accent 'I'm the storeman for the London Team. I have worked with Mitchell's bunch for years now. I've had my brief on what you need from me. So, let's get to it. One at a time, come in and we can comb through the nits of it. Then we can look at the cars. While you're waiting, there's a kettle down the hall. You can make yourselves a cuppa. Who's first?'

Mills gestured to Jim that he was more than welcome. Mills was heading off to the kettle before Jim had got through the arch doorway.

'Hi, I'm Jim.'

'Aye, I know who's who mate. You're the surveillance guy. The other is the Close Protection guy. I was doing your job when you were still shittin 'you nappy up your back mate. So here we are, I've got your money and weapons that you sign for now. I'll then take a shopping list from you. I can get you anything you want, within reason. You tell me you want a sniper rifle, I'll get you a sniper rifle. You want Claymores, I'll get you Claymores. You can pick it all up on Friday. I can't get you bedding or any shite like that. You have to buy all that with all this.'

Knocker leaned under his desk and pulled up wads of notes. The twenties and tens were bound by rubber bands.

'There's twenty 'K there. That'll start you off. Pay for everything in cash. Including rent. You need more, get a message to me and I'll get you more. I'll have more on Friday if you've spent this decking out your new abode.'

Jim took it all in his stride and nonchalantly put his signature on the chit Knocker produced for him, to say the cash had been handed over. Knocker offered Jim a choice of weapons to take with him. He opted for a Sig Saur 226. A standard 9mm pistol that fitted well into a belt holster, which sat on the inside of his jeans, in front of his stomach. It was well concealed by the untucked shirt Jim had on and could be drawn and fired very fast. He also took several magazines and boxes of ammunition. Knocker gave him a trendy looking briefcase-sized satchel to put his stuff in.

Mills went through the same routine as Jim. The same brief from Knocker. But when offered weapons, Mills went for a Heckler and Koch 45, with a silencer. With a shoulder holster. It fitted well with his frame and with a loose-fitting jacket, you'd never know it was there.

Jim was finishing his Tea when he heard the bell outside.

'Ay Jim, grab that for us? 'Called Knocker.

Jim got up and walked to the door. He opened it to see Mitchell stood there.

'Going OK?'

'Yeah, so far.'

'Have you got your cars yet?'

'No…?'

'Come on, let see if we can get them issued for you'

Jim didn't understand Mitchell's interest in the cars. But he let him lead the way to the arch.

'Knocker, shall we give them the cars?'

'Aye, if you want to. We can do the last bits after.'

Knocker led them all down a flight of stairs. Jim heard Mills offer up something about all they've done so far is walk down corridors and stairs, but the comment was lost on the other two.

At the bottom of the stairs, they turned in what felt like a U-turn, around a brick pillar. In front of them, was a huge subterranean garage and workshop. Workbenches along the sides had bits of cars and radios and wires and switches everywhere. At the far end was a ramp that clearly led up to and out of the double-garage doors they saw as they walked over.

In the middle of the garage were two brand new BMW's. M5's, if Jim knew his cars.

'Well gents, here's your new wheels. What do you think?'

Jim now saw why Mitchell was so keen to get the cars issued. They clearly were his idea. Mills and Jim walked over to a car each. They both moved around their respective cars and had a good look at the exterior, before opening doors, fiddling with levers and buttons and looking at the dash. After a couple of minutes, Jim who was sitting half-in half-out of the driver's door got Mitchell's attention.

'They're lovely.'

'They are, if any car can get you to the scene of an impending attack, it's one of these.'

'Yeah. I don't suppose you have anything…'

' Shitter? 'Mills finished Jim's sentence, as he was thinking the same thing.

'Shitter?'

'Shitter.'

Mitchell looked at Jim, who gave an empathetic confirmation nod.

'How shitter?'

'Well, I've always been a fan of a Passat 'Said Jim, 'Two to Three years old, petrol, manual, front-wheel drive.'

'Oh, right. And you, Mills, do you want a Passat?'

'No, I quite like Insignias. I need a bit more legroom. 'Jim gave a sideways look at Mills, tapping in to the ever-so light dig at the height difference between the pair of them.

'I see. Knocker, do you think we could, um….'

'I'll see what I can do! 'Knocker chuntered. And with that he turned and walked back to the stairs, muttering something like 'I fucking said this from the start.'

It wasn't long before Mitchell left them to it. Clearly embarrassed that he'd made the wrong decision on their behalf regarding the cars. The two men made their way up the stairs and to the store. This time, Mills went in first.

'Sorry to cause a stink about the cars…'

'It's no problem. I did say this to Mitchell at the time. He's a good lad, one of the most intelligent fellas I've never met. But he's just not an Operator, so he doesn't see it the way we do. But he's the right guy to be running this job. So let the car thing go. Anyway, I've got you what you want.'

'Already?'

'Aye, it's what I do. I'll be collecting it later mind you, so you'll have to pick it up off the street.'

Knocker opened a London roadmap book and thumbed to the right page. He pointed to a road in South London.

'Here. It'll be on this road, dropped off by me at 1900. Keys on the nearside wheel.'

'OK, thanks. So, what now?'

'Now, I need to get you accommodation. I've got a few fellas scattered around the city that I use for this sort of thing. They're not one of us, so there's no link to us in any way. So, you just go up to them and ask for somewhere to live.'

'OK, what's the catch?'

'No catch fella. Ask for a flat, you get the address and a key. You give them money and they ask no questions. They find accommodation for all sorts. Best you don't know, to be fair.'

'And there's no risk of them being turned?'

'What's the bigger risk, mate? Done formally through the MOD, with an audit trail linking the flat, letting agent and you. Or paid-by-cash for Landlords who house migrant workers and people who can't prove their income?'

'Not entirely sure, to be honest!'

'Trust me on this one, you'll get a decent place and no questions asked. That's the deal.'

'Ok, so where?'

Knocker opened an old notepad and showed Mills an address. Mills took out his notepad and wrote down the first line and the postcode. In return, Mills ripped out the page where he'd made his shopping list. He handed it to Knocker.

'Aye fella, I'll see what I can do by Friday for you.'

Jim went through a similar process. Knocker told him his car will be ready for collection at 1600 and gave him a road in West London. And the accommodation guy was a different one to what was given to Mills. After that, they were told to get on with it. It felt like a slow-burn start to a high-stakes operation.

Mills and Jim walked across the courtyard in silence. Both had a bag with money and weapons. Both had an address where they had to go to, to get somewhere to live. Both were picking up a car later. Both knew they were not to tell the other one anything. They got to the Gatehouse.

'See you Friday, then.' Said Jim, matter of factly.

'See you then.'

And that was it. They were already distancing themselves from everyone, including each other. Soon, they will be lost in plain sight on the streets of London. No team, no communication, no contact with loved ones. Nothing.

Jim got out of the taxi a couple of streets away from the address he'd been given. He wanted to walk the last quarter of a mile in. His satchel was slung over his shoulder with the strap across his torso, it banged on his hip when he walked. He felt the boxes of ammunition move about until they settled in a sort of curve in the bag, to sort of fit around his hip. The banging eased off slightly. He'd not be able to carry this much ammo in this manner when he was on task. He normally doesn't. He was looking forward to getting his car and filtering some of it out to the door wells and glove box. He walked up the street, eyeing up the houses and house numbers. Huge five-storey Victorian looking terraced houses, all divided down into flats. He found the house, and sure enough, it was divided into flats. To get to the front door, there was a flight of four steps, and at the top of those steps, there was a multi-flat intercom, with a buzzer button next to each flat number. However, the flat Jim wanted was the lower ground or basement flat. It had a low-level gate next to the main stairs and had its own steep set of stairs heading down. Jim walked down the stairs and was met by a steel gate across the front door. Nothing new there, he'd seen that every other door on the street was gated like this. He rang the doorbell. Only a short moment passed before the inner front door was opened by a smartly dressed man, who seemed to be in his late fifties. He unlocked the gate and pushed it open the first foot, indicating to Jim it was his job to open it the rest of the way.

'Round to the left.'

Jim walked in the hallway and immediately on the left, was a room that had been made out to be an office. If this was a normal owned flat, it would have been the master bedroom. Jim sat at the desk without being offered a seat. The man didn't seem to care and walked to the far side of the desk and then sat down himself.

'I have several places available. Any preferences I need to be made aware of?'

'Two bedrooms would be nice. A flat with an open terrace front, not in a block with your front door opening into a hallway.'

'Quite specific, anything else?'

'Not ground floor. First or second. With stair access, not just a lift. Nowhere shit, either. '

'I'll see what I can do.'

The man opened a drawer and thumbed through a few sets of envelopes holding keys inside them. He produced four. They all had the addresses on the front.

Jim looked at the addresses and selected an envelope with an address in West London. No real reason other than it didn't seem too far from the address he'd been given by Knocker for the car pick up later that afternoon.

'The deposit is £5,000 and the rent is £3,000 upfront. One calendar month from now, I expect another £3,000 put in the letterbox on the wall next to the front door. Miss the rent by one day, and my men will come to take it from you. '

'What if I'm busy on rent day?'

'I'm not interested. You do what you do, I do what I do. I got told you need accommodation and I have it for you. Do you want it or not?'

Jim didn't even engage in the conversation any longer. He took out of his bag his bundles of cash and put on the table a bundle of £5,000 and counted out a further three. He did ponder for a moment on who else this guy has for clients. But he couldn't ask, so dropped worrying about it. The transaction was done. He made his way back onto the street. It was still only late morning, so he decided to walk to the flat. By his guess, it was an hours 'walk away. And from there, another hour to the car. He still had plenty of time to 'settle in 'to the flat that was going to be his home for the foreseeable future.

Jim got to the estate early that afternoon. Built post-war, the blocks of flats were of good quality, made of brick as opposed to the prefabricated builds of the 1980s. The flats were only four storeys high, and each level had a balcony you walked down to get to individual front doors. 'Good Start 'Jim thought to himself. It just felt less claustrophobic to him, which seemed like a good thing.

His flat was on the first floor, accessible via stairs. Jim assumed there was also a lift to each floor, but it must have been down the far end of the block. Jim walked the balcony until he got to his door number: 6

It had a solid wood door, with a Yale-style lock. When he opened the door, there was the utility cupboard on the left, which came to waist height, meaning there was a shelf where you could imagine everyone dropping their keys when they walked in. Above the cupboard was a panel, next to the door. A point of weakness, Jim thought. If someone wanted to, they could pull the panel out, or break through it easier than the wooden door and simply unlatch the door from the inside. A small security risk Jim needed to sort out. Inside, there was the kitchen to the immediate left and a hallway leading to the living room at the back. At the doorway to the living room, the hall turned left and ran along the back of the kitchen. On the right was the bathroom. And at the far end, two bedrooms. One facing the balcony, one facing the inside of the estate, where residents parked their cars in allocated bays. Jim didn't think about parking. He wasn't sure if he was allocated a bay. He doubted it, and now he couldn't really go back and ask. Kerbside parking it was. Jim needed to buy everything. Fridge, microwave, bed, bedding. All of it. No wonder they were given a week to settle in. It was going to take that long to turn this place into something that resembles liveable accommodation.

Mill's guy was in South London. He got a taxi through town. He wasn't bothering with the underground. He didn't know the area, so couldn't work out if there was a station close by and didn't care to find out. The taxi dropped him off outside a taxi radio-office, of all things. So, he had to get out of a black cab and walk into a private-hire taxi shack. The place was a dive and Mills was pissed off he was there from the word go. It had a waiting area, with a desk at the far end. The walls all seemed grubby and stained from cigarette smoke. There were fruit machines tucked into the corners and there was a man standing at one, feeding pound coins into it. Along the walls, there were plastic seats. 4 along each wall. Each seat was taken. All nationalities sat in that waiting area. Mills walked up to the desk. The desk was close to chest-high and had a Perspex screen running from the desk to the ceiling. The only gap was a half-circle that was cut out of the Perspex, in the centre of the desk. Behind the desk, was a greasy looking man, heavy build, and wearing a grubby shirt and trousers. He had an ashtray next to him with a cigarette burning away in it. He didn't look up when Mills approached.

'Taxi?'

'No. Accommodation. '

'Everyone here wants accommodation. You want a job as well?'

'No.'

'Take a job, get closer to the top of the list for a bed. '

'I have a job. '

'You speak good English my friend. I could get you a good job.'

'Just accommodation.'

The man drew a breath in. He glanced at Mills and glanced at the other men in the room. He wrote down an address on a piece of paper and showed it to Mills, whilst distracting attention by calling out a fare over the radio to a taxi. Mills assumed it was illegal and parked around the corner, as there was no actual rank for taxis outside. Mills memorised the address which was a postcode and the number 4E. The man took back the piece of paper and wrote down the number 7. Mills took this as how much he had to pay. Mills had stored money all over his person. So, he took £1,000 out of each front pocket of his jeans. Then a further £2,000 bundle out of each jacket pocket and the last £1,000 bundle from the inside pocket of his jacket. He handed it all over and the man took it quickly and gave Mills another glance. This time, a bit more disapprovingly. He pushed some keys towards Mills.

'Rent due every month here. You sure you don't want a taxi?'

'I think I'll walk.'

'Suit yourself.'

The man watched Mills leave. He also saw two of his punters get up and follow Mills out. He shook his head and made another call on the radio. He didn't know who this guy was who needed accommodation. But he did think he wasn't that street-smart, taking money out in front of everyone like that.

Mills wasn't going to walk. He just didn't want to get a taxi from there. He didn't trust a soul and didn't fancy having a driver knowing where he lived. It was bad enough that the guy behind the desk did. But seeing as he was a contact of Knockers, Mills had no choice but to trust him. As Mills turned a corner at the end of the street, he had a glance down where he just came. Two men were following him. He saw them in the taxi shack, and he could see them eyeballing him. He continued along his path. He had his rucksack slung over one shoulder. So, as he walked, he slid his other arm into the strap and bounced it into a comfortable position on both his shoulders. He also instinctively unzipped his jacket by a couple more inches, so the zipper was somewhere between his sternum and his belly button. There was a small service road on the left and Mills turned into it. The pair closed the gap and followed Mills in. Twenty meters down the road, next to some large dumpster-style bins, Mills turned on a sixpence and confronted them.

'Who the fuck are you two?'

'We are nobody. We are just out for a walk.' Said the first guy, with a smile.

'We see you have money. We want your money.' Said the second.

'You've followed me out of that place, to mug me? Bollocks.'

'You talk too much. Give money now.'

The pair moved closer to Mills, positioning themselves for an attack. One face onto Mills, the second off to the side. Mills wasn't messing about. He drew his pistol from inside his jacket and held it one inch from the face of the first man. Attitudes changed instantly.

'Woah, what is this?'

'You tell me!'

'We are nobody, we arrive in the UK two days ago. We come here for work and a place to live.'

'I don't believe you.'

'It is true. We are what you say, economic migrants. 'Offered the second guy.

'And you end up here? How did you know about the taxi place?'

'Everyone knows. You come to the UK, you get told.'

'We have nothing,' continued the first guy, 'You have money. You seemed like you could share your money.'

'Are you taking the piss? Economic migrants and now you want to mug me? Who are you?'

'Who are we?'

'Russian?'

'No'

'Bollocks'

'Fuck Russia. We are Romanian. We mean no harm. You let us go, yes?'

'You just tried to mug me in broad daylight. Me! You could mug anyone. '

'No. This was a mistake. We will be good.'

Mills raced through the options in his head. Russians? Doesn't seem like it. Therefore, not after him, or they would have gone for it by now and not started talking. He couldn't kill them, he was pretty sure Phillips and his team couldn't cover that one up. Not before the job had officially started, that's for sure. Let them go, and they could mug anyone. They clearly had it in them. He lowered his pistol, so it was at the 4 O'clock position from his torso.

He pulled the trigger and a silenced round shot into the thigh of the guy in front of him. Mills heard the bone shatter. The man instantly crumbled to the floor. His left leg could not support him, and he folded in agony, holding his thigh. One hand on the front, one hand on the back. Mills looked at the second. He had taken a couple of steps back. But the angle he was at, meant all he did was put himself against the wall. His hands were up. Mills put a round into his shin. The sound of his shin shattering was quite something. It's enough to make you feel sick if you don't have the stomach for it.

Both were trying to hold back their cries of pain. Maybe out of pride, maybe because they were illegals and didn't want to go into the system. Mills didn't care. He'd wasted too much time on them already. He holstered his pistol and made his way back to the main road. Leaving them with a 'Now fuck-off home 'as a parting message. He knew full well that would never happen. But at least their introduction to the UK was one they will never forget and more importantly, might now think twice about mugging innocent passers-by.

Mills got out of the taxi round the corner from the address he was after. He watched the taxi drive off, before continuing on foot. All the houses on both sides were large Victorian-style buildings. Maybe even older? Georgian? Edwardian? Mills didn't know his period property, and he didn't care. Big houses, all with a multi-buzzer intercom system on the front. Indicating they were all separated into flats. Initially, that didn't sit too well with Mills. He had got out of the taxi at the wrong end of the road, and it took a while to walk the street and get to house number 4. He walked up the steps to the large front door and sure enough, there was an intercom system, with flat numbers on it. Flats 4A to 4H. Eight flats. Seven others. Seven flats filled with the type of guys in the taxi shack. He put one of the larger of the two key styles into the lock and turned. The door opened. When he walked through the doorway, he was pleasantly surprised. It was clean and in good condition. The two ground floor flats A and B had doormats outside and pairs of shoes, including children's shoes. As he walked up the stairs, the next floor looked the same, plus one of the flats had a kids scooter outside the door as well. The accommodation guy clearly knew who he was dealing with. Mills did wonder how much work Knocker threw his way. On the third floor were doors E and F. A smaller key opened the door to flat E.

Inside, his flat was clean and painted white. Not much of a hallway, doors led on to the kitchen and bathroom and into the living room. The bedroom was through a door off the living room. The view from the living room was the sidewall of another large house. Mills took off his bag and had a look around. When he looked out the bedroom window, he was pleasantly surprised. There running the entire height of the building, was an external fire escape. A metal-framed one, like what you might see in a movie based in New York. Mills had his escape route. He now could go down, or up if the front door was compromised. The fire escape had clearly been added in later years to meet multi-tenant regulations. So, the owner could turn the house into a letting business. Clearly climbing out a window was not ideal, but if there was a fire - or in Mill's case, a Russian Agent was after you - you'd not think twice about hitching yourself through to make a getaway. Mills paused for thought. He needed to go shopping. But didn't want to do too much until he had his car. He had time to kill. He sat himself down on the floor in the living room, took out his weapon cleaning kit he had got from Knocker and cleaned his HK.

CHAPTER 5

It was just after three-thirty when Knocker, in Jim's Passat, got to the drop-off road. He didn't want the car to be left for too long, but at the same time, in London, you never know how long you'll be looking for somewhere to park. He got lucky near a turning to the left. There was a space just before the turning and due to road markings, meant no one could park in front of him. Meaning Jim could get in and drive away hassle-free. Knocker parked up and had a brief look in all mirrors before getting out. He got out and had a brief stretch in the road, before closing the door, pressing the fob to lock the car and walking around the front to the nearside. He had a tired looking rucksack with him. In a slightly overdramatic play, to labour the point to accidental viewers, he looked down at an untied shoelace, gave a big huff, placed the bag on the floor and kneeled down to tie his lace. He then quickly slipped the spare key onto the tyre and grabbed his rucksack. The bit that wasn't part of the act, was the swearing at his knees when he stood up.

Jim was on foot all the way to the pick-up. He's been out for a couple of hours. He liked walking and was mapping out the area in his head as he walked. Timings from A to B. Noticing key landmarks he could recognise and use as a reference. Observing other people on the street as he walked. It all added to his trade. Even now, if he had to, without a road map, he could make his way back to his flat via three or four different routes. On foot or by car.

He walked down the right-hand side of the road and clocked

his car. He continued on his chosen path, preferring not to cross immediately and highlight himself. He gave himself some cover at the end of the street, by crossing over to the left-hand side and posting a letter in the postbox. It was just a plain envelope. Not even an address on the front, never mind a letter inside. But if anyone was watching, all they saw was a guy walking up to post a letter. This means in reality, they saw nothing at all. At the postbox, Jim gave a quick scan of the road. It was actually free from people. A car did drive down it and past Jim, but other than that, all was good. Jim headed towards the car. As he made his way across the side road, which was now on his right, he gave a look down it and used that as an excuse to look over his shoulder behind him. All quiet. Jim got to the car and with no fuss, picked up his key and walked around the front to the driver's side. Inside the car, he took no more than five seconds to familiarise himself with levers and handles, as well as adjusting the seat. He didn't bother adjusting the mirrors. He turned the key and was off. Jim had one thing on his mind. His flat. And more specifically, sleeping arrangements. He was off to find a retail park, or more preferably, a high street to buy himself something to sleep on, something to eat and basic toiletries.

At the start of the road, the opposite end to the postbox Jim used as cover was a small green space. Somewhere you could go to sit on the bench and feed the pigeons. There was a bin next to the bench. The green space had shrubs and bushes around the outside, by way of a border. Sat on that bench, with a tin of cider in his hand, watching everything through the cover of the shrubs, was Knocker. He watched everything. He gave himself a wry smile when he watched Jim use the sending-a-letter trick. Some things never go out of fashion. With Jim safely on his way, Knocker poured the cider away into the grass under the bench. He discarded the tin in the bin next to him. He grabbed his bag and was off. He had another collection and drop-off to do. His day was far from over.

Parking a car in the evening was trickier, but Knocker got lucky with a space on the right-hand side of the road. It did mean he had to walk into the road to place the key for Mills. And Mills, in turn, had to be in the road to collect it, before he could get in the car. But them's the breaks. No one said it would be simple. To give himself as much cover as possible, Knocker left his bag on the passenger seat, which gave him an excuse to walk into the road and open the passenger door. Once he had his bag, it was an easy manoeuvre to get the key onto the tyre.

Mills had been on foot for a couple of hours before the pickup, much like Jim. But Mills had the luxury of getting a meal and going to the shops, so he could buy the basics to survive the night. In his bag, along with ammunition and a small amount of trauma control kit such as a tourniquet and bandages, he'd bought himself some toiletries, coffee and milk and a multi-pack of socks and underwear. He'd also got a sleeping bag from an independent camping shop. He carried it in the plastic shopping bag given to him by the shopkeeper. It hit his leg when he carried it by the handles, so it ended up tucked under his arm.

He walked at a brisk pace and as he made his way down the drop-off road, he saw his car parked on the other side. Driver-side next to the curb. A bit frustrating, but he got it. Sometimes you have to just throw the car in wherever you can. As he crossed the road, a mum and a very tired young girl were walking down the pavement on the car's side. Because they were travelling in the same direction as Mills, he'd not seen them until he started to cross the street. No threat, but it would be weak of him to either change his course of direction now or be seen by them to collect a cached key. As he got close to his car, he dropped his sleeping bag on the road. That gave him enough cover to grab his key and pop open the boot, just as the mum and girl got to him. He acknowledged them as he threw the sleeping bag into the boot and said something about it being 'one of those days.' He got in the car and was away.

At the end of the street, off to the side, so out of the direct line of sight, Knocker was pretending to talk on a mobile phone. He saw Mill's charade. Job done. They had the rest of the week to bed-in. 'No doubt on Friday they will both be asking for another Twenty K 'Knocker thought to himself, as he started walking away from the area. The first few steps he took were a bit tight, from having to loiter for the last quarter of an hour.

Both men instinctively chose to sleep in the living room that first night. All was too new and makeshift to properly settle in yet. Jim had got himself a sleeping bag and an air bed. Mills was on the floor in a sleeping bag, with his jacket as a pillow. Both slept clothed and had their pistols next to them. The next morning, both men had a wash and with new kettles, made tea and coffee. The milk was already starting to turn. The next three days were going to be all about getting their respective flats as straight as possible. Now with cars, the idea of getting what was needed was less daunting. Jim started with the local high street. While Mills went for a large supermarket. The frustrating thing was, they needed everything. Normally when you deploy, you bring civvy clothes, a laptop, and bits of kit you've bought over the years. The kit you know you operate best with. But they had none of this stuff. Car boots and back seats were filled with tabletop fridges, bags of clothes and underwear. Folding beds and a half-decent mattress with bedding. Food. Lots of food. Once the essentials were covered, minds turned to passing the time. It had already been said that this could go on for a long time. And no one knew when they would be called into action. Mills bought a DVD player and a bunch of DVDs. Jim got a refurbished laptop. Deciding that if it's never connected to the internet, what harm can it do? Again, he bought a bunch of DVDs. Harder to come by than you'd think these days. He had to go to a budget store to get the volume he anticipated getting through. Exercise is always a key factor when you're deployed. And technically, Jim and Mills were deployed. So, both bought sportswear and some equipment. Jim opted for a pair of kettlebells. He always got a good workout swinging them overhead. Mills got a door-hanging pull-up bar and a mat to do sit-ups on. A few bits of 'domestic safety 'items were bought. Mills got himself a couple of door stops. One for his front door and one for the bedroom door. Jim saw a baby monitor. He decided that he could use the camera in the front bedroom, facing out the window. He could then have the monitor in the living room. He could watch the monitor before he left the flat. If anyone untoward was coming down his balcony at that time, he'd get a 5-10 second heads-up. Enough time to have his weapon drawn at the front door for when they got there. Minds were always on the job. There were too many questions. Retail therapy is a wonderful thing. But when you're buying to facilitate you being rested, fuelled and prepared for what was to come, it takes the shine off it. As with most things, shopping was a process. A necessary evil. By the end of Tuesday, both men were thoroughly pissed off with it all.

CHAPTER 6

It may seem like a wonderful idea, having time to yourself to just mong-out. But after literally decades of living like this on operational tours, there was nothing self-indulgent about the time that Jim and Mills had on their hands. When in a foreign country, whilst waiting for the next brief or operation, downtime was golden. Resting on your bed, watching a film or in more recent years, getting online to family was all part of the job and taken in ones stride. But in London, with certain liberties taken from them, the imposed isolation was a solemn beast sitting on their shoulders. Routines were similar, exercise in the morning, then head out for orientation and mapping your area. Either on foot or in the car, learning routes in and out of key areas was part of what they did in any other situation, so it made sense to do it here, too. Though in reality, they could be sent anywhere, so would always be working blind. But it made sense to them, to at least follow the drill of learning their routes. Though some food was bought in, most meals were eaten out. There's only so many DVD's you can watch in a day. And only so much wanking you can do.

Stephan Rushmere had been involved in drugs his whole life. Growing up in the tenement blocks of South Glasgow, weed and pills were never far away. Stephan's dad was a dealer and got sentenced to 6 years when Stephan was just five years old. Stephan's mum tried to smuggle prescribed meds into the prison once on visiting day and as a result, got a sentence herself.

Meaning from the age of eight, Stephan was in the care system. From the care system to the prison system; Stephan had been in and out due to low-level drug-related offences for years. It was all he knew. And it was how he came to be in London. He had been moved due to him dealing drugs inside one prison and he ended up in HMP Brixton. Once out, he named himself Snake and got to work for a firm based out of Wembley. Their plans were ambitious and wanted to expand into other gang territories. They used Snake and people like him, to make a foothold in someone else's patch. If they were successful and stole a few clients from the incumbent gang, then the firm would wade in and make an aggressive takeover. If the likes of Snake weren't successful and let's say, the rival gang got hold of him, then the Wembley firm would take it as read that they should steer clear of that area.

On Thursday, Jim had been out driving. He had been learning routes in and out of the city. He'd parked up two streets away and walked back to his flat. As he got to the balcony, there was a filthy-looking weasel of a man standing near his front door. As Jim paused for thought, the man started to walk up to him.

'Ah, there you are. I was wondering if you were just ignoring me knocking at your door.'

'Why would I ignore someone knocking at my door?'

'Maybe you were unsure of what you wanted. Unsure of who your supplier was?'

'I don't understand. 'Replied Jim. And he genuinely didn't.

'Don't play stupid with me fella. You're new here. And you need a guy to get you what you want. Well, today is your lucky day, my man. Because I'm your man. You buy from me. Understand?'

'I don't want to buy anything.'

'Don't be silly. Everybody has a little vice. A little coke on a Saturday night, maybe? To have some fun?'

'No.'

'Then maybe you need my help? Hmmm…? For a modest fee, I can stop my crew smashing down your front door and smashing up your back door if you get my drift?'

'Protection?'

'Look, this is my patch. And everyone on this estate buys something through me. Gear, protection, women, boys. You don't want to be any different. It wouldn't be in your best interest.'

'I'm tired. Can I get to my flat, please?'

'Listen. 'Barked Snake, stepping to one side to stop Jim from getting past. 'We can do this nicely, or we can do this not so nice. A little weed to relax in the evening is not a massive price to pay for your safety and peace of mind now, is it?'

'What's your name?'

'You were trying to get rid of me thirty seconds ago, and now you want my name? You think you're funny, do you?'

'Just asking.'

'The name's Snake. And this is my patch, and everyone buys through me. Including you.'

'Snake? Your mother must have hated you!'

'Now that's just fucking rude! 'spat Snake, as he pulled a

flick knife from his jacket pocket. Jim went full spectrum. When he saw Snake, he was worried. Then he was intrigued. Then he found the whole situation amusing. Now, he was being threatened with a knife, and Jim flicked the switch. Jim looked at the knife. He didn't need to look at Snake anymore, he'd already got all the information he needed.

'Aye, taking me seriously now, aren't you fella?'

Jim said nothing.

'Oi, look at me when I'm talking to you.'

Nothing. Jim didn't take his eyes off the knife. Not because he was worried, but he needed a break in the pattern to seize upon. Snakes failing was wondering what this guy in front of him was looking at. As soon as Snake took his eyes off Jim and looked down as well, Jim made his move. His left hand grabbed Snake's right forearm, just beneath the crease in his elbow. This stopped Snake from using the knife. At the same time, Jim's right hand grabbed the shoulder of Snakes jacket. He brought his left foot up and forward and twisted Snake slightly for a better angle, stamped down on the back of Snake's right knee. As Snake buckled, Jim helped him go down by pulling downwards on the jacket. The side of Snake's head hit the brick wall of the balcony. Not enough to knock him out. Snake tried to get up. Shifting his hand placement from Snake's forearm to the inside of his right thigh, Jim picked up Snake and threw him headfirst over the wall. Snakes 'bodyweight dropped and his hips pivoted on the wall, spinning him mid-fall. Snake spun a full rotation as he fell and landed on his left leg. Snapping it at a right angle. His Shinbone was sticking out of the flesh and had ripped through his jogging pants. Jim didn't even look over the balcony. He just made his way to his front door. As he opened it, he heard Snake shouting out 'Jesus Fucking Christ!'

'Na, Royal Fucking Marine.' Snarled Jim, as he closed the door behind him.

On a side road, facing the estate, with a full view of Jim's balcony, Kingston was sitting in his black Range Rover. Kingston, named after Kingston, Jamaica where his family originated, was the true head dealer in this area. And this estate, like many others in the borough, was his. His runners knew every person in each block and knew what they wanted, and when they wanted it. They knew when to push and they knew when to let them come asking. You could call Kingston a Yardie. But he was more than that. He wasn't a gangster. He was *the* gangster. An institution. Very little got past him. He was hard and smart. Business smart. He was ruthless. He knew the Wembley crew wanted to move into his patch. And he knew they were going to send Snake. He knew none of his clients would ever buy from anyone other than Kingston's crew. They wouldn't dare. But he knew Snake would try. Kingston was waiting to catch him in the act. And then, he would flay Snakes skin on his torso and send a video recording of it to the head of the Wembley crew demanding £10,000 to save their man. They wouldn't pay, so Snake would end up being cut into pieces, dropped down a storm drain and sent out to sea. That's how Kingston did business.

Kingston and his runner sat in the Range Rover, watching. They watched as Snake got in the face of this new guy. The guy who had been decking out the flat he'd just moved into. All week, he'd been bringing back furniture and boxes and bags from shops. And now, he's just seen this guy, who had a knife pulled on him, throw Snake over the balcony.

'Want me to go up and talk to this new white boy, Boss?'

'No, I want to do this one myself. Something doesn't sit right.'

'What about Snake?'

'Can't send a message, if someone has already sent it for us, can we? Stay here.'

Kingston got out of his car and walked over to the estate. As he crossed the road, he saw Snake propping himself up against the wall, attempting to hop away from the area. Kingston was impressed with this new guy. But also pissed off that he'd not sent his own message. He can't now take a broken man and say to the Wembley crew 'Look what we did - we did this after someone else got in first 'It doesn't work like that. Kingston made his way up the stairs.

Jim was sitting in the living room. He had already detuned from the Snake incident. All things considered, it was small fry. He'd been through a lot worse. And when he first saw Snake, he expected a lot worse. Jim was sitting on a foldaway chair, thinking, and watching. A figure passed the bedroom window and Jim saw it on the screen of the baby monitor. 'Here we go again, 'Jim thought, 'There's more than one of them. 'Jim had his pistol in his hand. To his surprise, there was a knock at the door. He thought for a moment. Then he went along with it.

'Hang on! 'He called, as he quietly got out of the chair. He threw a t-shirt over the monitor and had a quick scan to see if there was anything out that shouldn't be. Another knock.

'I'm coming.'

Jim walked to the front door, pistol in hand, already loaded and cocked. Across the panel above the utility cupboard, Jim had got some razor wire from a hardware store and nailed it across the panel. Not much-added protection, but it may slow someone down if they were trying to reach inside and unlock his door. Through a gap in the wire, he pointed his pistol at an angle towards the outside of his front door. He could do some damage if he had to. The chain went on, and he opened the door.

'Can I help you?'

'I notice you've recently moved in. I am just welcoming you to the neighbourhood.'

'You're not the first to do that today.'

'I know, our mutual friend? 'Kingston gestured over his shoulder to the wall of the balcony.

'What do you want?'

'A conversation.'

'I don't use drugs.'

'I guessed that. Can I come in?'

Jim weighed up his options. Right or wrong, he thought it might actually be easier to talk in the flat.

'Hang on.'

Jim closed the door. Quickly and quietly, he de-cocked his pistol and holstered it. He took off the chain and opened the door. He stepped back to the wall as he did, motioning to Kingston he should walk down the hall to the living room. Kingston obliged and Jim followed behind him. Kingston was eyeballing everything as he walked in. He gave Jim a sideways glance when he saw the razor wire. In the living room, everything was temporary. Like Jim had emptied his camper van out into the flat. The table was fold-up. The chairs were fold-up. There was a bag of clothes near the door, clearly ready to be taken to the launderette.

'I would say I like what you've done with the place.'

'Aye, I only moved in a few days ago.'

'I know.'

Jim started to try and place Kingston. How would he know? Who is he? Mutual friend? Police? Drugs Squad? Didn't seem likely. From the Estate? A rival gang? Drug gang? He's been watching. From where? View of the front door? From a car. Parked opposite? 'The black Range Rover across the street.' Jim concluded to himself.

'How can I help you?'

'I want to know who you are. When you started to move all your shitty stuff in, I guessed you were down on your luck. Just split up with the missus or something?'

'Yeah, not far off.'

'Hmm, and I would have been OK with that. I would have let you settle in before sending one of my guys up to do some business with you.'

'Why does everyone assume I'm want drugs?'

'I'm not saying that. But my man would have encouraged it.'

'I see.'

'But now I'm not so sure. Not after seeing how you did away with Snake.'

'You saw that? '

Definitely the black Range Rover...

'I did. So, it made me wonder. There's no way any user would throw a dealer off a balcony. That just doesn't happen. So, Snake must have said something really bad to offend you?'

'Snake isn't one of yours, then? I'm lost?'

'Snake is from a rival firm. He was trying to muscle in on my patch. I just needed to catch him in the act, and I was going to send a message back to his employer. But you seem to have beaten me to it.'

'You're welcome.'

'It doesn't work that way. But clearly, you don't know that, seeing as you have nothing to do with drugs, right?'

'Right'

'So, what do you have to do with?'

'Nothing. Exactly as you said, split with the missus. Lost the house. Starting again.'

'I don't believe you.'

'So don't.'

'And I don't like your tone. You need to understand who I am.'

'OK, go on.'

'Nothing happens in the area without me knowing about it. No business happens without me being involved. I run the streets and I run the networks. And I'm starting to suspect you are

Police. And If I'm right, you and I are going to have a very strong conversation, right now.' Kingston's attitude had shifted up a gear. Clearly turning on the intimidation. Jim was too old and too pissed off with life to allow himself to be bullied by someone he'd just met. Irrelevant of what he did for a living.

'I'm not Police.'

'Then what?!'

'Then nothing.'

'You need to start giving me more than that. I'm starting to lose interest in being so polite.'

'You came up here because I threw Snake off the balcony. Let's finish that conversation off, shall we? You asked what he said.'

'And?'

'Nothing. He said nothing of any importance. He pulled a knife on me. And I took umbrage to it.'

'Umbrage.'

'Yeah. When you came to my door, I was assuming it was some of his mates. Will they be coming to see me?'

'No. they won't try to come on to my patch unless Snake goes back with a couple of confirmed clients. I was going to send him back in a body bag as a message to stay away.'

'Instead, he's got a broken leg and a sore head. Not enough?'

'Not enough for me. But it'll no doubt make his firm think twice.'

'Messy stuff. Does everyone else on this estate use? And buy from you?'

'You'd be surprised.'

'OK, well I don't. So, leave me off your list.'

'I don't know what is pissing me off more, thinking you're Police or your lack of respect.'

'I said I'm not Police. And I don't understand what you want from me? To be scared of you?'

'Most are.'

'Well, I don't know about you, or your reputation. So why would I be scared?'

'If this is the bit where you give me the speech about you staying out of my business, and I'll stay out of yours, you're wasting your breath. You are on my estate, so you are my business.'

Clearly, Jim needed to move this conversation forward. He wasn't at all happy with someone being in his flat. But at this stage, better a drug dealer than a Russian assassin. And to be fair, after nearly a week, he was enjoying talking to someone.

'I'm really not that full of myself. Humour me though, if you thought I was the Police, why are you telling me all this?'

'Just to give you a chance to change your mind about sticking your nose into my business. Not many undercover cops fare well against me.'

'OK. So, look, if you who you say you are, then you can get some specific products, would that be a fair assumption?'

'I can get anything. Why, what do you have in mind?'

Jim did have it in his head that he may need some pain relief if things went bad. He had put a trauma kit down on his shopping list with Knocker. But to have a win/win at this game with the drug dealer stood in front of him, for the first time ever, Jim placed an order.

CHAPTER 7

Jim and Mills had been told to get to Regents Park Barracks at 1600. Jim had a reasonably easy drive in and though he wanted to be early, maybe just to level things out from Monday with Mills being in the lobby when Jim arrived at the Barracks, he actually got in a good half an hour early. When he pulled up to the barrier in the Gatehouse, the guard asked if he was WO2 Millbrook. To which Jim replied, 'Na, I'm the other one. 'Jim was told to go to the stores. It was clear they were going to get their shopping list before seeing Mitchell and the others.

Jim parked up and made his way to the door. He rang the bell. Knocker came to the door.

'Aye, you're a tad bit early lad. Grab a cuppa and I'll have your stuff laid out for you to sign for in fifteen minutes.'

'Cheers Knocker. How are you?'

'Aye, grand. Won fifty on a scratch card yesterday. I'm thinking of retiring.'

Jim smiled and went to make a cup of tea. Fifteen minutes later, the bell rang. Knocker asked Jim to open the door and come through to him. Jim and Mills greeted, Jim, let Mills know what was going on. Before Jim had made it to Knocker's store, he heard the kettle boiling.

On the storeroom table, was Jim's shopping list. A Heckler and Koch MP5 - a small and easy to conceal, semi-automatic weapon, which took a 30-round magazine. Ammunition and magazines to go with it. A medical kit. Grenades, smoke grenades and thunder flashes. Infrared head-worn scope. Ceramic body armour and various other bits Jim had asked for. No radio. No comms for this mission. Jim was still uneasy about not having a direct link to anyone.

'This should be about it, mate'.

'It looks like it, thanks. I have receipts for you as you requested'.

'Good man! You want more cash, then?'

'Please?'

Knocker counted out another twenty-thousand pounds in front of Jim. Jim signed for it.

To take his kit out to the car, he put most of it in a large sports bag, and then weapons and ammunition in a separate bag. He tucked it all together against the side of the boot, so it didn't move about when he was driving. He pottered around his car until he saw Mills come out and do something similar.

Knocker came to the door and looked at his watch.

'You may as well head over lads. The Brigadier is in, and Phillips should be here by now.'

'Cheers Knocker. 'They said in unison. They turned and walked over the courtyard to the DSF building. The same walk that took them less than a minute to complete at the start of the week suddenly felt like a mile long. Neither spoke. Both knew that when they walked out of the briefing room, it all was going to be real. The nice and relaxed pace of shopping and settling into accommodation and driving around orienting themselves will be a thing of the past.

Mitchell met them at the door again. He was happy to see the two of them. But his head was truly in the job. He missed the conversation when Jim tried to ask how he was and that they've got what they need from Knocker. Once back in the briefing room, things actually felt quite calm. The Brigadier was wearing a shirt and jeans - it was dress-down Friday, after all. Phillips was there, looking engaged with what was going on. He greeted the two with smiles and a good handshake. Asking how they were getting on. Pleasantries made, Mitchell relaxed a bit, it was The Brigadier that kicked off the meeting.

'Men, thank you for being here. I can only guess how many questions you might have. Can I assume you've both got somewhere to live, have had time to make it as comfortable as possible and have done any preparation you feel you might need?'

Both nodded.

'Good. And I trust that for this last week, you've been playing by the rules? No comms in any way to anyone? No smartphones, no internet, no documentation linking you to anyone or proving you are in the Military?'

Again, both nodded and gave a quiet 'Yes Sir'

'OK, Mitchell, they're all yours.'

'Thank you, Brigadier. OK, so let's get straight to it. Because as brief as this might sound, time is now not our friend'.

Both men were fixated on Mitchell. He actually felt uncomfortable with them staring at him the way they were.

'The signal that GCHQ picked up on, the one I told you about. It's been confirmed that it was a Russian field agent. The interesting part was that the communication came from London and went to Moscow. I'm certain it was destined for the Kremlin. Ordinarily, communication of this type comes from Command to the Agent by way of Orders. It's not a conversation. It's Direction. Espionage is not a 2-way street. Agents act upon what detail they are given. They are not there to question or retort. Radio communication, a dead letterbox, a coded message in the daily paper. It's all the same thing. So, communication going from the Agent to Command is interesting.'

'And it means? 'Asked Jim. One of them had to.

'Well, that I can't confirm. But I can make a pretty good guess. And this is where it gets interesting for you two. I think I eluded it before, that it didn't seem right the explosion on the line and Compton's death were so far apart. They almost had no impact whatsoever. Not on the scale that was intended. It does lean to the idea that there is only one Agent. BUT - for whatever reason, something didn't work out. He should have been more on the ball. My initial thought was the communication going from London to Moscow was him explaining himself. But that goes against protocol. It goes against training and orders and processes. What our guy in Moscow has said is there is a buzz around the Embassy. Something is happening. He thinks it's a mobilisation. I now think more are coming to support the Agent here.'

'Because he's fucked it, somehow? 'Offered Mills.

'Quite. He could be injured. That would sit well. Maybe he realised to get the impact they want, things need to be timed better. So, an act of sabotage and an assassination attempt happening at exactly the same time? It wouldn't surprise me. Not now.'

'How many then? 'Asked Jim.

'I don't know. But I'm expecting to have that confirmed within a few days.'

'OK, all this is great, but how are we going to find out where we need to be to stop them?'

'Fair question. Orders still have to come via the Kremlin to the Agent.'

'Agents. 'Said Mills.

'Yes, Agents. The good thing is, GCHQ now has the frequency of their radio transmissions and are listening out for it 24/7. We will be able to intercept the frequency and decrypt the message.'

'Isn't the point of encryption that things like that can't happen? Otherwise, all comms will be useless?'

'Well, to be honest, all encryptions can be decrypted. It stands to reason, no? What keeps messages safe is a process. Changing the encryption daily, for example. Not giving anyone time to decrypt it, before the information in that message is old news. Or only using correctly controlled environments to keep information secure once the message has been delivered. Like a Tempest-secure room like this. You follow me?'

'To a point 'said Jim, 'Kinda heard that before, but not really thought about it. But you're saying you can decrypt messages if they're out in the open?'

'Well, not me. GCHQ. Yes. So as soon as they pick up on the signal, every resource will be allocated to decrypting the message and let you know who or what the targets are.'

'Pardon me for saying, but it sounds a bit thin? 'Said Mills.

Mitchell paused. Maybe for effect. Maybe it was what he learned in training. Maybe it was his solemn belief.

'The espionage game is as thin as tracing paper, Mills. We work on threads of information and rely on professional judgement and gut feeling to make a plausible theory that we can act upon.'

'I understand. I wasn't trying to be a nob about it.'

'It's fine. But these are the stakes we are dealing with. No one wants to lose, do they?'

'And so, you decipher the information, feed it to us via the old school way you do, and we decide how we deal with it?'

'Absolutely that.'

'And you think it'll be what we need? The targets and locations?'

'I'm certain of it. You must remember; this is still being orchestrated by Moscow. They still give orders. Every radio transmission is exact information. It always has been, so why not now? I do believe when we pick up on the next signal, and we can decipher it in time, we will know who and what is being targeted'.

The rest of the meeting was mostly Jim and Mills trying to understand moot points. And often the Brigadier would move the conversation on. Detail is always important. But not at the expense of focus. The bigger picture is always more complex than we care to admit. Going down a rabbit hole over 'what if ' is only going to distract you from the 'what is. 'And the 'what is ' for Jim and Mills, was that they were being delivered to a scenario where all they had to do was kill the enemy. That's what they do. The background to how it's known where the enemy is, what support is in place, the collateral damage, all of it, was not their concern.

Individually the men handed their addresses and spare keys in sealed envelopes to Phillips and got the location of their first letterbox from Mitchell. The walk back to their cars was a sombre one.

Back at the cars, there was no pep-talk between them. No more chuntering over lack of information or questioning the bigger picture. Both had been around long enough to know that as bizarre as all this may seem, it was reality. They parted company by giving each other the unofficial SF mantra of 'Happy Hunting'.

And with that, they left Regent Park Barracks.

CHAPTER 8

The plane landed early hours on Sunday morning. The red-eye flight. Though only four hours from Cyprus, the agents had been on a long journey well before they boarded at Larnaca. Sat in the middle of the Mediterranean Sea, surrounded on 3 sides by Europe, The Middle East and Africa, Cyprus has always been an international hub. A Spy's wet dream. You can walk the streets and pass Agents from twenty different countries, and no one bothered one another. A safe place. And a forward mounting base for those with an onward journey and agenda.

Carrying only a daysack on one shoulder, Serg had been mobilised from Ukraine. He had been dormant for 2 weeks. Ordered by radio transmission to keep out of sight after a successful assassination of a Ukrainian Police Commissioner.

Dima was on an assignment in Islamabad, Pakistan when he was ordered to drop everything and go to the UK. Fucked-off that nine months of hard work had gone to waste, he decided to have himself a good drink before he left. After all, he'd been to the UK before. There was no way he was going to drink their warm Ale.

Noticing each other instantly at Larnaca, they ignored each other and made sure they boarded as spaced out as possible. After Cyprus, 4 am in London was a cold and miserable place to be.

Mitchell got the call from GCHQ on the secure phone he kept in his bedroom. It rang and after scripted pleasantries, Mitchell produced his encryption key and on the count of three, turned it. There was a crackle and a pause, and then the same voice spoke again.

'It's come through.'

'Are you sure?'

'Absolutely. We will start to decrypt it now. It's going to take time.'

'How long?'

'We've never tried this one before. A few days?'

'Could be too long.'

'Well, unless you want to try yourself, I guess you had best let us get on with it and we will call you when it's done?'

'Yeah, call the office, I'll be there.'

Mitchell hung up and took out the encryption key. 'It's started. 'Mitchells only real concern was that it'll take too long to decrypt the signal and they will miss the chance to stop whatever is being planned. He got dressed and headed to the city.

Jim and Mills were waiting. They had been waiting for over a week now all-in. But this weekend was painful. Not knowing anything. No contact with friends or family. Boredom is a killer in its own right. Both kept themselves busy with exercise, packing their kit and wanking. Pissed off, both were looking forward to their first letterboxes on Monday. A snippet of intelligence to act upon. Or direct targets to protect. Both were hungry for some action. They had moved to another place in their heads. Now, duty had kicked in. They wanted to fight. They wanted to perform. They wanted to get this shit over and done with.

In the office, Mitchell paced in front of the secure Diplomatic phone. He wanted to call his link in Moscow. But was not sure if what he was about to ask for, was an ask too far.

He picked up the receiver, paused, and then pressed the pre-set button for Moscow. It answered after only one ring.

'Quicker than I thought you'd be if I'm honest. 'Came the voice at the other end.

'I was never a good sleeper. 'Mitchell offered back by way of trying to keep it light.

'GCHQ got a transmission?'

'Yes. And look, I need to ask you something. Could you maybe get the crypto ID for me, so I can give it to them?'

'One step ahead of you mate. I have it and I have a transmission to another agent, on the same crypto within the last 12 hours. Fully decoded for you. The mission is nothing for you to worry about, it's something to do with Taiwan. But the point is, it's fully decoded. And GCHQ will be able to decipher your transmission instantly.'

Mitchell was nearly lost for words.

'My God, how? I mean, Thank you…'

'It won't happen again, OK? But time is of the essence, as they say. I can confirm there are two agents mobilised. If this signal gives the targets, then you've got what you need, right?'

'Absolutely. Thank you again.'

'It's fine, but I need to lay low for a bit now. Be squeaky clean. Write this down.'

He said four words that represented letters, followed by '544 689 309'

Mitchell knew them as Russian letters. He thanked his contact, and then the phone went dead.

Mitchell put the receiver down. He needed to call GCHQ back. But that was on a different line, with different encryption. He walked to another room. Adrenaline pumped through his body. This was real. He got the encryption key ready for when he needed it, picked up the receiver and made a call.

Vladislav's back was still in agony. Red-raw from where blistered skin had died and fallen away. But for today at least, he had a new focus. When he opened his laptop and downloaded the message that was on the radio, he was euphoric in delight. Two of his comrades were coming to support him - though he did not actually know who they were, he didn't care. They were all on the same side. The targets were set. And it was happening Tuesday night. Thirty-six hours from now, the wrongs will be righted. The message will be sent to the world. Vladislav will be back!

Vladislav checked the incoming flights. He didn't know what

one they would be on but knew it would be from either Cyprus or Dubai. Both had departures within the last few hours. They will be arriving soon. He started to tidy the place up.

A short while later, there was a knock at the door. He checked the CCTV camera he had focussed on the doorstep, and sure enough, there were two men. His men. He rushed to open it to them.

Both looked tired. Vladislav offered coffee, but both refused. They needed sleep. It was agreed that they would wash and sleep, while Vladislav called upon his contacts to get them what they needed for their respective missions. Their brief was that evening. Which gave them time to prepare. Vladislav had already decided who was to get what mission. Dima will be tasked with rendering a new 'Green energy 'Power Station in North London unviable. And Serg's target: The Secretary of State for Environment. For the two Agents, this was nothing special. A task was a task. But for Vladislav, this was momentous. He left them to it. Trying to look as uninhibited as he could due to his injuries, headed out for operational supplies.

CHAPTER 9

With the crypto ID and the already deciphered message, it took GCHQ minutes to match the coding to the transmission to London. They had it. The direct orders from Moscow to the London agent, now agents. Mitchell didn't know if he was impressed or enraged when he read the message. It gave a date, an address and a title. The date was for two days 'time. Tuesday. 'Thank God we got the deciphered message.'

In all the frantic excitement, Mitchell had nearly forgotten all about the letterboxes. They had to be deployed before Monday morning. The lads will be expecting to collect them any time after 0800. Lots to do. Mitchell had told each of them in private where their letterbox will be and what it will look like. He also gave them a brief on what the message will look like inside. He generated two messages. One for Jim and one for Mills. Giving the day and the target. That was it. He had nothing else to go on. He added the date and time for the next letterbox, but that was all. But for Mitchell, it was all solid intelligence, and it proved his theory. He needed the messages out. Late on Sunday night, Mitchell got in his car and set off to deploy the dead letterboxes.

Jim made his way to Maida Vale early Monday morning. He drove to the area, parked up and put two hours of parking on his car. He found a smart looking cafe overlooking the canal. He had poached eggs on toast for breakfast, and two cups of tea. All paid for in cash. He walked to Maida Vale underground station and stopped to buy a paper from the kiosk. As the kiosk clerk was getting Jim's change which, he gave a tut at having to do, because Jim had paid for a newspaper with a ten-pound note, Jim ran his fingers on the underside of the Kiosk serving ledge. Sure enough, there was a one-pound coin, stuck to the underside. Just like he was told there would be in his brief. Jim prised it off and smiled as he took his change from the kiosk clerk. In broad daylight, in front of half a dozen people, Jim had just got his first message from MI5. He was used to being hidden in plain sight, but this was a new level. He smiled at himself as he made his way into the underground station. He was going one-stop, getting off and walking back to his car.

Mills made his way to the Oval cricket ground. Situated on a main road in South London, it was quite an overpowering sight in the local area. He needed to make his way round to the service area and locate a security Portacabin. His message was going to be in a pound coin, stuck to the underside of a bench, opposite the cabin. Mills got himself a Coffee when he got to the area and walked along the road, with the Oval on his right. Before long, he spotted a side road that led him to the back of the cricket ground. Sure enough, there was a service area that had bins and recycling. There was a barrier that let in service vehicles and next to the barrier was a security Portacabin. Across the road, was a bench. Mills walked over and took a seat. He did think at first, he was being tested, having to find his note in front of a security post. But as it went, the hatch of the cabin faced away from the road, and therefore the bench on the far side of the road that Mills was sitting on. No one else was around there. And so, when he was comfortable to do so, he reached under the bench to locate the pound coin. With a bit of pressure from his thumbnail, it came away. He finished his coffee, got up and disappeared from the area.

CHAPTER 10

The best way to get to the message inside was to use a razor blade and gently press it against the side of the coin. Once open, the paper was so thin it was translucent. On one side was a typed message. The men read theirs through a magnifying lens. Information was limited but exact. Jim's message was a Grid Reference and a date. Mills got a name and a date. The dates were for the next day. Time was now against them.

Though most of the equipment had been checked and rechecked, both men started their final battle preparation. Completely in the zone. This was how they earned a living. Weapons were re-oiled, and magazines checked for serviceability. Body armour laid out. Jim checked the Grid Reference against a London road atlas. It was in North London.

Mills was given a name. A Politician, he thought. But he wasn't sure who. He didn't pay that much attention to most Politics. He knew who the PM was, the Defence Minister and the Home Secretary. The rest didn't come up on his radar. He headed to an internet cafe to do some homework.

Jim got to the area Tuesday morning. The target, for all he understood, was a Power Station. A new one. A biofuel Power Station. He circled it in his car the best he could, examining any entrance points. The problem was, it was a Power Station - more secure than any prison you'd find. 'How the fuck are they planning to do this? 'He parked up, and with his satchel of ammunition and grenades slung over his shoulder, went on foot to find one guy in the whole city.

Mills was right, the target was a Politician. The Secretary of State for Environment: Annabelle Thornton. A progressive politician who was pioneering in her approach to tackling Climate Change. She was giving a speech as part of a conference at the ExCeL centre that Tuesday evening.

Dima knew his job. And he was good at it. At state college, he studied Industrial Electronics and mastered in engineering. Not just a saboteur, he was employed by the Government to design and oversee the building of domestic electricity networks to hard to reach villages. Like Britain's National Grid system, but on a Soviet scale. He was recruited by The Kremlin when he was invited there to be decorated for his efforts.

Dima already had his plan in his head, but after a bit of research on the internet, he knew exactly how to make the power station unviable. 'Legkiy. 'He thought: Easy.

Despite his years of service, Serg had never been to the UK before. Not that it phased him, but he did need to understand where he needed to go, how to get there and his escape routes. Politicians have protection, so that had to be considered. Despite Vladislav being very supportive and supplying all he could for the Agents, he could not get hold of a sniper rifle. So, a long-range hit was out of the question. This was going to be a close-up assassination. Not a problem, but the more you know about your target and the situation before you go to work, the better. Vladislav got Serg an Underground day pass and some half-smart looking clothes. Serg wanted to look like he belonged at a function when he was in the ExCeL centre. There were several different conferences going on, and between Vladislav and Serg, they agreed he should be attending one about Sustainability in the City. Various White-Collar companies were meeting to openly discuss the most cost-effective way to reduce their CO_2 emissions. A great strategic move, seeing-as The Secretary of State for Environment was in the same building giving a speech about the same subject to Government suppliers that very same day. What these companies wanted to do was facilitate their CEO's a chance to mix with Annabelle Thornton's office and pick up a couple of Government contracts themselves.

Serg got to the ExCeL centre early in the afternoon. He had a fair bit of reconnaissance work to do. He had no problem with being there for so long. There were so many people about, he'd not be singled out by security officers. He didn't mind the idea of CCTV seeing him either, that was nothing new. By the time all the chaos was over, and the Police started looking on CCTV, he would be out of the country and on another task.

Serg walked the length of the huge open hallways of the conference centre, looking at the places to eat and the title of the conference that was taking place behind each set of doors. He smiled at those who smiled at him, as they passed each other in close proximity. He got a coffee from a coffee kiosk. His English accent was better than that of the Portuguese guy behind the counter. He continued to walk.

He finally came to what he was after. Sectioned off, and with a fat security guard sitting on a chair to one side, was a set of double doors that led to a conference room. Same as all the others. But this set of doors had a small information stand in front of it. And on that information stand Serg could see, just, the crest of the British Government. To the untrained eye, it would mean nothing. Maybe not even noticed at all. But Serg did not have an untrained eye. And though this was his first assignment on UK soil, he had dealt with British Ambassadors and their staff many times before. He knew exactly what he saw. Plans started to build in his head. Access in and out, security, location of the hit. He needed to see entrance routes to the back of that conference room. There was no way a Politician was going to walk the route he just walked to get to the conference and onto the stage. Serg threw his coffee cup into the general waste bin instead of the recycling bin as he walked out the glass doors and to the outside public areas. He was on the lookout for service roads. He soon found them and pacing out the distance, he casually strolled past the back of the hall he was after. He took it all in - the doors, the access routes, steps, blind spots. He carried on walking, not pausing at all. If he was caught walking down the service roads, he could say he was lost. If he was caught eyeballing private entrances to conference halls, it would be a different conversation.

Jim was already pissed off with the whole situation long before he got out of his car. It started when he got told to come to London the other Thursday. Then being given the vaguest brief about some Cold War scenario, then having to tell his wife he was off, again though, in reality, he was less than an hours drive away from home. He was pissed off at having to live like a tramp in a shitty flat. He was pissed off at the fact some Russian Agent was about to try and ruin everyone's day. But mostly, he was pissed off that he had no idea who the guy was or what he looked like and here was Jim-Bastard-Davidson, walking the streets of London searching for him.

As he got out of his car, Jim put his bag on the ground briefly and used that as cover to place a strip of sticky tape across his door and onto the body of the car. Low enough not to be seen if you were trying to manipulate the lock and break into the car. But Jim would know that someone had if the tape had been pulled away from the body. It wasn't much, but it was a little bit of comfort to know he was doing something to secure his vehicle.

Jim walked and walked. He had nothing better to do. He was waiting. Watching. Profiling and looking for any hint that someone amongst the hundreds in his immediate area was the guy he wanted. He 'petaled 'in and out of the power plant. He would walk towards it from one direction, walk along next to it for a short while, scanning for any sign he could, and then walk away from it. He would then walk two streets down and then walk towards the power station again, so he could search a new area of the perimeter wall without spending too much time on target. If this was a farm building in Northern Ireland, Jim would use this method - moving in and out of the natural cover - until he had completed a full 360 of the building. If the building was the centre of the flower, then his movements would draw the outline of the petals. Hence the name. The intent was to not be noticed by the security guy on the main gate. It wasn't an easy task at all, and roads are never perfectly straight, so he had to use a bit of best judgement to get himself back on track once or twice. Always using whatever cover that was available, he went into several shops to buy drinks or snacks. He had to have a reason to be in the area. A reason to be close. He was watching everyone. Everyone was a possible Russian agent. At one point, he was walking along the West wall of the plant, looking for access points when he came across a timeline of the construction of the plant. Clearly a bit of a PR spin by the energy company. It showed the site under construction and timelines for key milestones. It showed children smiling with the engineers, wearing their site PPE for a photo. It showed the local wildlife and stated how many natural resources the energy company has saved by being biofuel and not a fossil fuel. It was all there, for any passer-by to read. It did nothing for Jim. It didn't tell him who was going to try and blow it up at some point later that day.

Jim continued to patrol the area. He moved away from the power station again. He didn't want to be the guy that got mistaken for being the baddie. He walked down a street and turned left, with every intention of turning left again, to make his way back towards the power station for another pass. He did wonder where Phillips and his team were. They couldn't have been too close, Jim would have spotted them by now. Jim was about to go into another shop, to buy another snack when a mum walked out of the shop with a kid in tow. The child was crying. In his hands was a toy. A broken one by the looks of it. The mother clearly had enough of her sons crying, snapped at him as they got out to the street.

'Will you stop. It's not my fault you broke your favourite truck.'

The boy gave a shout 'It's not a truck, it's a Transformer!'

Jim looked at the toy. It was a Transformer. Optimus Prime. Jim had something similar when he was a kid. Because of the films, Transformers were big business again.

Jim froze. The blood ran out his face. Transformer?

Jim took off back along the route he came down. Holding on to his satchel of ammunition, he angled as he took the corner of the road that led him back to the power station. He ran across the street with no care given to the cars that had to brake and swerve to miss him. He got back to the timeline images. He scanned. There it was - a National Grid substation. Were they transformers? He didn't know and he didn't care. All he knew now was he was right, he just knew it. Blowing up a power station was ludicrous. But to disrupt the electricity getting to hundreds if not thousands of homes and businesses would be massive news. The Russian won't be at the station, he will be there. Stoke Mandeville Road. That's where the substation is. But where the Hell is that? Jim raced to his car. He opened the door without checking the tape. No threat of a Russian agent tampering with his car if there was no Russian agent in the area! He got out his London road atlas and used the index to find Stoke Mandeville Road. He thumbed the map and the route to help memorise it. It was only two miles away. Another reason to be pissed off. Wrong location. Granted it was the information given, but it was wrong. And not having a smartphone for maps and finding shit out, was another reason to be pissed off. But Jim couldn't dwell on that now. He slammed his car into gear and was off.

CHAPTER 11

Dima always had the substation in mind. They were textbook targets. One well-placed device could take out half a city or an entire region. If the message gave an exact grid reference and that was of a power station, then the intelligence unit was wrong. They didn't understand what a field guy had to do. Vladislav and Dima agreed instantly on moving the target to a substation. Vladislav facilitated by getting a car and a weapon for Dima. Along with makings for an incendiary device.

Dima arrived in the area around midday. He cruised the streets for a while, surveying the area. There was normal traffic on the road and pedestrians walking the streets. He drove past the entrance to the substation. It was relatively understated, with a metal gate and a sign saying it was the property of The National Grid and trespassers would be prosecuted. There was a single CCTV camera watching the entrance. The perimeter fence was five meters high with razor wire across the top.

About fifty meters past the front gate, Dima found a place to park. Facing away from the substation, so he could get in the car and drive straight off after he'd completed his mission. He got out of his car and headed towards the substation. He couldn't just walk right up to a Utility asset like a substation and waltz through the front door. He had some work to do first. Dima was focused on his task ahead - thinking about the CCTV camera, thinking about the bolt on the front gate. Thinking about making his way to the back of the facility to leave his device, making sure it had a full impact when it detonated. Lots to consider, lots to focus on. Even more so, seeing as the attack had to happen today. 'Segodnya dnem, 'Vladislav told him: Today, during the day. Clearly, there was a message to be made, but Dima was not told exactly what it was. His orders from Moscow didn't tell him. Nothing new there. But Vladislav didn't mention the politics of this mission either. Which Dima did think was a bit off. Dima was focused on the substation. He only looked in the direction of the substation. Not interested in anyone or anything else, he had no way of noticing a dark blue Passat passing the junction at the far end of the road.

The timing was going to be critical for Dima. He needed a first pass of the gate to look like just anyone was walking by. But he needed to be close to the gate. Close enough to touch it. Eyeballing everyone coming towards him, he spotted an old lady on a mobility scooter. Going at a pace only just quicker than someone on foot. She was closer to the gate than he was. He picked up his cadence and got a glass container out of his pocket. As he got closer to the substation, he held the glass container in his left fist. It had the circumference of a small energy drink but half as long, so it fitted perfectly in his fist. Using his thumb, he prized off the glass lid, which was only held on by very thin welding, so the lid popped off with relative ease. He made a point of moving to the inside of the pavement, next to the substation and making eye contact with the lady so she knew his intent. He even managed a small smile. The kind of smile people give when they have that awkward moment on the street where they're accommodating each other so they can pass without contact. As they did pass, Dima turned side on and gave a gesture with his right hand, opening up the way for the lady to scoot past. With his back to the gate, and the bulk of his torso shielding the view from the CCTV camera, Dima poured the contents - acid onto the top of the padlock on the gate. Plenty fell off onto the gate below and the floor, but enough hit the arm of the padlock and went into the workings of it. Dima walked on. Though there was a small amount of smell, no one would notice it on the streets next to car exhausts. And the faint smoke-like residue that came off the lock as the acid corroded away at it was too faint to be picked up by the CCTV.

Pass one complete. Dima walked to the end of the road and turned left. He continued on that course, turning left at each junction. He was making his way round to the front again, for pass number two. He had already spotted an area to get changed when he was cruising the streets in his car. When he got there, he did a cursory glance behind him and then got his bag off his shoulder. Still walking, he got a Hi-Vis jacket out of his bag, which was stuffed next to the device. He put the jacket on and slowed his pace down. In his mind he saw an engineer walking to the site, not very impressed that he got a call out. So, marching along wouldn't fit the look. He relaxed into his charade. He needed to give the acid time to work, anyway.

In the left pocket of his jacket was a pair of rubber gloves. The type you'd see a labourer wearing on a building site. And in his right pocket was a pair of hand-sized ratchet cutters. As he turned the last corner, he put on the gloves. Making sure no one was walking in the opposite direction, as he got close to the gate, he took out the cutters. He slowed to an almost crawl as he got into view of the CCTV and whilst keeping his back to it as much as possible, to give himself as much cover as possible, used the cutters on the weakest looking part of the padlock arm. It took three hard squeezes of the cutters to get through it. Each squeeze was held in place with the ratchet system and though it was a hard effort on his hands, to get through the lock took maybe a second and a half. Cutters back in his pocket, Dima casually opened the gate and stepped inside. Making sure his shoes didn't touch the acid on the floor. Gate open, Dima inside, gate closed. Six seconds.

City substations are larger than you may think. Banks and banks of towers and thick industrial cables that hummed with energy, which led off to pylons that transported the electricity to houses and businesses. And in the centre, was the transformer. In this case, the size of a small outbuilding. Dima had seen bigger, much bigger. In Russia where they need to service the remote towns, they are huge. But this isn't Russia. And there are restrictions in urban areas. The humming was almost deafening this close-up. But that was fine. Dima knew what sounded right and what did not. A car passing on the street sounded OK. An acceptable secondary sound. He wasn't expecting to hear much else. So, when he heard the faint sound of someone running, he took note.

Jim was thoroughly pissed off. He didn't like being on his back foot at all. He didn't know enough about what was going on in his own mission. He was now taking plastic toys as a lead. 'The espionage game is as thin as tracing paper.' He tried to comfort himself with Mitchell's words.

He drove down the street, looking out for Stoke Mandeville Road. Eyeballing where the road names might be - on a street sign at ground level, or high on the side of a building.

Stoke Mandeville Road had a street-level sign. As he passed the road, he clocked the sign and confirmed that's where he needed to be. He passed it, to have a look down the road before he went wading in half-cocked. As he looked down the road, he didn't see anything untoward. A couple of pedestrians. He carried on driving. He needed somewhere to park. He scanned for a space to throw his car in. He was watching everyone and everything. Nerve endings on high alert. Eyes on fire, watching, profiling. A group of lads leaning against a wall, smoking something they probably shouldn't be smoking out in public. A pensioner on a mobility scooter. Mums with prams. A site worker. A young lady walking a stupid-looking dog. Jim parked up.

'This could go on all day. 'He thought to himself.

He needed to get to the substation but didn't want to make it too obvious. He needed cover. His brief look down the road didn't fill him with hope. There was no cafe, there was no shop, there was no postbox. No reason to be walking towards the substation. Unless you were working there.

Jim's eyes widened. A site worker? He turned in his seat to look down the road behind him. Gone. He turned back and looked ahead. If a guy was working at the substation, they'd drive up to it? Or, if they have to park up and walk in, there would be a van? No van. 'Fuck.' Jim got out of his car, ammo satchel over his shoulder. He instinctively tapped the handle of his Sig in its holster as he crossed the road to the side nearer the substation. He then took off, running towards Stoke Mandeville Road.

He got to the gate and saw the padlock had been cut. And it was still corroding. The gate itself underneath the lock was also corroding. Jim took his pistol out and used the end of it to push the padlock out the gate lock and onto the floor. He pushed the gate open enough to step inside. Pistol raised and finger on the trigger. The hum of electricity was annoying. He had no idea who he was up against. He had no idea where to start looking. So, he kept his back to the perimeter the best he could and faced inwards. He stepped gently on the loose stony ground.

Dima had not had time to leave the device at the transformer in the centre of the substation. When he heard someone running towards the substation, he backed against the perimeter and tucked in behind a junction unit. His bag was on the floor. He was hoping the running would go straight past the front gate. But it didn't. It stopped. There was a clatter at the gate and the gate opened. This much he knew. What he didn't know was who he was dealing with. A security guard that had got mobilised from the CCTV security company. Young lad, keen to impress? Most probably. So, unarmed. This was good. Dima didn't want to be shooting anyone if he didn't have to. That would change his plans altogether. He wanted to be back on a plane and out of the UK that evening. He heard a faint footstep coming his way. Dima decided he would knock the guy out and carry on with the mission. Once the guy was knocked out, Dima needed 30 seconds to get to the transformer and place the bag. Another 30 seconds to set the primary charge. And he would then have 2 minutes to get out of the area before the device went off. If the guy woke up at that time, he could get out of the area too. He wouldn't stay after being jumped. If he stayed, it's unlikely he would die. The device wasn't a fragmentation bomb. It was just high amounts of explosives with a copper slug that once detonated, would shoot up into the underside of the transformer. If the guy was still inside the compound, he would get a massive shock and have his eardrums burst, but that would be it. If he tried to be a hero and deal with the device himself, then that would be on him.

Jim moved along the perimeter. He came to a junction unit. About 2 meters by 2 meters and maybe 3 meters high. He stepped forward to move around it. Keeping his weapon raised.

There's a brief pause in time that comes before a threat to life. If you think about it, the moment passes without you having a chance to act upon it. You must rely on your primal instinct. It even comes before adrenaline kicks in, and the 'fight or flight ' choice is made. For a split second, all sound leaves the air. Everything becomes super-real. Like you're the only living soul around and everything else is on TV. Jim felt it. His prehistoric being came to the forefront and he knew he was in danger. Training took over. Movements and responses he had drilled and drilled and drilled over the years. He turned to the left and started to drop to one knee. His instinct was right. His drill was wrong.

From around the corner, came a thumping roundhouse kick. Clearly aimed for his ribs, to wind him. But as he was already dropping to one knee, the boot caught him on the shoulder. The force sent his arm inwards and the momentum of the kick sent Jim crashing into the junction unit. His arm momentarily lost all feeling and his pistol fell to the floor.

Dima came square on to Jim. He raged at the sight of someone with a weapon. This was not a dog-shit security guard. This was someone after him. Dima grabbed Jim by the head and jaw and dragged him into the open. He dropped Jim down and pulled his satchel off his shoulder and discarded it. Jim started to get to his feet. Dima gave a hard right-hand punch to the top of Jim's head. Stars exploded in Jim's eyes. He dropped back down to his knees. Stones dug into his kneecaps, making him buckle further. Dima lined himself up for a boot to the ribs. As he kicked Jim, Jim braced his torso to absorb as much as he could and grabbed on to Dima's leg. It was a hard kick, so Jim did move along the ground, but holding on to Dima's leg meant the leg went with him, throwing Dima off balance. Jim kept his left arm wrapped around Dima's ankle and put his right hand on the outside of Dima's knee. Jim pressed as hard as he could, and the knee buckled inwards. Dima's body weight came down on top of Jim. As Dima came down, his fists came out. Hard heavy punches were directed at Jim's head and face. Some Jim had to absorb; most he was deflecting. Jim was a ground fighter. What Jim needed to do was manoeuvre himself into a position he could start doing some damage to Dima. Right now, he was under a lump of a guy who was throwing everything at him whilst Jim himself was laying on sharp stones. Another reason to be pissed off. The trick is to never stop moving. Jim was targeting Dima's elbows. If Dima was throwing a punch with his right hand, Jim would use his left hand to reach out and get Dima's elbow and push it to one side. This would mean Dima would miss his target, throw him off balance and waste his energy. Then Jim needed to find the leverage to get out from underneath. That moment came when Dima decided shooting inside a substation was a good idea after all. Dima leaned back and drew his pistol. He held it in his left hand and pointed it at Jim's head. Jim reached up and grabbed the back of the weapon and Dima's hand. Jim had got his finger wrapped around the hammer. No matter how hard Dima squeezed the trigger, if that hammer could not go back, Jim was not getting shot. To ensure his grip on the hammer was as tight as possible, Jim went against every human instinct. He started to pull the pistol towards him. As the pistol got closer to Jim's face, his grip got stronger, and Dima's got weaker. Jim then let rip the hardest left hook he could and planted it on Dima's left bicep. The impact and the dead arm knocked Dima's hand off the pistol and the pistol itself went flying over near the humming electricity cables. With Dima's body opened up and his left arm temporarily out of action, Jim put a right hook into his ribs and then pushed him off to one side. Both men were on the ground. They squared up like wild animals. Dima launched first, going high with a fist. Jim stayed low and shot his whole body into Dima. The pair went over into another grapple. Only this time Jim was on top. Fists were planted into eye sockets and Jim then tried to end the mess by targeting Dima's throat. But he underestimated his opponent. Dima started to punch back. He reached to one side and found a stone to use as a weapon. He crashed it into Jim's face. Jim lost the advantage again. Both men got to their feet. Both trying to eye up the closest weapon. Both squared up to the other. Both not wanting to lose the psychological edge. Both wondering who the fuck was in front of them. The only thing they both knew right now, was that one of them was going to die.

Dima advanced first. He had re-composed himself and he came at Jim, fists high looking for a fight. Jim shuffled around as he ducked what blows he could and absorbed what he had to. As they closed in again, knees came up and overhand punches became hooks and uppercuts. Jobs, Politics and Nationalities no longer mattered. This was now a street fight. Dirty and nasty in any language.

As they moved around, they got closer to the plant equipment. The hum of wires got uncomfortably loud.

The towers that held the cables all sat on concrete sleeper platforms. About six inches thick. Jim caught his ankle on one as he was evading another of Dima's iron fists. Jim needed to work an option to get back on the ground. No fight is won by trading punches. Your hands are just not made for it. It's different when you're boxing, and your fists are wrapped. But punching a skull with bare knuckles needs to be left in the 1800s.

Jim waited for a low punch. As it came, he caught Dima's arm between his own arm and his torso. Jim turned and pulled Dima closer to him. Jim got his right arm around Dima's neck and tried to pull him to the ground. By now, Dima had sized up his opponent and he slipped the neck hold. As he stepped back, he produced a knife. Jim didn't even see where from. It was a big knife as well. Dima waved it in front of Jim. Panting, gasping for air, Jim eyeballed the knife. The second knife he had pulled on him in a matter of days. Jim composed himself, gave Dima an ever so slight nod of acknowledgement and put his right hand inside his trouser pocket. Jim had cut the pocket lining out. Strapped to Jim's thigh, was a blade of his own. Jim grabbed the handle and produced his own weapon. Though not as big as Dima's knife, Jim had produced a dagger. The Commando's fighting knife. Dima for the first time realised exactly who he was dealing with. It took this to win the psychological edge. Jim had no intention of taking a cut anywhere. He'd been cut before and it's a scarier wound than a bullet. Which he'd also taken before. Jim was littered with scar tissue.

Dima came in fast. Lunging straight at Jim's torso with the point of his blade. Jim held his nerve. For the first time, Jim noticed his opponent was left-handed. His left hand was holding the knife and he had lunged left foot forward. Jim stepped in, leading with the right. He dropped, letting Dima's knife go over his right shoulder. Jim went low and thrust his dagger through the side of Dima's calf muscle. Dima screamed in pain and dropped his knife. Again, Dima collapsed on top of Jim, punching out of rage and desperation. The fight wasn't over. Jim muscled Dima over to a concrete platform and the two exchanged more punches. Jim was exhausted. Again, where he could, he would lever Dima's arms out the way, so he missed and used up more energy. Finally, Jim got both hands on the sides of Dima's head. He pulled his head up and smashed it onto the concrete. Dima took another swing. Jim squeezed Dima's head again in his grip and pulled it higher, so Dima's shoulders came off the platform. Jim smashed the skull down on the concrete. Dima's body movements slowed. 'One more. 'Jim pulled his opponents head up as high as he could muster and putting his whole body weight into it, smashed Dima's head onto the concrete. The skull cracked. It was a sickening sound. It gave a hollow echo and Jim felt the back of the skull move as bits of bone caved inwards. Dark blood poured onto the platform. Jim collapsed on top of his opponent, panting for all he was worth. He sat up and pulled in some big breaths to try and compose himself. He got off the body. Jim stood on the ground. With the body on the concrete platform, he was easier to inspect. Jim had a quick pat-down of pockets, to see if there was any intelligence he could gather for Mitchell. There wasn't. He took his knife back, pulling it out of the calf and wiping it on Dima's trousers before stowing it away. Jim took stock of his own wounds. He looked at the corpse for a moment, before going to collect his satchel. He walked in pain and with a limp back to the body. He opened his bag and rummaged through. He produced a strip of blotting paper with a scale on it. He dabbed the paper into the body's blood. Not the blood from his skull, but from a wound on his body. After a few seconds, the paper gave a reading. Jim tutted and dropped the paper onto the body.

Jim tried to tidy himself up. He limped over to his weapon and put it back in the holster. Now the adrenaline was easing off, his whole body was screaming at him. He needed to go. He was wounded and he needed to administer himself. He didn't even think to look for a bomb or an incendiary device. He hoped Phillips 'team were on the ball and had worked out where the target location really was. He hoped they'd be there soon to clear this up. That was their job. He'd done his. Jim sucked up the pain and walked with as little limp as possible out the gate and back to his car.

CHAPTER 12

Mills wanted his car with him at the ExCeL Centre. He had his kit in the boot and wanted the option to get away quickly after - after whatever was going to happen. Parking was controlled and though Mills found a man-managed car park near the ExCeL, it wasn't close enough for his liking. Too far to be of real getaway use. It also took away his option of opening the boot to get more weapons and ammunition if he needed them. But it was all he could find, so went with it.

He walked from the car park, along the main public access to the West entrance of the conference centre. He scanned all the conferences going on. Mostly to do with the Environment, which made sense. He did wonder if Phillips and his team were close. He knew they wouldn't be in the centre, but if this went off in a bad way, they would want to be close.

Mills walked at a decent pace. The irony was, if Security was going to think someone was suspect, they would pick him. After a while, Mills found what he was looking for. The same conference hall Serg spotted. Mills also saw The British Government crest. He just recognised the general shape and the Lion - he wasn't an expert on these things. He used the bathroom across the hall, by way of a reason to be in the area. On his way out and back the way he came, he had one last look at the security guard on the door. 'Any chance that's him?' Mills shook off the idea. This wasn't Hollywood. The conference was due to start, and the halls were filling up with business folk. The kind of folk Mills had no time for. He needed to get in. Or, better still, work out when Annabelle Thornton will be turning up. And where she will get into the conference. Surely, she will not walk through the front door. And will she have some sort of protection? Not of the same Level as the PM. Special Branch does him. And Mills has looked after Politicians and Dignitaries overseas. The Environment Secretary was not important enough to have that level of spend put into their protection. She will have a Security company looking after her. Guys who have done five minutes in the Police or Army and fancy themselves as some hotshot bodyguard. Or worse than that, some weirdo who just did the Close Protection course because they see themselves as Ex-Army who wants to be a bodyguard....

Mills took a walk around the outside of the building. The same route that was walked by Serg only a couple of hours earlier. A vulnerable area, possibly. But she would have some level of protection. Would an assassin try their luck here? Or inside? Back inside the hall was filling even more. But this time, as well as the suits and ties, there were hippy-looking types. A generalisation - but they were younger than the others, and were clearly not there for commercial functions. Security was looking twitchy. The guards who were posted on the doors were facing inwards and looking uneasy. Talking to each other on their radios. Mills headed back towards the conference that Annabelle Thornton was due to be speaking at. As he got close, the security guard noticed Mills.

'Can I help you?'

'Not unless you know what is going on?'

'Extinction Rebellion 'The guard said, 'Despite every

conference here today being about the environment, they still want to come and protest.'

'That's weird.'

'Yeah, they say companies should be making environmental changes for the good of the planet. Not for commercial gain or to get contracts.'

'Like with the Government? 'Mills nodded into the conference hall.

'Yeah. I hope this lot gets cleared out before The Environment Secretary shows up.'

'And when is that?'

The guard changed his tone slightly.

'None of your business, mate. Unless you have a pass. And besides, I saw you walk past here before.'

'Oh, you did?'

'What does that mean?'

'Nothing. It's fine. We are on the same side mate. That's all that matters.'

'Who are you?'

Mills said nothing. He just shook his head in a way that suggested the guard drops it and looked back to the Extinction Rebellion children having their little song and dance in the main hallway.

Annabelle Thornton was briefed about the gathering, in her

car on the way to the ExCeL Centre. She gave a retort about it being healthy to let the public voice their concerns and it would be good for them to understand the Government's position. 'After all, we all want the same thing.'

She was delivered to the Service entrance round the back of the hall, with precision timing. Her car door was opened and the door to the hall was opened in perfect unison. She stepped out and made her way into the hall. She had minutes to go before she was on stage. Her security, all two of them, not including the driver, walked a pace behind her.

When she took to the stage, she was greeted with rapturous applause. Cameras were rolling, for PR purposes, not for the general public or the News. In the audience were Chief Executive Officers and Chief Finance Officers of industry companies who either had a contract with the Government or who had not got a contract but had rubbed shoulders with the right people to get a seat. All wanted to know the same thing - What are we going to have to spend, to be compliant?

Outside Mills was getting more and more pissed off at the racket going on. He was in a shit situation. He knew a hit was going to be made. But didn't know the first thing about the guy making the hit. He couldn't get into the conference hall to see what was going on. There was a little riot kicking off in the public areas, which was being fanned by agitated security guards and suit-types goading them. When he heard the applause, he knew The Environment Secretary was on stage. And still alive.

The noise from the hallway could now be heard inside Annabelle Thornton's conference hall. It was distracting. Not to her, but to the people in the audience, who turned to look at the doors, as if they were expecting it all to stop just because they gave a filthy look in that direction. However, people looking at the doors was distracting Annabelle Thornton. It frustrated her no end that whatever was going on the other side of those doors seemed to be more important than what she had to say.

Back outside, some of the Extinction Rebellion protesters had started to take things to the next level. They started preaching with megaphones about the hypocrisy of the Government and the blood on the hands of the corporations. How the World has no future because of how we are acting. How our children will suffer. How there will be no fish left in the sea. The noise went through Mills. And that's all it was to him. Noise. He couldn't work out if they were genuine or they had been planted. A distraction? Surely not?

Annabelle Thornton finished her speech and stepped off the platform. She received a standing ovation. To be expected. But she didn't care for it and did not give a friendly wave to her supporters as she marched off the stage.

She made her way to the rear exit.

'Just get the car ready. 'She ordered anyone who was listening.

Her two-man security detail raced ahead. One got the partition door for her to walk through, whilst the second ran in front to confirm the car was waiting on the other side of the exit.

Once she was through the partition door, the security officer also ran ahead, out of the now open door. Presumably to try and be in some sort of position for when The Environment Secretary exited the building to get in the car.

Annabelle Thornton had maybe twenty steps before she was out the building, in her car and away.

Hysteria feeds hysteria. The Extinction Rebellion crowds were getting more extreme in their voices and actions. The security guards were reacting to provocation, which in turn fired up the crowds even more. Mills saw the doors open to the conference hall and people starting to make their way out. A couple of Extinction Rebellion supporters tried to make their way in, only being stopped by the security guard at the last moment. That was enough for Mills. Right or wrong, as far as he was concerned, they were part of this whole farce. They were planted. They were a distraction, and they were stopping Mills from doing his job. He made his way to the door. The Extinction Rebellion pair were trying to bully the security guard. Mills came up behind them and in full sight of the security guard, punched one in the side of the neck. The attack on the man's nervous system and blood vessels set off an explosion in his head and he passed out instantaneously. Mills put a hard headbutt to the second guy's right eyebrow and he too dropped.

'Let me in. 'Mills demanded.

'I can't.'

Mills pointed to the two men on the floor.

'I said we are on the same side. Let me in, or I'm going in without your consent.'

The guard nodded and let Mills pass. There were a few stragglers in the seating area of the hall. Mills passed them without even looking at them. He was fixated on the stage and beyond. He picked up the pace. He bounded up the stage stairs and out the back. Because he had walked down the service road at the back, his bearings kept him on track. He saw a service corridor that could only lead out to the road. He upped his pace again.

When Annabelle Thornton stepped through the exit, she was expecting to be greeted by her car with the driver at the wheel, one security officer opening her door and the second roadside, scanning the area. What she got was a car, with the driver shot in the head, slumped forward on the steering wheel. A perfect round hole in the windscreen with a spider-web looking pattern round it where the glass had fragmented by the shockwave, but not shattered. There were also her two personal security officers, both lying dead. Both face up, both with a single bullet hole in their heads and pools of blood coming out the back of their skulls.

Mills got to the door and instinctively turned right. He was behind Annabelle Thornton. He slammed his left foot into the back of her right knee and with his left hand, reached across to her right shoulder. As she buckled, he pulled her to the side, pushing her towards the car. In a matter of half a second, he had replaced her body with his. He drew his pistol just as Serg came round the corner. Serg had ducked out of sight for a moment after shooting the security team. When he came back around after hearing a woman's footsteps, he was expecting a perfect execution. What he got was Mills. Serg pulled the trigger first. The round hit Mills square in the chest. Mills fell backwards and let off two rounds of his own. He missed. Serg disappeared.

The security guard from the door came through the exit.

'Keep her safe and call the police.' Ordered Mills.

The guard nodded and reached for Annabelle Thornton. Mills got to his feet, he pushed the ceramic plate off his body armour forward, trying to get some space for his ribcage to move. He grimaced at the blunt pain that was all around his ribs. He gave the body armour a thank you tap and took off after Serg. He was acutely aware that his body armour was not going to keep him alive a second time. The ceramic had shattered, as it should do when it absorbed the round from the Russian. Mills needed to be careful. He took off in the same direction as his assailant. He instinctively went low as he rounded the corners of the service area walls, with his weapon forward. He was waiting for another round to come his way. It never did. Mills was in pursuit, but he was now not sure where he was heading. The penny dropped hard - his mission was to stop the assassin. The assassin's mission was to kill the Environment Secretary. There was every chance the Russian had got back into the building and was still after her. Mills would be. Your mission is your mission. He turned right to square on to the building. He needed to get his bearings. In his mind, he was two conference halls down from the one Annabelle Thornton was in. There was a service exit, the same as the one he had run through a few minutes ago. It had an outside handle. He unloaded half a dozen rounds into it and forced the door open. No alarm sounded. He ran through the conference hall to the inside hallway, looking to make his way back to where this all started.

The alarm did sound. It sounded in the security control room. There was a 2-minute delay before it went public, giving the security team a very small window to confirm if it was a genuine incident. The shift supervisor ordered a guard to the area as he started to search on the CCTV for smoke or worse. With the chaos in the main hall still going on, he was pretty sure it was one of the protesters fucking about. He had yet to hear about the incident in the service area.

Mills ran full throttle towards the hall, missing Extinction Rebellion protesters as he passed by an inch, if that.

Inside, the guard was trying to console Annabelle Thornton, keep her safe, which right now was hiding in the back of the hall, seeing as his first assumption was the attack came from an extremist protester. He was trying to raise Control on the radio, but with everything that was going on, now including a fire alarm going off, no one seemed to be listening to him. Neither of them had any idea the Russian was in the hall.

Serg heard them and started stalking to the area, keeping a wide arc.

The security guard deployed to the area that Mills had re-entered the building, soon panicked when he saw a forced door and what looked like bullet holes in it. He called over the radio as loud as he could 'MAGPIE MAGPIE', the codeword for an incident that takes priority over every other incident or event that is going on. Control heard him, as did every other guard on the network. The shift supervisor had just seen a man running from that exact location towards the conference hall the Environment Secretary had just been in. It all started to add up. He ordered all guards to the hall.

Serg was closing into the back of the hall when he heard someone enter at the front. He ducked out of cover and watched. It was the same guy he shot at. And the fact it was him, meant he was wearing body armour. He wasn't in a black suit like the others, and he had a silenced weapon. 'Who is after me? Who knows about me? Special Branch? MI6? 'Right now, it didn't matter. Right now, Serg simply needed to kill him and kill his target.

Mills knew he was there. He was in full instinct mode. Hunter-Killer. The only thing that mattered was to return the gesture and put a 9mm round square in the chest of the Russian. He heard Annabelle Thornton breathing heavily, trying to control her emotions. 'She's still alive.' If she was at the back, to the left as Mills stood, the Russian must be lining up to shoot her. Back right. Mills unloaded two rounds in the general direction of where he would be if he was going to shoot her. Two rounds came back. Mills moved for cover. Again, two rounds and move. Rounds came back, and Mills started to second guess where the Russian would be. Not much was between them, tiers of chairs, tables, media equipment. Mills caught sight of the Russian first and tried to land a well-placed shot but missed by a fraction. Serg took that as an excuse to unload the last of his current magazine in Mills 'general direction. Tables splintered and Mills got caught by one the size of a pen in the arm. He gave a muffled shout in anger. Serg had already changed his magazine and was up, moving in for the kill across the open hall when the doors flung open. He was faced with a group of security officers. Serg turned, he needed to assess where the threat was, it took him a split second to realise none of them were carrying. He turned back to Mills, but it was too late. Mills was up, he had time to adopt a perfect shooting stance and though he had a splinter in his left shoulder, brought his weapon up and held it on aim with both hands. As Serg pivoted back to him, Mills double-tapped him in the chest. So quick in succession and so controlled, his weapon hardly moved, and the two rounds hit the Russian's torso only millimetres apart.

The security guards turned with wide eyes to Mills. For all they knew, he was the bad guy. Without speaking, Mills made his way over to the Russian. He patted him down, looking for anything to give over for intelligence. There was nothing. Eventually, one of the guards spoke.

'The Police are coming. You need to put your weapon down.'

'I don't. 'replied Mills.

'You don't want to shoot us all, do you? Put it down.'

'No. I need to go'.

'You can't. The Police are coming.'

'I know. I need to go. I can't be here.'

Annabelle Thornton and her guard came from around the corner. Clearly distressed. When she saw the Russian, she broke down again. Maybe in relief. Mills took the opportunity to work his route out without anyone trying to stop him.

'Can you tell these guys I'm not the baddie here?'

'It's true. 'Said the guard, 'This guy saved the Environment Secretary's life.'

'The guy in the car park, is he one of yours?'

'Yes.'

'Please radio him and tell him I'll be there in a few minutes, and he needs to let me out without question.'

The guard nodded. The others just stood there. No idea what was going on and was in no position to stop the guy with the gun anyway. Especially as they just witnessed his capabilities. Mills took off at pace. The whole world had just seen his face and what had happened. He felt uneasy about it. He had no idea how this day was going to go. But somehow, he didn't see it going like this. He got to the car park and ran past the guy in the security box. The barrier was already up. The guard gave a gormless look as this big guy with a wounded arm came running past. His car revved in high gears as he sped out and down the road.

CHAPTER 13

The CCTV camera on the gate of the substation was on a remote monitoring system. When Jim left, he left the gate open. After three minutes, with the gate not in its correct panel on the sensors, the alarm was triggered to a remote monitoring station. When the alarm went off, the first procedure for the guy monitoring all the remote alarms was to find out who the client was and call them. In this case, it was the National Grid's engineering subcontractor. Once it came back that they had not sent an engineer to the site recently, the alarm monitoring company dispatched a mobile security officer.

The officer got to the substation over an hour after Jim had left.

The officer was clearly moved when he saw the body. It was wounded everywhere and drained of colour. He called control and made them call the Police.

Phillips 'team were three miles out from the Power Station. Sitting. Waiting. Phillips himself was trying to work out if he was best placed near the ExCeL centre. Having two incidents to react to was bad enough. But not knowing when or exactly what he will come across was bothering him greatly. He had deployed a two-man team to the area of the ExCeL centre early in the day. And they had been reporting on the hour every hour that there was nothing to report. Phillips wasn't expecting anything yet. He knew when the Environment Secretary was going to do her talk. But nothing was rock-solid. It was only a theory that the assassination attempt was going to be there. 'Paper-thin.... '

Tuned into the local police forces 'radio, Phillips and his team of an additional three were listening to the comings and goings of the regular Bobbies on the street. Then the call came, 'IC1, deceased at the Stoke Mandeville Road substation.... ' Phillips didn't need to hear anymore. 'Thank fuck I didn't leave. ' He thought to himself. He was annoyed that he didn't realise that the Power Station was an impossible target. But how would he know any better? The grid was the intelligence given.

He got to the substation moments before a patrol car turned up. Phillips had parked across the front of the gate and got out. His team had parked across the road, and all were making their way over. When the officer in the patrol car wound down his window, Phillips flashed his badge.

'This is a Special Branch issue mate. None of your concern.'

'Sir, we got the call from the Station. I've not been told anything about Special Branch.'

'Well, now you have. Stand down, one of my team will brief your Station.'

Reluctantly, the officer did as he was told.

Inside, Phillips didn't know if he was impressed with the fact the Russian had been killed, or a bit disturbed at the sight of him. If this wasn't a mission sanctioned by MI5, the person who did this assault would be going down for a long time. He didn't know which one of the lads did it, and it didn't really matter. All that mattered was right now, they were one-up. No disruption to the power grid in North London. All Phillips had to do now was to process the body. Being a hands-on leader, he was involved in bagging the corpse. They found the incendiary device and made sure it was disabled before having it put in a container for transporting. The body and the device were to be taken to Thames House, the home of MI5.

With the immediate concerns processed, Phillips focus moved to the ExCeL centre. He left two of his team at the substation and the rest made their way to the same area as his two pre-deployed officers. There, they will wait again. And this time, he hoped they were right and therefore closer to react.

The scene at the ExCeL centre was carnage. Extinction Rebellion had whipped themselves up to such a frenzy, that they were impossible to move. The other conference halls had evacuated. The guards were trying to secure the hall with the dead body in it. There was not enough of anyone to control anything. The Police had been called. Cars and vans turned up. Phillips and his team, after waiting for the rest of the day, were relieved to be called into action.

The scene was completely different to the substation when they arrived. The idea of anonymity for the Operator was blown out of the water. There were too many people and too many cameras. Phillips got it - if the Russians, KGB, SVR or whoever could tap into any of the camera footage or maybe even the live phone feeds that was now going on, then they would see one of the lads. From that point, identifying them would be easy.

As with the substation, Phillips took ownership of the hall where the body was. The Met Police were tasked with disbursing everyone else. Inside and alone, Phillips looked at the body. Two gunshot wounds to the chest. A sniper couldn't have landed them closer. Annabelle Thornton and the guard with her needed to be debriefed. Again, that would have to be at Thames House. Phillips resisted the temptation to ask what the 'other guy' looked like. As much as he wanted to know, it would have blown his cover. Phillips was too far down the rabbit hole to ask a naive question like that. He would have to check the CCTV himself if he wanted to know the answer to that one.

Jim made his way into his flat. The drive back was painful. All he wanted to do was get his clothes off and see to his wounds. He wanted a drink. He didn't know how today was going to go. He had mentally prepared for the worst. But now that he'd done what he had to, he was again pissed off. 'I'm too old for this shit,' went round in his head in a loop. Clothes were bagged for burning. One by one, Jim looked at each wound. Cuts and bruises on his head and face. Swollen knuckles. Bruised ribs. A swollen ankle. He necked some painkillers that he had asked Kingston to 'prescribe, 'and washed them down with a full tin of beer, without even pausing to catch his breath. After a while, the pain eased off and he composed himself. He pulled on a pair of shorts and got down to business. Administering himself was his life. Tending to wounds and cleaning weapons and recharging magazines. The only bit missing was the Operational debrief. But his next letterbox was to be a live one with Mitchell. So, Jim guessed they would have that conversation then. Jim had done his bit for the day. When he sat down, he finally wondered if Mills had done his.

Mills had got out of the area as quickly as he could. But then calmed down to a normal driving pace. He needed to think. He needed the splinter out his arm. He had a minimal amount of trauma equipment in the boot of his car. He pulled over in a side street, once he was back in South London. He opened the boot of his car and looked at his weapons and equipment. He had bought himself quite a supply over the last few days. He had his issued weapons and magazines filled with rounds. A large machete-style blade. Rope. Plastic zip-ties. Medical supplies and a change of clothes. He got his medic bag and a new jacket and got himself back in the front of his car. The wound was still bleeding. Probably because he was constantly moving, and his blood had not been given a chance to start clotting. He wrestled out his jacket and looked at the splinter. Wood. proper wood. Not MDF or prefabricated rubbish. Which, to be fair, could have been worse. If that went into his arm, it could have disintegrated and got deeper down and become more of a process to get out and clean up. No easy way about it - Mills got hold of the splinter and calling himself every name under the sun, pulled it out. Blood poured out the open wound. He quickly covered it with a bandage and pressed it in place for a moment. He then got out a bottle of iodine. He needed to sterilise the wound. Holding onto the steering wheel as tight as he could with his left hand, he poured the iodine onto the wound. He gave a shout of anger at the pain of it and then set about trying to wrap his shoulder the best he could. He wrestled himself into a new jacket and headed back to his flat.

Inside, his process was the same as Jim's. Clothes off, wounds, weapons and alcohol. Mills drank whiskey straight from the bottle.

Mills also had a live letterbox coming up. But it wasn't for a couple of days. Both men knew that this wasn't a one-night stand. With the effort going into accommodation and the cars and the money. There was to be more work coming up. Which said to Mills that there were more of them out there. And they were now looking for who stopped them in their tracks. Before

Mills went to bed that night, he put a doorstop under the front door of his flat.

CHAPTER 14

Vladislav sat in his safe house. Waiting. He was expecting a result to have been reported back from Dima by now. Though no real time frame had been discussed. He was hoping to see something on the News. 'Half of London in blackout 'would have been nice. But nothing. As time moved forward, his frustrations grew. He wanted the results to come in and he wanted to plan the next attacks. Dima and Serg were planning a hit and leave. Get out of the country as soon as possible once their missions are over. But Vladislav wanted to keep them for more attacks. Really put the boot in. However, right now, he needed his first success to come in. It wasn't until the evening news came on, that he realised something bad was happening. It started well. Reports of chaos at the ExCeL centre, London's biggest conference facility. Extinction Rebellion in protest. The Environment Secretary giving a speech.

And then it hit - 'It has been reported that an assassination attempt was made on Annabelle Thornton'

'An attempt!' Which to Vladislav meant only one thing. Serg had been intercepted. An assassin of his calibre would not have missed. He would not have changed his mind. He could only have been stopped. The News did not report anyone being taken into custody. Though it was a possibility. Vladislav watched the News like a bated dog. There were images of the protests and video footage captured on personal phones that had been sent in.

And there was CCTV of a man running. Not Serg. Vladislav knew instantly Serg was dead. And therefore, so was Dima. His head went into overdrive. Who knew? How did they know? Who was this person? He's killed two Russian agents. He must be an agent himself.

Vladislav's skin got goosebumps at the thought of it all. The implications. The reaction. The political picture. The failure. This wasn't right. 'How did they know? '

There was nothing he could do. Not now. And not for Dima and Serg. They were either dead or they were in the hands of the Police or Military Intelligence. Both of whom would not hand back their new prizes. Not even if Vladislav asked nicely. He had some thinking to do. Thinking meant drinking. He opened a bottle of vodka, to toast fallen comrades.

The next letterboxes were live. So, both Mills and Jim were to meet Mitchell face to face for a debrief of sorts, an intelligence update and to cover off any admin such as ordering replacement equipment or get more money.

The problem was for them both, the letterbox was a couple of days away. It made sense. Let the dust settle. But in the meantime, the men had nothing to do. After waking the next morning and being very stiff and sore from their operation the day before, there was very little to do. Both instinctively knew they had to lay low. This was the 'off the grid 'bit of the job. Both had spent years in camps or safe houses waiting for their next task. But being stuck on UK soil doing an isolation routine seemed different. It made the whole process harder. Both ate to put energy back into their system. Both sorted out their equipment. Both exercised. Jim used the kettlebells he bought, Mills did pull-ups, push-ups and sit-ups. More eating. More tending to wounds. More wanking. More listening to the radio.

It was early hours the next morning when GCHQ picked up on a burst transmission coming in. It was intercepted and quickly recorded for decoding. Nearly an hour later, a return signal - from the UK outwards. Undoubtedly intended for the Kremlin. They made reference amongst themselves about the 'Operation with no name'.

When the Duty Officer called Mitchell, he was already awake.

'Good morning. Sorry, did I wake you?'

'Not at all. Too much going on. Have you got something?'

'Yes. Two messages. Not an hour apart.'

'Jesus, OK, go on...'

'The first message said - You failed.'

Mitchell paused. The cogs in his mind started to turn. 'You failed.'

'And that was it, two words?'

'Yes. Just those two words.'

'And that was the first message? No chance a message went out from the UK first?'

'A chance, maybe. But not likely'.

Mitchell pondered at the wording. If no message went out from the UK first, then the Kremlin must have been watching the News. They would have seen that there was an incident, but the

Environment Secretary was still alive. And no National Grid outage. Two words. The brutality of it. No room for compromise. Failure and it is your fault.

'You said there were two messages?'

'Yes. A reply.'

'OK, what was it?'

The Duty Officer paused. And then with no hint of emotion or irony in his voice, said 'Send more.'

CHAPTER 15

The first round of live letterboxes was done in a London black cab. A proven way of doing such business. Mitchell didn't like being out for so long and being stuck in the London traffic didn't help. Mills was first. Mills got in the back of the taxi when Mitchell pulled over on the side of the road to 'pick up a fare'. It was all very awkward, as there was no way any real taxi driver would have pulled over the way he did, almost hand breaking into a space where his 'fare 'was. He received a few beeps on car horns and a couple of hand gestures that he didn't appreciate at all.

Mills was OK, all things considering. His first comment was 'Nice to be out the fucking flat.'

They spoke at length as Mitchell drove. They spoke about the coincidence of Extinction Rebellion being at the ExCeL centre. They spoke about the security at the centre and Annabelle Thornton's security detail. Mills said they were nothing compared to his team. Mitchell thought it to be a bit crass to speak that way of the dead but accepted the point to be no doubt true. Mitchell drove Mills to the South side of the river and dropped him off half a mile from his flat. Mills had given over his shopping list, which started with new body armour. They said their farewells and Mitchell went off to meet Jim. Mills went off for a coffee.

Jim was waiting on the side of the road, looking like he'd just been jumped. His face was still cut and bruised. The bruises had not yet started to run, so there were patches of deep purple and blue all over his face. One taxi pulled over on a punt, seeing if he could pick up a fare. Jim waved him on. After seeing Jim's face, the taxi driver seemed relieved that he didn't want to get in. Mitchell pulled over in a more controlled manner than he did with Mills. Jim got in the back.

Mitchell tried to acknowledge Jim's state, without sounding too condescending.

'I'll live! 'Was Jim's opinion on his injuries. Again, they spoke about the job in detail. The acid on the padlock. The incendiary device. The ability of the Russian. After that, as with Mills, formalities were discussed. Before Mitchell dropped Jim off, he checked again if he was OK.

'I promise you, mate, I've had worse. 'Was Jim's answer. And with that, he got out of the taxi.

For the first time in a long time, Mitchell didn't know what to do. His gut told him there would be some sort of sustained attack. That was what all the precautions were for, to protect the lads. But now it was a reality, he felt anxious. It had been a few days since he found out about the 'send more 'transmission. It was evident to Mitchell there was someone in London running these operations. But who? He knew most of the agents from all the big-threat states. His ally in Russia had gone cold. When he saw Jim and Mills at the live letterbox meets, they looked fed up and Jim especially looked like a bag of shite. The intelligence from them wasn't great either - no reflection on either of them - but the two Russian agents had nothing by way of intelligence on them to gather. And Phillips 'team took DNA samples which both came up negative, meaning they were not on 'the system'. At some point, the bodies will have to be repatriated back to

Russia. Which will be the job of the British Ambassador to tactfully bring up. The stark irony of all of this is that despite their attempts to kill and disrupt our way of life, we still have to walk up to them and say, 'Guess what, we've killed two of your failed assassins and now you can have them back.' The layers upon layers of how international politics, diplomacy and tolerance works, was still often a wonder to Mitchell. Mitchell wondered how the lads were doing. He guessed boredom was getting to them. Both said they pass their time OK, by learning routes around London and shopping for food and exercising. But animals like Jim and Mills are caged in a city of millions. Without the ability to talk to loved ones or even have regular intelligence catchups, he knew they felt isolated. And that only fed the rage. All the reassuring that it was for their own good, did not help. When Mitchell ran that one past Jim the other day, it was received with a stare and a clenched jaw.

Mitchell had received shopping lists from both men. Ammunition and body armour for Mills. Money for both. A request for smartphones, despite knowing they wouldn't get one. Mitchell put the lists into Knocker who turned them round in less than an hour. He called Mitchell on an internal line to say they were ready for collection whenever he was ready to come over. Mitchell was thinking about every single detail. Including the security of the lads. He was too aware of how much Mills had been exposed at the ExCeL centre. Mills knew it too. But Mills seemed to care less than Mitchell about being exposed like that. After all, Mills made a living with a gun.

Vladislav was waiting on something from the Kremlin. Anything. And in the meantime, he was searching the internet and archives and Deep Net for the man he saw on the News in the ExCeL centre. The man who spoiled Vladislav's mission. His plan. His reputation. The man who killed Serg and Dima. He was also scanning every radio transmission he could and trying to find some sort of pattern on search engine maps. But nothing came up. No name. No face. No conversation on the radio or insecure text message. Nothing. The guy had to be an agent. But it made no sense. How did they know? Vladislav questioned himself over vodka. Did he make a mistake? He knows first-hand how good British Intelligence is. But are they that good? Was the Compton thing that much of a giveaway? Maybe so? But even so, it changes nothing. There is still a lesson to be taught. And Vladislav was to deliver it. Nothing changes. All he had to do was wait. The agents would be sent. And this time, there will be blood and chaos on a truly Cold War scale.

The next round of live letterboxes was to deliver on the requests that came two days ago. No intelligence update. Mitchell would simply hand over the shopping list. A confirmation of the date and location of the next dead letterbox would be in with that. Then there would be a dead letterbox every two days until intelligence came and they would again be set to work.

Jim's letterbox was in Portobello Market. Near the junction that fed on to Ladbroke Grove was a Hair Salon. In front of the Salon was a series of stalls, some food, some tourist trinkets, some clothes. Mitchell had Jim's shopping list in a sports bag. The exchange was easy. Mitchell felt reassured to see Jim's face looking less swollen. When Jim got in the taxi before, Mitchell felt a huge amount of guilt. Now, he had put that to one side and was back in work mode. Mitchell walked up to a clothes stall on the market and placed the sports bag to the side of it and got the attention of the stall owner. Jim simply walked past and picked it up. Jim spent another hour walking around the market before he went home. An hour with fifteen grand in his bag. There were also a few more grenades and some medical supplies. He also requested a second pistol. Just in case.

Mills had to go to Brixton for his letterbox. To a Superstore. While he was there, he did a small amount of food shopping. On the way out, he saw Mitchell walking across the car park to a car in the far corner. He had in each hand, a reusable shopping bag. Mills scoffed at the idea of having to walk back to his car which was parked on the road a few streets away, with shopping bags. His shopping list was ammunition and body armour. He knew the weight of them but appreciated the fact Mitchell would have balanced the weight out between the two bags. Mitchell got in his car and drove off, clocking Mills walking towards him across the car park as he did. He had left the bags tucked against the hedge. Mills picked up his pace, walked up to the bags, picked them up and walked out of the car park to the path that had the bus stop on it. He got himself in the crowd as much as possible. Nestled amongst them, you could not tell him apart from anyone else. When the bus came, he just walked around the back of it, crossed the street and headed off to his car.

It took a few days for the next batch of Russians to arrive in the UK. Vladislav was frustrated because of waiting so long. A few days to him felt like an eternity. Like he wasn't being respected by the Kremlin. He wanted results immediately. The first arrived by passenger ferry from France. Aleksi was a smart-looking man with an air of sophistication about him. It was clear he was posted to France for this reason. He looked the part. But he was also deadly. He had undertaken missions against the French Foreign Legion in West and Central Africa with results that resonated across the whole world. His reputation preceded him, and Vladislav was keen to finally meet him. Aleksi came through customs at the Port and spotted Vladislav immediately. He wasn't expecting a reception party but was not going to turn down a lift. They got in the car before they spoke. As Vladislav pulled away, Aleksi was first to break the silence.

'Have I got my mission particulars yet?'

'No. But I am expecting it anytime soon. Now you are here, and the other guy later today, the transmission will come.'

'I understand. And you have all we need?'

'Nothing I cannot get.'

'Good. If you don't mind me saying, it is a pleasure to meet you. You are from the era that inspired me to be who I am today.'

'And that is quite an accolade coming from yourself. I have heard about your work. I am glad you are working on my operation.'

The men said little more during the journey back to London. Every now and then, Vladislav would wince as the tight skin on his back stretched when he moved his arms around the steering wheel. Aleksi saw but said nothing. He had received enough of a brief about Vladislav and his failed missions so far. Aleksi was annoyed at being called in to pull Vladislav out of the shit. But a mission was a mission and Aleksi did not fail.

Ilya and Grigor also arrive by sea. But their journey was not as pleasant as Aleksi's. While he was on the top deck of a ferry, watching the Great White Cliffs of Dover come majestically closer and closer to him, Ilya and Grigor were - for cover, they were told - transported from Turkey along with six others in the back of a truck. They were, as far as the driver was concerned, being trafficked to the UK for labour purposes. The other six, all thought they were off to the promised land after their families had paid a huge sum to the organisations that arrange such journeys. When they finally make it to UK soil, they had no idea that the freedom they so longed for would be taken from them and they would be put to work. Two were male. They were to be taken to a construction site. The two older women, and by older, they were in their early twenties, had already been sold to a brothel. And the two teen girls were earmarked for the streets of Manchester. As the six of them spoke, Ilya and Grigor knew none of them had any idea about their fate. They joined in the conversation. They spoke of being repressed back home and how their extended families scraped together enough money to send them away so they could earn real money and repay their debt to the family, and then bring them all over to the UK legally to start a new life. Ilya and Grigor both heard sincere optimism in the voices of the six.

The journey across Europe took a day and a half. And then there was the sea crossing from Europe to the UK. And in the UK, they still had a few hours more in the truck before they were delivered to the compound. At this point, the two Russians were to be met by Vladislav and they would just disappear. The driver could protest as much as he liked, but he wasn't going to stop them.

The truck stopped in the early hours of the morning, at a quarry somewhere in the Midlands. All eight were tired, cold and hungry. The fresh air felt like being born again. Grigor spotted a car outside the gates of the quarry and indicated to Ilya that that must be Vladislav. They started to walk off. The driver, seeing his cargo leaving, called to the men who were there to take receivership of the new workers. One gave a sharp whistle to get their attention.

'You. You two, you stay here.'

'We are not part of your consignment. 'said Grigor

'You came in my truck, on my expenses. You have a debt to pay. You stay the fuck here. You are mine, now.'

The man was joined by the other three. They got close. To intimidate. To bully. Ilya had them as Albanians. He despised Albanians. Their transmission was specific - use the cover to get to England. At no point did it say they were to cause a drama with the criminals conducting the trafficking of people. But then again, it didn't say not to. On any other day of the week, neither of them would have cared about young girls being trafficked for sex. But they had just spent two days travelling with them. There was a connection. Ilya and Grigor had nothing. No weapons. Not even food in their stomachs to fuel a fight. But they had training and adrenalin and they were fucked off. Grigor struck first. Shooting an arm out at an angle to catch the man on the right of the foursome. His thumb went straight into his eye socket and Grigor clasped his hand tight around his head and bent his thumb, locking it inside the man's skull. The man screamed and as he did, Grigor pulled him down and brought up a textbook uppercut to his throat. One man down. Ilya had struck an instant after Grigor. He went for the man running his mouth off. Ilya hit him several times in the face, but the man seemed to absorb the strikes. He came back for his own attack. Sharp straight punches, he fought like a trained fighter. Ilya had to take some punishment before he could work on a counter. Grigor was faced with the next guy, who had pulled a knife. Grigor raised his hands and crouched into a semi-wrestler pose. He eyeballed the guy. The guy struck out with the knife. Taking aimed shots. Grigor had to dance about and gesture with his hands to try and deflect attention, so he could work on getting close enough to bypass the blade. Ilya was taking a beating by two of them. But he was a seasoned fighter. And nasty with it. He was parrying as many shots as he could, which frustrated the two attackers. Ilya was also a great chess player, and in this situation, he needed to sacrifice a Pawn. He let his left-hand drop, opening up a clean shot for the guy on his left. The guy took the bait. He threw an overhand right at Ilyas' chin. Ilya bent his knees and dipped his head at the last moment, absorbing the shot on his cheekbone. As the shot landed, Ilya grabbed the guy's wrist and pulled it off his face, and back past Ilyas head, so Ilya was closer to his opponent. Once inside his guard, he grabbed the guy by the hair with his other hand and pulled him in. He leant forward and bit him on the nose. The guy screamed and threw futile punches in an attempt to get Ilya off. Ilya pushed him off and kept the guy's nose in his mouth. The man stopped and tried to feel for his nose, before seeing it in Ilyas mouth. Before he could do anything else, Ilya hit him on the chin and knocked him out cold. Two down. Grigor had got inside his guy's guard and was trapping the hand with the knife between his arm and torso, whilst putting his fist into the face of his opponent. The guy struggled back and got Grigor in a hold, but Grigor threw his opponent over and when he hit the floor, Grigor stamped on his face until he stopped moving. Three. The last guy was back on Ilya. Ilya had the other guy's blood coming from his mouth and his opponent was duly cautious. His hesitance was his downfall. Ilya struck him straight in the face, knocking his front teeth out and cutting his lips. Ilya came forward and got his thumbs on the inside of the guy's cheeks. Ilya pulled his arms wide and his opponent's face split open. He screamed like a little girl until

Grigor came up behind him and hit him on the back of the head with a thumping right. Four. In four minutes. Not bad.

The two gave each other a knowing look and made their way back to the truck and the six now-truly free immigrants.

'You were going to be trafficked for sex and labour. 'Said Grigor, 'So go. Do everything you said you would and keep your promises to your families.'

The driver was hiding around the side of his truck.

'I didn't know. I'm just the driver.'

'But you called those cunts over when we started to walk away, didn't you? 'Sneered Ilya, still dripping with blood, 'So you are a cunt, too.'

The driver tried to run past Ilya, forgetting Grigor was standing two feet behind, at the front of the truck. As the driver ran, he ran straight into a left hook by Grigor. The driver's head bounced off the front of his truck and was knocked out. He would come round OK. He could explain to the Governor what the fuck happened at the quarry and why his men were in the state they were. There was every chance the driver was going to take a bullet for this anyway. Grigor and Ilya had nothing else to do here. They walked to the edge of the compound, towards the parked car.

They got in. Ilya in the front, Grigor in the back. At first, Vladislav said nothing. He started to drive back to London.

'There are bags on the seat next to you in the back with clothes, food and weapons. The rest we can get for you in London.'

Ilya eyeballed Vladislav.

'You didn't think to come and lend a hand? Not with one of those weapons you just mentioned?'

'You were doing fine by yourself. Besides, I don't think your brief was to upset the Albanians and their trafficking operation.'

'And what were we supposed to do? Ask them nicely to let us go?'

'You are Russian agents. You didn't need my help. But it could cause problems upsetting the Albanians. That is all I am saying.'

'And who will they complain to? 'Asked a sarcastic Grigor, 'The Russian Embassy?'

'They were your transport. That was all. Their business is not yours. But it is done now. We are still waiting on the transmission. To be honest, I am surprised there are two of you.'

Ilya looked out the car window as he spoke.

'We got told this job has to be a success. No matter what. We are each other's assurance policy.'

CHAPTER 16

Back at the Safehouse, the three agents were telling stories. Ilya and Grigor told of their 'horse shit 'trip to the UK. Aleksi gave an empathetic chuckle at their misfortune and teased them by saying how shockingly limited the selection of hot mains was on the ferry over from France. Vladislav brought them food and drink and tried to be part of the conversation. But he felt excluded. Much to his annoyance. He was happy when he checked his radio and laptop and found a transmission had been made. He felt his skin tingle with excitement.

Again, the order was brief and exact. The three agents instinctively split the tasks. Aleksi was to do the hit. Ilya and Grigor the attack on the infrastructure. Plans were starting to be made. They had two days. Vladislav showed the images of the ExCeL centre. All three got the image of Mills locked in their heads. If he showed up, he too would die.

Vladislav insisted the assassination and the sabotage attack would happen at the same time on this operation. If this character was going to try and stop Aleksi, then Ilya and Grigor would undoubtedly succeed. Aleksi scoffed at the idea that someone might stop him in his mission, but he understood the point being made. Discussions went on for hours after that, and Vladislav was included in them all. He had vehicles and more equipment to source. They now needed him.

Mitchell was sitting looking at the phone when it rang. He answered before the first electronic ring had finished.

'Hello.'

'Mitchell, do you ever sleep?'

'Do you?'

'I get more done if I don't. Are you ready for this one?'

'Go on.'

'Another transmission, as expected. Another target for destruction and another Politician for assassination. They are not messing around.'

'Who? What is it? 'Mitchell was desperate to know.

'It's the Chancellor. And I've checked the grid location. It's Canary Wharf. Specifically, One Canada Square. They are going to try and cripple our Finance sector in one fell swoop.'

'When?'

'Two days'

'Fuck me. OK, I've got a lot to do. Thanks.'

They both hung up without saying goodbye. Mitchell got his head around the magnitude of it. Environment Minister and cutting electricity to half of London. That would have been devastating. That would have made the point. But that was a failed mission. Now, they are coming back for bigger targets. To make a bigger impression. There are more agents in the UK. That was clear. But he had no idea when they turned up. He also knew they would be looking out for his lads. And he was hoping they were OK and lying low. He knew both had a rough time last time. There had been no visual contact with them since the shopping list collection. The dead letterboxes were being collected every other day - saying 'Nothing new '- so he knew they, for now, had not been identified. The next dead letterboxes were set for tomorrow morning. And this time, they will have the next targets. For no reason other than it was his 'turn', Mitchell assigned the protection of the Chancellor to Jim. Which meant Mills got tasked with stopping a sabotage attack on Canary Wharf.

Boredom was starting to get to the two men. Routines were established. Morning exercise. Food. Out the door to learning more routes and go shopping. Collect a letterbox if there was one that day. Both were getting bored of the letterboxes coming up with nothing. If they were going to be living this monk-like existence, then at least have some work to do. Not that either wanted an exact repeat of what happened last time, but they were in the zone. They needed to perform.

Both were sick of eating out, so kitchens were being filled with utensils and fresh food. Both went out driving and walking in the evening, to recognise routes in the dark - lamps, pub lights, they all had value in recognising where you were. Weapons were oiled and serviced, equipment in car boots was added. Anything to keep your mind on the game.

Relief came by way of the dead letterbox the next morning. Jim's last message had said 'Nothing to report', followed by the location of this letterbox. Which was in Leicester Square. Similar to the others, he was to find a coin under a bench next to the Theatre ticket booth on the North-West corner of the Square. Sure enough, there it was. Jim got a coffee and headed back to his flat.

Mills 'last message was exactly the same, only the location of today's letterbox was obviously different to Jim's. Mills found himself out for a stroll in Clapham Common, homing in on a piece of modern art. He found himself face to face with a rainbow painted cow made of plastic waste. He knew it all meant something, but he didn't care. He found his coin and walked on.

Back at his flat, Jim sat in his chair in the sitting room and watched the monitor of the baby camera that was looking out the bedroom window. He wanted to make sure as he always did, that no one was following him home. After five minutes, he took his eyes off the monitor and got the coin out of his pocket. Again, the same as before, he scored along the edge of it with a razor blade and got to his message.

It read 'Chancellor of the Exchequer. Tomorrow. 'The second line was the location of his live letterbox. His face-to-face meeting with Mitchell, to debrief after this mission. Jim's eyes widened. 'They're not fucking around 'he thought to himself. He gave Mills a quick thought and guessed he was picking up the infrastructure bit this time. And guessed it must be something like the Bank of England. But that was Mills ' lookout. Jim had homework and preparation to do.

Mills sat on the edge of his bed. It seemed to be his go-to perch for opening his coins. He was expecting another 'nothing new. 'When he saw 'One Canada Square, Canary Wharf. Tomorrow 'He was overjoyed. He quickly balanced it out in his head. 'Not a name, so not an assassination. A building, so a bomb? 'He had some homework to do. He knew of Canary Wharf. But One Canada Square meant nothing to him.

Jim was not sure if he was impressed with the audacity of the Russians for going after the Chancellor - after all, he was guarded by armed Met Police in most cases - or he was just pissed off that it meant another hard day at the office. Tomorrow, as well. Not long to prepare. He needed to find out where the Chancellor would be, get himself in the area and not spook the Chancellor's personal protection detail. It also meant the assassin would have to do the same. The proverbial needle in a haystack. Jim started to get his kit together. He re-assembled his pistol, again. And loaded magazines. Lots of them. He had decided after the substation incident that no matter what, he's shooting the next guy. He's too old to be playing silly buggers like he did the other day. He still had marks on his face where he'd been hit with rocks and his shins and arms had deep bruises. They were just starting to turn green and yellow as the dead blood finally started to disperse.

He was also hungry, so taking ammunition and grenades in his satchel, to dump in the car, he headed out to his now-local internet cafe to do some homework and then it was only a couple of minutes walk to a parade of shops and restaurants, where he could get himself a curry. He walked out of his door and down the balcony. He gave a nonchalant wave in the general direction of where Kingston normally parked. He didn't look to see if Kingston was there. He was. Kingston didn't react, he just watched as his newest customer went out. Again.

Mills sat in his internet cafe sipping on a black coffee in a lidded mug as he brought up a search engine. It did occur to him that he should use different internet cafes to avoid setting a pattern. But seeing as he was completely off the grid as far as anyone was concerned, coming to the same place every few days didn't seem that much of a risk. Besides, the girl behind the counter at this cafe was better looking than the one down the road.

He had a browse for One Canada Square. The website he came to brought up Canary Wharf and what he was after was part of that website. 'So, they're after hitting our Stock Market? ' Mills thought to himself. This was huge and potentially disastrous. The only way he could see this happening was by a bomb. How else would they do it? This felt bigger than an under-the-radar espionage mission. Why couldn't everyone be called in to stop this? Mills was getting pissed off with the lack of information around the targets. Both his and theirs. But he knew nothing was being kept from him. It was just the way it was. He read more about Canary Wharf. When it was built, what it was for, the social scene, the underground shopping arcades, the canal boats, the light railway running overhead. There were too many options. Eventually, Mills focussed back on One Canada Square. To get in there would be a task for any agent, he decided. His gut told him that if a bomb, a high-density plastic-explosive bomb was placed somewhere in the stairwell in the shopping arcade directly underneath the building, it would do enough structural damage that the whole place would have to be evacuated. Probably for months. That would be enough of a disruption to make the news. And then if Jim failed, someone from the finance world would die, the point would have been made. The Russians would have got the result they wanted. So, it was down to Mills to stop a bomb from going off, by finding the agent and killing him first. Mills sighed and got up to order himself another coffee. There was a different shift behind the counter. The girl had gone and some fella with his hair tied up in a bun took his order. Twice. Because he needed to confirm that a black coffee was an Americano.

CHAPTER 17

Vladislav showed Aleksi the trick with tracking someone's Google account to see their current location. Aleksi knew how to do this, but let Vladislav have his moment. The Chancellor was in Brussels. Undoubtedly still fighting with his EU opposite number about the UK's Brexit divorce bill. But tomorrow he had to be back in London, to sit in on PM questions. A very public show of British politics, where Members of Parliament get to grill the Prime Minister on current political affairs. And the PM's closest allies were always there, including the Chancellor. So that was it when the Chancellor was moving from the airport or Eurostar back to Westminster, Aleksi would take his hit. Aleksi smiled at the idea of it. Time was not their friend and there were many factors to consider. Aleksi gave Vladislav his shopping list, which included a motorbike, a fast one. Appropriate motorbike clothes and helmet. A submachine gun and a thousand rounds. Vladislav was a bit taken back by quite a demand. But then he loved the idea of such a hit. He picked up the phone to make a few calls.

Ilya and Grigor didn't have much to go on. Just take a building - this specific building - out of operation. Stop trade coming out of it. That was enough. Clearly, they wanted to do the job well. So, requests for C4 plastic explosives and sealed cylinders went in. Vladislav was already anticipating their requests and had a contact who could supply all they needed to make a high-density bomb. They also wanted a car each. To open up their options. And when they saw that there were underground car parks and shops directly beneath the target building, they agreed a second bomb was needed, to hit the building in two areas. Their plan was simple. Park up and take one bomb as high up into the structural foundations of Once Canada Square as possible, and then both leave in one car. Leaving a car bomb and the planted bomb to go off when they are long gone.

CHAPTER 18

The Chancellor arrived back in London via Eurostar mid-morning. His car and security detail were waiting for him in the secure lobby of St. Pancras station. His personal bodyguard walked two steps behind him until he got into the car, then sat in the front next to the driver. Their destination was Westminster. The Chancellor had to brief the PM on what action points had come out of his meeting with the EU finance minister before PMQ's - as they are known, later that day.

Aleksi was on a black Japanese motorbike, dressed in blue jeans, a black bike leather jacket and a blue helmet. He fitted-in on the streets well. His bike had a bag that was secured to the fuel tank. In that bag was his submachine gun, magazines of ammunition, two grenades and a flare. He waited. He didn't need to wait long; he knew exactly when the Chancellor left Brussels and timed the rail journey perfectly. He didn't know exactly where the Chancellor's car would emerge from, but it had to come out of one of only three possible exits he had surveyed earlier that morning.

Jim was in his car. His method of working out how the Chancellor would be getting back into the UK was a little more basic. After lots of bad media coverage about Ministers ' expenses and spending too much of the General Public's money,

Jim decided a private jet wouldn't be the done thing. So, he hedged his bets and parked up in the area of St. Pancras station. He had been in the area since 0800 and had already been spoken to by two different Traffic Wardens. But Jim needed to be close. He had memorised the arrivals from Brussels as best he could so he made sure he was not moving when he knew a train was coming in. The one advantage Jim had was that he knew where the exit for 'VIPs 'was. It was something he learned when he was helping the London team. The exit was out the back of the station on York Road. It ran north away from the busiest routes at the front of the station. Jim watched everyone. Everyone was a suspect. Every person's walk, clothing and action were analysed. He needed to find that one thing that made them Russian, made them an assassin. After the first time he got moved on, Jim joked to himself that the Traffic Warden nearly got two rounds in the chest when he knocked on Jim's window.

Nothing changed for Jim. Not for hours. Then a motorbike went past. Nothing new there. There had been hundreds of motorbikes passing him throughout the morning. However, as this one passed what Jim knew to be the exit that the Chancellor's team would use, he noticed the rider's helmet turn ever so slightly to the left, as if it was looking down the exit. A few moments later, a black Jaguar car exited and turned on to the road, heading north. It was followed by a support undercover Police car - Jim could spot them a mile away. It was without a doubt the Chancellor. Which meant the rider on the bike could be the Russian? 'Paper-thin, Jim. Paper-thin. 'He muttered to himself.

It was enough for Jim to go on. The bike was long gone, up the top end of the road by now. Jim was now fully expecting an ambush. Time was against him. Jim pulled out onto the main road. He mapped out in his mind how many exits came off York Road before they got to the main road running East to West at the top. There were three. He knew the driver would stick to the main routes, as they were the quickest. He needed them off that route and for the driver to get the Chancellor out of the area. He couldn't exactly go up and knock on the window, though he did consider it. He followed the Jaguar and the support car under a bridge and past a junction on the right. 'Two junctions to go. ' Jim thought to himself. In a situation like this, the only wrong decision is indecision. Jim got a Thunderflash out of his satchel. He opened his car window all the way down. Jim took off the safety clasp of the Thunderflash and pulled the pin with his left thumb, holding it tight in his right hand. He held his hand out the window of his car. A car passed on the other side of the road. Jim had to wait. They passed the second junction. The next was on the left and the last option for the driver to get off the main roads and away from certain death for him and his passenger. Jim dropped the Thunderflash. Three seconds passed and there was a deafening explosion behind him. Only just quieter than a real grenade. The shockwave caught up with his car and he felt the air compress around him.

The hint was truly taken. Both vehicles upfront switched on their blue lights.

In the Jaguar, the driver was talking on the closed-radio net to his support vehicle.

'Two hundred meters to left turn', he said. Giving the running commentary of his route.

'Roger 'Came the reply from the support vehicle.

The perceived explosion behind them sent the blood running from their faces.

'Stand-by, Stand-by! 'Called the support vehicle. 'Possible compromise!'

'Roger', confirmed the driver, 'getting off the main now'

Blue lights on and a drop in gear gave the car a menacing sound. The engine revved as it picked up the torque and the driver pulled the car around the corner on the left. They were now in an evasive manoeuvre, getting the Chancellor back to Westminster as fast as possible and via unknown routes.

The intent of the support vehicle was always to go with the Chancellor. As the driver looked out his rear-view mirror, he saw a car speeding up behind them. It looked like it wanted to pass, to get to the lead car. The driver swerved in the road over to the right to block the cars way.

Jim was only halfway through his mission. Though the Chancellor was temporarily out of harm's way, there was still the matter of an assassin on a bike that he had to deal with. He needed to pass the support vehicle. He closed the gap and looked to overtake, assuming the car would soon be turning left to support the Chancellors car. But it swerved in front of Jim, blocking his way. Jim touched the breaks, pulled to the left and then hit the gas. He undertook the support vehicle exactly on the left turning. Jim had blocked the way for the support vehicle to do its job. Jim pulled away as fast as he could to find the man on the bike. The support car followed Jim. As far as they were concerned, he was the one making the attack.

Jim was in low gears and the engine was pulling hard. It pissed him off that the support vehicle was now on his case.

Amongst everything else, they could get caught up in the crossfire that was inevitably going to go down. He assumed they were Met Police, so wanted a bit of whatever action was going on. Jim pulled on to the main road fast and took the corner wide. A car swerved to get out of his way. Fifty meters down the main road, tucked in on the far side, was Aleksi, sitting on a revving motorbike.

Aleksi had to sit on his motorbike near the front of St. Pancras station for only a few minutes before the Eurostar pulled in. He covered his actions by pretending to send a text message. His tracker pinged the Chancellor's smartphone as soon as the train emerged from the tunnel and Aleksi had been monitoring it all the way into London.

He timed his move best he could. When it was obvious the Chancellor was in a car and making his way to an exit, Aleksi got round to that exit as smoothly as he could. As he passed, he gave a quick glance to see if he was right. Two cars were coming out of a secluded slip road. The tracker, the timing and the confirmation by sight. Aleksi had his target. He continued to ride up York Road and checked his mirrors to make sure the cars were following him up. He got to the top of the road and turned left - the general direction of the Centre of the City. He found a spot behind a closed-down petrol garage to park up and wait.

Moments later, not too far away was an explosion. Or at least it sounded like an explosion. Aleksi's eyes widened. Something was not right. He heard engines revving loudly. He waited. Seconds seemed like hours. A blue saloon car came round the corner. High revs and tyres screeching as they slipped on the tarmac. Aleksi eyeballed the driver. 'Is that him? 'Not two seconds later, another car came round the corner, clearly in pursuit. Blue lights were showing through the front grill. 'The Police escort?' But no principal car. Aleksi was enraged. Not getting the opportunity for an easy ambush was one thing, but now he had to get this guy whoever he was, kill him and relocate the target. Aleksi pulled away and chased the car with the flashing blue lights.

Jim was pulling fast down the road, scanning for a motorbike. The blue-light car was behind, chasing him. And little did Jim know it, the motorbike he was after, was chasing them. For now, the Chancellor was safe. That part of the job was done. But not closed-off for good. If he didn't find this motorbike soon, he would have to go on a pursuit for the Jaguar. 'This is why I need comms.... 'He thought to himself, as he raced through options in his head.

Aleksi needed the escort vehicle out of the way. He wasn't sure why they were chasing the guy in front, but it clearly had something to do with the explosion. Aleksi closed in on the car and weaving in and out of traffic and past road junctions, pulled alongside it. He took out his submachine gun and let out a short three-to-five round burst into the tyres of the car. The car swerved as the driver tried to keep control of it. They hit the central reservation and were taken out of the pursuit.

Jim heard the rounds go off. He searched in his rear-view mirror to see what had happened. He saw the escort vehicle go into the central reservation and emerging from behind was the motorbike. Jim put his foot on the gas. Upfront was a large junction, with traffic lights and lane markings. He got on the car horn to warn those upfront. He sped into the junction area and pressed down on his clutch. As he did so, he put a quarter-left turn on the wheel and pulled the handbrake up as hard as he could. The rear end span. He spun over 180 degrees and was facing more the corner of the shops than square-on to the road that he just came down. But that was perfect, as his window was still open. He got out his pistol from the holster on his belt and held it straight-armed at the motorbike rider.

Aleksi was closing in on his target vehicle when he saw it do an impressive manoeuvre in the middle of the road. Then he found himself staring down the barrel of a gun. Time for his own manoeuvre. The rear brake went on and he skidded 90 degrees to the left. He pulled onto the kerb as the first two rounds zipped past him. Aleksi wasn't dealing with some fanatic or an opportunist. This guy - the guy from the CCTV that Vladislav showed him? - was in the trade.

Jim pulled the trigger twice in fast succession. The motorbike had moved out of line-of-sight and Jim couldn't follow up with more shots. He clearly didn't want a stray round to hit a civilian. The motorbike barged past pedestrians on the side and was still heading towards Jim. The rider had a weapon and, in a few moments, will be behind Jim to take a shot. Jim put the car into second gear, over-revved the engine and pulled away fast but controlled, with very little wheel-spinning and the need to over-correct his steering wheel. He pulled straight onto the side road that fed into the junction. A road with small shops and residential houses. The motorbike was in pursuit. Jim needed options. He got a smoke grenade out and pulled the pin. He held it down outside the window for as long as he could before it started to burn his fingers. A white cloud followed him down the street.

Aleksi rode straight into a white-out of smoke. He had to slow to an almost crawl to get his bearings. Aleksi manhandled his bike to the left and again mounted the kerb. He rode along the pavement until he passed the smoke grenade in the middle of the street, before getting back onto the road and picking up his pace. His target had put some serious space between them in a matter of seconds.

Jim drove as fast as he could, turning left and right down small roads. He needed to give himself an advantage. He needed to be face-on to the rider to be able to shoot him. The roads were opening up, he had pushed north and was coming up to the North Circular - a large trunking road that runs across the top of London. No option to turn here. Jim put his foot down and hit the road at an increasing seventy miles an hour. The motorbike was mere seconds away. Too far at this pace to be of any use with a handheld gun. But he was closing in. 'Options, Jim. Options.'

Jim got into the centre lane. The road was surprisingly quiet, and Jim decided he needed to take more drastic actions. He took out a grenade from his satchel. He flicked off the safety catch and then pulled the pin out. He held the grenade in his hand and let the fly handle go. He gave a very quick count to three before dropping the grenade out the car window. A second later, there was a shocking bang as the grenade went off. Jim looked out his rear-view mirror. Through the smoke came the motorbike. The rider now had his submachine gun in his hand and was closing in fast.

Jim took out a second grenade. Again, safety catch, pin and fly handle. He counted to three at a slower pace this time. But playing dare with a live grenade in your hand is a fool's game.

He dropped it out the window. Less than a second later, it detonated. The noise was deafening, and the shock wave lurched his car slightly, and some fragments from the grenade hit his rear window.

Aleksi was in hot pursuit. His principal target was long gone. He knew that. Vladislav would be angry with how this has unfolded. But as far as Aleksi was concerned, he would go back and take out the target another time. Right now, he needs this person in front of him dead. Or better still, alive so he could be tortured. Pulling out onto the main road, he was a good eight-seconds behind his target. But that could be made up fast. The target pulled into the middle lane and was moving from seventy miles an hour upwards. Aleksi put his head down and pulled on the throttle. A moment later, something was thrown from the car. And a split moment after that, an explosion. The target had dropped a grenade in the road. Aleksi was too far behind at this stage for any of the fragments to do any damage. But the noise was deafening. The guy in front clearly wanted a fight. Aleksi sat up, got out his weapon and moved up for shots at the car. He was a few seconds away when the second grenade came out the window. This time it went off almost immediately. Some fragments buried themselves into Aleksi's jacket and jeans. He felt shards of hot metal cut at his flesh. He screamed in rage and pain and pulled on the throttle to get too close for another grenade to be an option for the guy in the car.

Jim's second grenade didn't serve its purpose either. And he was now in trouble. The motorbike was maybe three seconds behind him. Jim was close to a hundred miles an hour and still losing ground. Rounds hit the back of his car and rear window. The window shattered and Jim instinctively ducked. Enough was enough. Jim broke as hard as he could at that speed and as he lurched forward, he saw the motorbike go racing past him. He dropped to third gear and using the forward momentum of the car to help the engine, pulled away hard and picked up a pace of eighty miles an hour quickly, before moving up gears and back to over one hundred.

Aleksi was pissed off at being caught out by such an easy trick. He gained distance between him and the car. He saw a slip road off the main carriageway and took it. Jim followed. Aleksi slowed enough to launch an ambush. He came off the road and into some wasteland. As the car came racing off the slip road, Aleksi came up beside the driver and tried to fire in through the open window.

Jim saw what was about to happen. The motorbike was now coming along beside him, and the rider had a submachine gun in his hand. He pulled hard to the right and pushed the motorbike off the road and onto the pavement.

Aleksi revved the bike and started his pursuit again.

Jim was now the one being chased, again. 'Options, Jim. Options.'

He kept heading north along residential roads. Trying to get away from the public as much as possible. There had already been too many near misses with civilians, as far as he was concerned. He needed space. What had gone on so far resembled more of a World War Two dogfight between a British Spitfire and a German 109, rather than two assassins having it out.

Up ahead, Jim had made out a construction site. A crane towered above the landscape. Maybe he could take this off the street and get the space he craved to manoeuvre his car. Jim dropped a gear to put the car into high revs and high torque. He braced against his steering wheel as his car breached the gates. He skidded to a halt on the open dusty ground. Before Jim could even turn to look, he heard the revving engine of the motorbike.

Aleksi closed in on the car as fast as he could. It was driving in a straight line towards what seemed to be a dead end. He couldn't make out what the car was aiming for. When the car rammed through the gates of a construction site, it was clear to Aleksi that the driver wanted a fight. There was no time to get his weapon out again, so Aleksi pulled on the throttle with the intention of getting in the compound and finishing this once and for all. He was inside the gates no more than a second after the car. The car was already pulling to a halt. Aleksi was vulnerable. He kept the power on and shot past the driver's door and took the bike around the back of a bank of generators and portacabins.

Jim opened his car door and got out. He got down on one knee behind the open door, in a fire position. His weapon was pointing through the open window, in the direction of the generators. He listened. The motorbike was idle. He could hear it, but it definitely was not moving. It did occur to Jim that the site was quiet. Empty. Why? What day was it? Was it the weekend? He couldn't think why, but ultimately it didn't matter. He listened. He watched. He waited.

Aleksi had stopped behind the portacabins and taken his helmet off. His leathers were wet from his blood. His jeans were stained. He took off his jacket and looked at his T-shirt. It was peppered with slits where the fragments had penetrated.

He had an advantage, he was behind some sort of welfare portacabin, the canteen, maybe. There were windows at the front and rear. He had visibility on the car. He looked through as he inspected his clothes, keeping an eye on his adversary. He was down in a fire position behind his car door. Aleksi felt the fragments from the grenade in his skin as he moved. The initial pain had gone, but the grating under his flesh gave a bitter ache and it enraged him. He took off his T-shirt too and looked at his torso. Tiny cuts scattered his body. A child could do a dot-to-dot drawing on him. Dry blood had stained his flesh red and pink. He looked through the windows again. The guy was moving.

Jim couldn't stay still. He was the target if he did. He heard the motorbike idling behind the portacabins, so decided he would head to the left and go round the generators. Weapon high, he crept round his door and passed the front of his car. He stalked round in a big arc, continuously facing the direction of the motorbike. Aleksi decided to use the noise of the generator as cover. He got on his bike. He knew he was shielded by sound and rode the length of the portacabins towards the far side of the generator. At the end of the portacabins, before the generators, there was a gap of maybe two meters. Aleksi jumped off his bike at this point and let the bike carry on along the far side of the generator.

As Jim closed in to the end of the generator the motorbike came charging out, running alongside the back of it. Jim tracked it to the left, he let off six rounds. All aiming for where the rider should be. The motorbike carried on for another twenty meters before it went off balance and crashed to the floor. Jim stopped. Everything stopped. The dead-still of nothing came over him again. He had just been fucked. He didn't even turn to look as he dropped his weapon down and back in an arch, like he was drawing a perfect upside-down rainbow with his pistol. He fired off the remaining rounds out his magazine as he ran to where the motorbike had just come from, round the back of the generator.

Aleksi had timed it perfectly. He came round the front of the generator a split second after he heard the rounds go off. Rounds going off into thin air. He even took his time to hold his weapon in both hands to take aimed shots. He should be aiming at the back of a dumb-ass Brit who fell for a basic trick. However, as he cornered around the generator, bullets came flying at him. It was an act of God that he wasn't hit directly in the stomach. In retaliation, he let off several rounds himself, but they too missed. Back to a stalemate.

Jim changed magazines. He was two meters in line of sight to the other guy. All that was between them was an industrial-sized generator. Aleksi was moving. He crept back round to the two-meter gap, wanting to take on his opponent from behind. Jim saw it coming, his last thunder flash was in his hand. He flicked off the safety catch and tossed it against the sidewall of the portacabin on the far side of the gap. It hit the wall and bounced down into the gap. It landed behind Aleksi. The noise nearly blew his eardrums. Not knowing it was merely a Thunderflash - it was training that made him throw himself to the ground - to get away from any grenade fragmentation. Though there was no fragmentation this time, the drill saved his life. Jim came round the corner and fired two shots into thin air. Aleksi seized the moment. He pushed up from the floor and with all his might, hit Jim square-on in the bollocks. Jim buckled and as he did, he was picked up and was tossed against the generator. Aleksi had a grip of Jim's jacket and jeans and bounced him off the portacabin and generator until they got to the front edge of the gap. He threw Jim like he was a ragdoll into the open. Jim's weapon flew out of his hand and landed a few meters away. Jim shook his head to focus. As he looked up, there stood a fearsome sight. Aleksi was ripped to the bone. He clearly worked hard on training his body and keeping it in good shape. His abs and obliques showed and he had large veins running over his biceps and down his forearms. Jim bet his last quid it wasn't all for show, either. And to make a scary sight absolutely intimidating, he was scattered with bleeding cuts from the grenade fragments, making his body look like a child's painting that had run after it had been left out in the rain. Jim was in the shit. Again. He was expecting another boot to the ribs. Instead, the monster in front of him bent down and grabbed him by the throat and picked him up. The pressure instantly built-in Jim's head. He was high on tiptoes and struggling to breathe. The Russian squeezed as hard as he could. Jim's only defence was to try leveraging himself into a body position that the Russian couldn't hold. He brought his left arm up inside the arms of the Russian and twisted it so his forearm was on the outside of the Russian's arm. Jim bent his arm so he could get his hand downwards below the Russian's arm, he then grabbed his left hand with his right. Then, using all his might, pulled his left hand down, buckling the arm of the Russian. His grip went and Jim fell to the floor. He was free but still on his back foot. Jim started taking punches to the head, long before he could start to focus. Jim scrambled his arms, to deflect some of the attacks. He then saw the wounds on the Russian's torso. Cuts were still bleeding. With all his might, Jim got a finger and punched it inside the biggest cut he saw. His finger went in almost to the knuckle. The Russian howled in pain and anger. Jim stood up fast and started his own attack, throwing head-butts and punches. The pair fell to the floor, and both were hitting with rage at the other. Aleksi took the punches, rolled the Brit onto his back and got his hands back around his throat. Jim wasn't strong enough to keep the guy down. He found himself pressed to the ground being choked out for the second time. It was almost a divine moment when he remembered he promised himself he would shoot the next guy he met. Jim bent his legs and drove his heels into the ground. He arched his back and bridged all the way onto his head, taking the weight of the Russian on his neck. He went all the way back so he could see through his eyebrows at the floor behind him. There was his pistol. He reached back with his right hand and turned his palm downwards. With a final push of his heels, he grabbed the pistol grip. He collapsed his legs and brought his right hand down. With his left hand, he grabbed the Russian's head and pulled it to one side. Jim pressed the pistol into the Russian's body, next to the collarbone, facing down the length of his torso. He pulled the trigger. The Russian's torso went rigid for a split second and then collapsed down on top of Jim. Jim let a second-round go. This time the body did not go rigid, it just shifted slightly as the round passed through it. Jim lay there a beat, panting heavily. His breathing was laboured because of the now literal dead weight on top of him. He suddenly felt weird about it. Not often does he have a man in any context, laying on top of him. He tried to move the body, but he had no leverage to do so. So, grabbing the Russian where he could with his left hand, he brought his right heel up and drove it into the ground. As he did so, he pulled with his left hand and then pushed the body with his right. Eventually, the body half-rolled, half-slumped onto the floor next to him. Jim sat up. He felt the Russian's blood drip down his face. He looked at the corpse. There was blood all over the Russian's upper body from the fragment wounds and now the double bullet holes. Jim looked up. The rounds had exited the Russian. Out his arse. There was blood and shit splattered all over the generator. Which was still powering away in its unimpressed rhythmic grunt. Jim thought for a moment. He confirmed to himself that he kept his promise. 'I said I'd shoot this one. 'If he, had it in him, he would have smiled. He looked up at his car. He got up and made his way over. He opened the boot. Inside was all the equipment that he had either bought, or Knocker had supplied. He found his medical pack. He took out a strip of blotting paper - the same as he did with the first Russian. He went back to the body and dabbed the paper in some blood. Whatever Jim was looking for, he found it. When the paper indicated a match in the blood group, he raised an eyebrow and forced a pained smile. He quickly got out the rest of the kit; A needle attached to a tube that led into a bag. At the other end of the bag was a second tube. As crude as it was, Jim knew from the start that if it came to it, he would have to be his own A&E. He needed to bank some blood. With no etiquette at all, he pushed the needle into a vein on the corpse's arm. Then, he put his lips around the second tube and sucked as hard as he could. Blood started to pool in the bag. Not a lot. Maybe half a pint. He tied off the bag and disconnected it from the needle. Quickly, he did a second. He had maybe a pint before he decided enough was enough. He went back to his car and changed his t-shirt and jacket, wiping his face with the old jacket in his car wing mirror before throwing it in the boot. He inspected his car. It was shot-up and smashed to fuck. In the distance, he heard police car sirens. He couldn't drive out now. He looked at his weapons and equipment and made a decision. Phillips should be on his way, or at least his team. 'That really should be them, now…. 'Jim took out a couple of full magazines, took his money and his satchel. He closed the boot. He then went to the front of the car, took the key out of the ignition and closed the front door. As he used the fob to lock the car. He smiled at the absurdness of it all and discarded the key and fob back into the car through the open window. He set off on foot. As he left the compound through the gates, he busted open, he gave one last thought to where everyone was, then dropped it and walked on.

CHAPTER 19

Ilya and Grigor's plan was a simple one. Crude, but simple. They wanted to have two bombs. One placed as high in One Canada Square as possible. A room near a server would be ideal. And one in a car in the car park underneath the building. The bombs would be simple high explosives to generate as much of a shockwave as possible. No need for fragmentation. A charge would be set for two hours and there would be a 30-minute delay between the two devices going off. The first would do enough damage to empty the building. That was for sure and with any luck, do some long-term damage to the structural integrity of the building. The second would definitely do some damage to the structural integrity. If the foundations are compromised due to the second device going off in the underground car park, then it will be weeks if not months before the building can be re-occupied. And if there are emergency services or even the Army already in the building after the first device goes off, then so much the better.

They opted for propane gas cylinders as the housing unit. The size you would use for a garden BBQ. Vladislav provided them. He also sourced them a car each and the C4 explosive and the detonator timers. Ilya and Grigor spent all that night preparing. The cylinders were emptied of gas and the air-tight valves were unscrewed. Patiently, they moulded the C4 into sausage sized lumps and fed them into the cylinders. Dozens of lumps went into each one. After five or six lumps the cylinder would be gently rocked back and forth to get the C4 lumps to shuffle into place and create as much space as possible, so the cylinders could be filled to the absolute top. The valves were glued back in place with metalwork two-part cement. The timers were also glued into place, at the top near the handle. To set the two-hour delay was a bit tricky. The device had to be opened and the timer manually set. Once closed though, all the operator had to do was move a sliding button from 'X' to 'O'. The romantic images of a clock counting down to zero as you'd see on a Hollywood film were not reality.

They agreed to go in some sort of cover clothing. They researched the contractors to that building and found the Cleaning Company online. They fashioned the brand logo and labels to put on their overalls. Not a perfect match, but enough to throw someone off the scent long enough to allow them to do what they needed to do. The plan was to take a bomb each. Once in the car park, they would leave one bomb in the boot of Grigor's car. They would both go up the stairs and lifts and gain access to the service corridor of One Canada Square. Once high enough up the building - They generally agreed floor ten would be enough - they would turn the device on. They then made their way back to the cars, which they guessed would take them twenty to thirty minutes. They would turn the second device on and get in Ilya's car and disappear. All things being equal, they would be watching the News live as the second explosion goes off.

Mills was overthinking his task. Why did he now have the sabotage attack to deal with? Why not the assassination attempt? Did he do something wrong last time? If he did, Mitchell didn't say so. And if Mitchell thought he did, then fuck him. Being back inside a large landmark building again bothered him, too.

He didn't like the hordes of people. But he guessed Extinction Rebellion were not too focussed on the Finance sector, so the worst he would face would be masses of City Bankers all flapping around when the shit goes down. Wanting to keep his car close again, he planned to park up at Canary Wharf and play the hunting game on foot again. He didn't know any timings. So, that morning as early as he could reasonably justify, he left his flat, gave a nod to the mum and her kid on the second floor as he has done almost daily for the last two weeks, walked to his car and drove off to Canary Wharf.

It may sound Textbook to plant a bomb inside a building at night. But in fact, two strangers walking through an empty street and up to a building like the target building in the early hours, just sends alarm bells ringing to any half-switched-on security guard on duty. So, they agreed to start the mission after 9 am. They wanted the place full of busy unassuming bankers. They forward-mounted themselves close-by beforehand, so they could get into position as soon as they saw fit to do so. They parked on a regular road, two streets away from Canary Wharf. Ilya faced towards the target area and Grigor had manoeuvred round to face the way they had just come and was parked on the opposite side of the street two cars down from Ilya. They had eye contact with each other. They didn't need it. They had phones. But there was no damage to the integrity of their cover this way, so they were both more than happy sitting and waiting like this. They watched as bankers walked to Canary Wharf. A sea of suits and dresses and bags and phones and heels and coffees. Cars made their way into the area too. Some really expensive cars that made Ilya whistle to himself. Some not-so-expensive, which clearly belonged to a regular worker in the area. A coffee shop waiter, or a receptionist, or someone who works for the bank, but is not a banker. All in cars similar to what they were in. Grigor gave

Vladislav credit for not putting them in a bright pink VW Beetle. A saloon car came past Ilya. Grigor saw it face on. The driver looked different. He was not young, like a waiter. He was not a receptionist. He was not dressed like any office worker that Grigor had seen over the last twenty minutes. He wasn't in an old hatchback car or a snazzy sports car. It just didn't fit. *He* didn't fit. Grigor avoided any chance of eye contact with the driver as he passed, by looking towards the pavement and took a huge gulp of coffee from a throw-away mug. As the car got level with him, he had a quick look at the driver's side-profile. Ilya saw Grigor look. The pair locked eyes. This was why they were parked opposite each other, no need for a call. Ilya watched the car turn into a car park. 'Their car park. 'He gave Grigor the slightest of nods and pulled out onto the road. He was four cars behind the Insignia and even as the car turned and before it went underground and out of view, there was no way the driver could see him now. Grigor waited for another four cars and did a U-turn in the road to follow behind.

Mills drove down the ramp into the underground car park. Though a new development, it still felt close and not open enough for comfortable driving. He was minding his corners and he turned. The last thing he needed was to take out an Aston Martin or a Porsche. The car park was maybe half-full. Mills didn't know if that was normal or not. Most of the cars were parked near the lifts. There were glass walls where you could see from the car park into the lift lobby. There were people standing waiting to get into the lift. Down the far end, the car park was pretty much clear. The service lift and stairs were there. That is where Mills decided he wanted to park. He found a bay in the middle of the car park, not up against a wall. For some reason, he took note of his area. 'Zone G 'was painted on a pillar. He got out, fobbed his car to lock and walked over to the service staircase. Ilya crept through the car park looking for the car. Grigor had caught up as not all the other cars were going the same way and was only one car behind Ilya now. They saw the Insignia parked up and its driver disappearing up the service stairs. It confirmed for them what they were thinking. Somehow, someone knew what they were up to. The only leak could have been Vladislav. Why? They did not know. But it was part of their transmission that once their mission was complete, they should eliminate all links back to them. They took this as 'eliminate Vladislav.' That, however, was not for now. Now was to kill the British assassin and plant the bomb. Ilya slowly drove his car to the back of the Insignia. He parked it side-on, so his passenger door was almost touching the rear bumper. He got out and walked to his boot to get out the sports bag with the cylinder in it. It was heavy and bulky, but he used the shoulder strap to carry it and it didn't look out of place. Grigor circled the cars and came to a stop at the front of the Insignia. Again, the passenger door touching the bumper. From above, the three cars looked like the capital letter 'I'. Grigor got out of his car. The two had a brief discussion about their options. Plant the bomb and go? The Brit will either be in the building when it goes off, or he won't. What difference would it make? But what if he's on to them and is setting up an ambush? The pair quickly decided that he had to be taken out. It just made sense. They could hide the body and leave it. With all the drama that was about to follow, it might be days or weeks before someone finds him. And that way, a clear message would have been sent to the British Authorities. They moved at pace to the service stairs.

The service stairs doubled up as a fire escape. Mills climbed one flight and opened the fire door to the underground shopping mall. It was unreasonably bright. Everything was white, the walls, the floor, the ceiling. Clearly making up for the lack of natural light. The shops were all designer names. Mills hadn't really seen something like it before. He'd been to shopping precincts and streets with top brands on them, obviously. But here every single shop was high-end. The businesspeople of Canary Wharf liked their labels. He was about to close the door and start climbing again when he heard movement below. He didn't turn to look. He didn't know if it was friend or foe, but right now, he didn't care to find out. He pushed back through the door into the mall. Ilya and Grigor got to the top of the first flight of stairs just as the door closed behind Mills. Ilya had the bomb, so Grigor went after the Brit. Ilya continued to climb the stairs.

Mills got out into the bright lights. Mixing with the suits, he stood out like a sore thumb. He was dressed for a fight, not to buy Stocks and Shares. He knew he was going to be seen by whoever came out that door after him. He was still hoping it was nobody. But instinct said it wasn't. The fight was coming to him. He walked past a floor plan of the shops and saw the mall was in one big square. If he kept turning right, he'd get back to the fire exit and the service stairs. If no one was after him, he'd then be behind the Russian going up to One Canada Square and he'd be hunting. The position he'd rather be in. If the Russian was behind him right now, Mills would see him as he turned the corner and get a glimpse of who he was up against and maybe work out the best way to deal with him. If it was a spin on his heels and shoot it out, so be it. Mills turned right. He gave the cursory look as he did. He saw nothing. Suits, heels and a cleaner. Keep walking.

Grigor saw the Brit turn the corner. Grigor was trying to avoid eye contact, so was looking away and didn't see the same sign as Mills did. If he had, he would have done things differently, for sure. He followed around the corner to the right. He held back slightly as the mall was longer on this side. Or maybe it was just because he was on the corner, as opposed to joining it halfway along as he did when he came out of the fire escape. He pulled into a Jewellers doorway and watched as the Brit turned right again. Grigor followed.

Mills saw nothing suspicious as he turned the corner. He relaxed the idea that he was the hunted and re-focussed on getting to the Russian. He needed to work out what was happening and where. Maybe there was a generator they were going to take out with some fancy engineering? A server they could shut down? Or God forbid, they had a bomb? Mills picked up the cadence of his walking. He turned again. Nothing. He was one length of the mall, plus one turn and half a length away from the fire escape. He turned and looked. Shops, suits, a cleaner. He carried on and got to the fire escape. He went through and looked up the stairs.

When Ilya got to the top of the next flight, there was a clear distinction between the shopping mall premises and that of One Canada Square. Most notably, that of an alarmed fire escape. The mall doors were not alarmed, but from one property to another, Ilya understood why this one was. But he needed to get through it. He was prepared. He had on his person battery-powered circuit loops. He slid the metal plate of one circuit loop between the magnetic connectors on the door. That sent the signal from that sensor back to the server. He then pushed the second loop in place, this time with the connectors facing the door frame. Circuits complete. Ilya opened the door and slid through. He couldn't take the loops with him, he couldn't do that from the other side of the door, the risk of the alarm going off was too high. So, he had to leave them. But with Grigor on the case with the Brit, he didn't see the need to worry too much.

Ilya was breathing heavily by the fourth floor, with the weight of the device hanging off his shoulder. He placed it down for a moment to catch his breath. Just then, a cleaner from One Canada Square came through the service door, probably looking to use the service stairs as a quicker way to get from one floor to the next than walking the length of the office block to use the office lift. He was an old guy, working well into retirement. He was shocked to see someone in the stairwell.

'Jesus lad, you scared me half to death there! What are you doing out here?'

Ilya said nothing. He just stood and stared at the man.

'Are you new, I don't recognise you?'

Ilya clearly had a problem on his hands.

The man leaned in, 'That uniform, it's not ours, is it?'

With that, Ilya let go with a right hook that crashed into the side of the man's head. His head hit the wall and his knees buckled. As he slumped to the floor, Ilya put in a left uppercut for good measure. The man's teeth smashed against each other, and his head snapped back. He was unconscious before he hit the floor.

The fourth floor it was. Ilya didn't have time to carry on climbing now. He got the bag back on his shoulder and to help his cover, he took the cleaner's blue cloth he had in his hand. Ilya walked out to the office. He turned left and walked down the corridor with the blue cloth visible in his left hand, ready to wipe something if someone passed him. He found what he was looking for. An open cupboard that was next to a structural wall. Ilya went in and closed the door behind him. The bag came off his shoulder and opened to show the cylinder. He put his finger on the slide switch and pushed it up to the 'O 'position. He checked his watch. He zipped up the bag and left the cupboard. He took his phone out of his pocket. He needed to tell Grigor the device was set, and he wanted an update on the Brit.

Mills had made it to the fire escape door with the circuit loops. All it did was confirm he was right, and he was on the right track. He did think about taking the loops off and sounding the alarm, but that would no doubt escalate things to a level he couldn't control. Maybe the Russian would detonate the bomb instantly and therefore, Mills would have failed. Mills went through the fire escape and left the loops in place. He made it up a few flights of stairs and came across the cleaner bringing himself too, next to a fire escape door. His mouth was bleeding.

'You OK there? 'Asked Mills.

'Do I look OK? 'retorted the man, as he spat a tooth out.

'What happened?'

'New fella. Not seen him before. I thought he was lost. He just came at me, hit me on the side of the head and hit me on the way down.'

'New fella? As in, one of you? A cleaner?'

'Yeah'

'Where did he go? '

'No idea. Why?'

'Don't worry about that. You just look after yourself. Go to the hospital about your head and teeth.'

With that Mills went through the door. He looked right and left but saw nothing. He flipped a coin in his head and turned left. He was a few paces down the corridor when a cleaner came in to view, with a mobile phone to his ear.

Grigor kicked himself when he realised, he had walked a full square and had lost the target back into the stairwell. He flew up the next flight as quickly as he could. He went through the fire escape with the loops, recognising them to be theirs. He strode up the stairs, taking three at a time until he came across a man wearing the same type of uniform as he was wearing. Grigor saw what had happened. The cleaner was on his feet, bleeding from the mouth and looked alarmed to see Grigor. Grigor paused in front of him.

'You have phone? 'Grigor asked.

The man nodded.

'Drop on floor. Now.'

The cleaner obliged.

Grigor stamped on it. The phone screen smashed. Grigor put his finger to his lips and gave a silent 'Ssshhhh'. Grigor's phone started to ring as he walked through the door.

The penny had dropped with Mills. The cleaner in the mall. The beaten-up cleaner in the stairwell and now a cleaner in front of him. The Russian had used a disguise to mask his way around the building. Then the penny dropped further. Not Russian. Russians. Plural. Behind him, he heard a mobile phone ring. Mills turned to see a second Russian in the same uniform as the first guy. He turned back and started to draw his weapon. Then Ilya rushed Mills, grabbing his wrist and pushed him backwards. Grigor came forwards and grabbed Mills from behind. The pair of them muscled Mills back to the fire escape. The three of them burst through the door. The cleaner couldn't believe what he saw. But all he knew at this stage, was the two guys in the fake uniforms were the baddies and the guy being manhandled in the middle of them was the goodie. He took a swing at the first guy. Grigor hardly felt the punch land on his chin. But in retaliation, he threw his arm out, which sent the old boy flying backwards. Again, his head hit the wall. Again, he was knocked out. He slumped down on the ground. Grigor releasing his arm like that gave Mills an angle. He kneed Ilya in the nuts and head-butted backwards into Grigor's nose. He's bought himself a couple of inches of space. Fists went into the guy in front of him. Fists then went into the back of Mills 'head and ribs. Mills dived to the side to get away from the punishment. Again, he tried to reach for his pistol. Again, he was stopped. His arm was pressed against his body. Not only stopping him from drawing his weapon but taking that arm out of the fight as well. Clearly a Russian tactic. Another fist came swinging towards his head. The Russian in front of him went to draw his own weapon. Mills twisted it out of his grip and holding it by the barrel end, smashed the guy in the face with the grip. Mills cut the guy badly above the left eye. The Russian raged and picked Mills up and threw him against the far wall. The weapon fell out of Mills ' hand and as luck would have it, landed in the cleaner's mop bucket. Mills was winded and couldn't defend the boots that came into his ribs. He was stood up by the Russians and was head-butted several times. A second weapon was pulled and aimed at Mills 'head. He was about to be executed at point-blank range. Mills spat a mouthful of blood into Grigor's face. Grigor instinctively covered his face. Mills let off a rally of punches at both of the Russians. He got hold of Grigor's hand and tried to aim it at Ilya. He didn't succeed. Ilya stamped on Mills 'knee and Mills went down again. He came back up, diving into Ilya, who fell back against Grigor. Mills got on top of them and gave a crushing right hand to Ilya's throat. He wasn't as successful with Grigor, who still had his weapon in his hand. Mills had to try and keep the weapon away from him, whilst being on the receiving end of Grigor's rock-hard fist. Eventually, Mills got in close enough. He bit Grigor on the cheek. Grigor screamed and dropped the pistol.

Mills took off down the stairs. The Russians picked each other up and went after The Brit. As Mills went through the fire escape with the circuit loops, unintentionally he knocked one off. At the bottom of the stairs, there was a small alcove, so the stairs didn't lead straight into the car park. Mills stuck out his right hand as he got to the bottom of the stairs and put it on the corner wall of the alcove to use as an anchor and help him turn a sharp right, into the car park. When he got into the car park, he was going to get in his car, put some space between him and the stairwell alcove and using his car as cover, shoot it out with the Russians. What happened in reality, was that he stopped in his tracks when he saw he was boxed in. He had to think. He heard the Russians coming down the stairs. He ran forward and got in his car. He watched the stairwell as he turned the engine on. He put the car in first gear, kept the clutch down and revved the engine hard. The counter was pushing six thousand revs when Ilya and Grigor got to the bottom of the stairs. Mills took his foot off the clutch and kept the pressure on the accelerator. He had the car in a full lock right turn and the wheels spun and screeched on the car park floor. Ilya and Grigor turned the corner and came out of the alcove. Grigor had his weapon raised. Mills ' car started to shudder as the front wheels made sporadic traction with the floor. His car shook itself out of its incarceration at a perfect right angle. Mills had to over-correct the steering slightly, but when he was square-on to the Russians, the tyres took grip, and the car flew at them at maximum torque. Grigor was in front of Ilya. He let off a wild shot that went nowhere near Mills. The car smashed into Grigor's upper legs. His body bent forward onto the bonnet of the car and his face was pressed against the windscreen. Mills kept going forward. Less than a meter behind, Ilya was hit by his comrade and both men felt the force of the car. Mills was only stopped by the walls of the alcove. It was wide enough for people, but not wide enough for a car. Both corners of the car hit a brick wall. The front lights and indicators smashed. The Russians were propelled backwards and flew the three or so meters to the back wall. Ilya's torso hit the wall and a split second later, the back of his head hit it. A split second after that, Grigor's head came smashing into Ilya's face, sending his head back against the wall again. For a moment, both men stood upright, and all Mills could see was Grigor. Then, like layers of damp wallpaper, Grigor peeled to the floor, exposing Ilya, who too fell to the floor. Mills got out of the car. He walked around the open door and to the front corner where it was rammed into the wall. He looked over and saw the two dead Russians. There was no way they survived that. But not one to be taking a risk now, Mills took out his silenced pistol and put two rounds into the torso of each man. He was aware of the commotion above him. He could only assume the police had been called. He was hoping Phillips 'team were close.

CHAPTER 20

Phillips had clearly got the brief about the Chancellor and One Canada Square. The head of the British Economy and the flagship building for Financial Services. On the same day. He had to split his very small team and send them off to two different areas of London. He sent only two to support the Chancellor mission. Phillips 'thinking was the Chancellor has a protection team anyway, which was a good start. And if the assassination attempt was out in the open, then maybe they can control the crowds and the Met police better than in a building. Which left him plus three to get to Canary Wharf. He felt like he would need more to control that sort of situation if it all went down. And going by the track record of Jim and Mills so far, it was going to go down, and go down hard.

The two-man team knew the Chancellor was going to be arriving back at St. Pancras. The Special Branch can ask questions like that, and the Chancellor's office will happily give that information over. So, in one car, they deployed to the area. They parked up two streets south of the station. When the Chancellors Eurostar pulled in, they prepared to move to the area. Expecting an assassination attempt straight away. They were expecting Jim to do his job at the station and be long gone before they showed up. Then, building on what they did before, they would take ownership of the scene, keeping London Transport Police at bay, while they assessed who they had got, bagged him, tagged him and got him to Thames House.

What they weren't expecting to hear was an explosion that

sounded like a grenade going off on the road outside the station. There was a fight going on. They moved. At pace. They listened to the '48 - the London police radio network. They heard another explosion before they heard anything being reported. They raced north. Soon the calls were coming in as fast as the next explosion. 'A high-speed chase in Holloway.' 'Gunshots heard. ' 'One IC1 in a saloon car, one motorbike in pursuit.'

The pair were not actually sure if they were now on the correct call. They were waiting for a report in the station, or on the Chancellor's car as a minimum. Soon the transmissions changed and there were reports of gunfire at a construction site. The pair closed into the area, hoping to be one beat ahead of the Met police.

When they got to the construction site. With the exception of the generator growling away, all was quiet. They walked round to the far side of the portacabins to see a corpse in a pitiful mess. Beaten, half-naked, covered in blood, peppered with cuts all over his torso and shot through the length of his body. It was enough of a sight to make them question exactly what the fuck happened. They looked over at Jim's car. This was going to be quite a clean-up operation. As the Met police got to the gates for the construction site, one of the pair went over to brief them that this was now a Special Branch operation and they could stand down, while the other got on the phone to Phillips.

Phillips had himself and his team in two cars, a couple of miles apart, at places where they could get to Canary Wharf pretty easily if they had to. They too were just playing the waiting game.

Part of Phillips was really happy he was involved in this mission. As 'not good 'as it all was, this was the way of the dark world of espionage, sabotage and assassinations and he loved being part of it all. Another part of him was a bit pissed off they were just the clean-up crew. He did offer up his team to do the job of Jim and Mills. He told Mitchell how good his undercover officers were and argued the Special Branch was in a better place to deal with this mission than Special Forces. It was only when Mitchell explained the sensitivity of the intelligence coming to him, and the fact that the Russians were deemed Military themselves, that Phillips had to concede that it wasn't technically a National Security matter, but more a Military-coated Diplomatic one. He understood the politics of it all as much as the next man. And the next man, from what Phillips saw, understood fuck all.

He was only just off the phone to the lads in North London when things escalated for his team. He didn't need to call Mitchell about the construction site. Reports from the Chancellors driver would have already got to Mitchell. And right now, as long as the Chancellor was alive, then Mitchell had done his job. If the assassin was dead, then Jim had done his. If Jim was dead, then Mitchell had a lot of paperwork to fill out. That's how Phillips saw it, anyway.

Over the Canary Wharf police radio, Phillips heard that the fire alarm at One Canada Square had gone off. That was enough for him. He gave the call and the two cars started heading towards the location. He called on the radio for more information. It trickled in, frustrating Phillips.

Mills gave his car a quick once over. Though damaged lights

and dents in the front wings, the car was drivable. He eyeballed the two Russians cars. Why two? He still had his weapon in his hand, when the police arrived. They turned up mob-handed. Generally, they have an easy time on the Canary Wharf posting. Almost glorified security more than the police. But this time, with it all going off, every man and his dog had turned up to the party. The officer closest to Mills spotted the pistol and pulled a Taser on Mills.

'Taser, taser! Place your weapon on the floor! 'He shouted in a very well-drilled - but never used in anger until now - voice.

'I can't do that, mate. 'replied Mills.

'Police. Place your weapon on the floor and step back from it, or I will be forced to Taser you. 'Again, it sounded like the police officer knew the words, but wanted to cry. His voice was about to crack. Maybe he's not seen a dead body before. That was no reflection on him. But Mills was getting impatient, waiting for someone grown-up to take over.

'I can't. I can't let you have it. I'm not a threat. I can't explain right now. But if you would just relax and let me holster it…?'

It was too late. One of the dog handlers was patrolling the area and had made his way to the Russians cars. The dog sat next to one of them. Mills saw it. He knew exactly what it meant. The handler piped up.

'We have a confirmed in this car.'

All the officers' eyes widened. And all of them as if on cue, pulled their Tasers. Now, Mills had six pointing at him.

'Time to do as you're told, Mills…' He thought to himself. As he was slowly complying with the latest demand to put his weapon down, he looked up to see a team of four walking towards him. The man leading the four was Phillips.

'Officers, thank you for taking control of the scene. However, I will take it from here. I am Superintendent Phillips of the Special Branch, and this is now my operation.'

'Sir, 'Piped up the Sergeant 'I'm not sure about that. He's just shot those two men there and there is a suspected device in the boot of that car.'

'Sergeant, I am telling you to stand down and take control of the situation upstairs. If you want to challenge my authority, we can head down the fucking pound now, and we can thrash it out. But I assure you I will take your job, your pension, your soul and your fucking wife if you do. Do you understand me?'

'Yes Sir.'

With that, the Sergeant signalled to his teams and they all re-holstered their Tasers and with the dog in tow, headed back to the main lift lobby and back up to the mall.

Mills holstered his pistol.

'Thanks for showing up…'

'To be fair Mills, you should be long gone.'

'Aware of that. But your pals had something to say about it.'

'Not my pals.'

'Ah come on Phillips, you were just like them once.'

Phillips didn't even grace the comment with an expression, never mind a retort.

'What's going on here then, is there a device in that car?'

'I assume so, 'said Mills, getting in his car. 'And I reckon there is another in 'Canada Square as well. Fourth floor.'

'OK. You want a lift, and we can deal with your car?'

'No ta. It's kind of in-keeping with where I'm staying. I'll be fine until I can get Knocker to square me away with a new one. But thanks.'

'Fine Anything else I need to know?'

'There's a cleaner on the fourth. In the stairwell. He helped me. Please look after him. Other than that, those two are yours.'

And with that, Mills reversed his car, turned it towards the exit and drove off.

CHAPTER 21

Jim took a long time to walk home. He was hurt. His body was sore, and he felt drained. He needed to take on fluids. From doing a metaphorical head-to-toe as he walked, he guessed he had no wounds that wouldn't heal. Nothing broken. Nothing damaged beyond repair.

He got himself home by walking small streets and along the canal. He avoided eye contact with everyone. He didn't want a conversation. He got home and sat himself down in his chair. He took a moment to compose before he started to administer himself again. His body screamed out in agony. He took more of the painkillers that were supplied by Kingston. He stripped off and went for a shower.

Mills got back to his flat after parking a street away and walking in. He got into his flat and put the doorstop under the front door. He needed a drink. He opened a half-drank bottle of whiskey and poured it into a coffee mug. He drank it down in a couple of gulps. He pulled a face as it burned down his throat. He breathed in through his nose as he felt the heat leave his stomach and course through his veins. He felt good. He started to administer himself and his kit. Wounds were tended to, and magazines recharged.

Vladislav was sitting and waiting. Stewing. He had several

radios tuned in to police networks. He had the news on, and he had two mobile phones sitting on his desk. Neither of which was ringing. Things were not adding up. He had heard over the police networks of explosions near St. Pancras station. That was Aleksi in action. But he had not heard on the News anything about the Chancellor. He had not got a call from Aleksi confirming the kill. He had not heard on the News about an explosion at Once Canada Square. Why had Ilya or Grigor not called? What was going on? How can he run an operation if no one communicates with him? It also did not sit well that both missions were appearing to have been foiled, by one man. The man in the CCTV. It was becoming more and more apparent to Vladislav that someone was on to him. But who? And how? Who would have access to the sort of information that would lead them to stop his missions? These questions had been bugging Vladislav for days now. The same questions. Someone must be giving the information over. Someone from his side. Someone from the Kremlin. Someone *must* be a traitor. Or a Mole. And worse than that, they are now actively hunting him and his team. There must be a team of them. There is no way this is a lone operator. No chance both missions have been stopped today by just one person. Last time, maybe. Not today. No way. He felt like he was being watched. He was a caged rat and he hated it. He felt insulted. If he had failed again, and it was starting to look that way, the next transmission from Moscow would not be a good one. Agents are an expensive resource. And they would be booked up for other missions. The impact of failure would be felt far and wide.

Vladislav stewed and festered. What was he missing? Why could he not achieve what he needed to achieve? Who was stopping him? His mind was on a loop. Who was in control here? Where did he need to turn now? He could not stop. He was one of the Soviet's greatest. He needed to re-assess. He needed a plan. He listened to the radios. He watched the News. He thought. He schemed. He planned. He replanned.

One Canada Square came on the News. He froze. He watched. 'An evacuation of Canary Wharf's One Canada Square took place this morning 'The reporter started, 'A fire alarm sounded during the morning's trading. '

Vladislav watched with bated breath. The News was not what he wanted to hear. The News reporter finished with the line 'There was no suggestion this was terrorist-related. 'Vladislav raged. He picked up the TV and threw it against the wall. Whatever happened, it was stopped and now, again the world will see. It didn't happen. He was officially fucked. There may not be a transmission. There may just be a hit put out on him for failing. Again. He had to think. Think. 'No suggestion this was terrorist-related. 'The blood drained from his face. Terrorist. Maybe that was the answer. Maybe that was why the agents were failing. They were assigned to assassinate and destroy. As per the old ways. But the old ways, *their old ways* were not the ways that got to the UK. What got to the UK were acts of terrorism. Vladislav sat in his chair. It was as if he'd just had an epiphany.

Vladislav took himself to the Embassy. Unannounced. This was not common practice. Even though he was known there and welcome, it was not the norm for agents of any stature or operational activity to just turn up on the doorstep. But it didn't matter. Vladislav, the former Soviet KGB great, had everyone's attention.

'Give me a line to the Kremlin. 'He insisted.

The clerk that greeted him wasn't sure what to do. It would be out of place to point-blank refuse, but it was not common practice to call the Kremlin unannounced.

'Give me a secure line, now. 'He insisted. Vladislav was still standing with a subtle twist in his torso where his skin was tight from the burns. He looked tired and he was half-cut. He looked like a psychotic homeless person.

The clerk looked over her shoulder to a Diplomat. He nodded and led Vladislav to a private office.

CHAPTER 22

Mitchell's head was too full of ideas and pieces of the puzzle to focus on anything else. He almost didn't hear the secure phone ring. When he realised it was ringing, he stared at it for a moment, before rushing over to answer.

'Hello?'

'James. Sorry for the call out of the blue. But you need to know this.'

'OK, go on?'

'The Kremlin got a call today. From London. As I understand it, there is one guy orchestrating all the attacks. And he's pissed off mate. Big time.'

'OK, right, an agent we know?'

'I don't know mate, but we'd assume so. Anyway, he's worked out you are on to him. So, he's changing tact mate. Whatever the conversation was - and James, I'm only working on what I can glean from my contact here - he got approval from The President himself.'

'He spoke to Putin?'

'No…. he got approval from him. He asked for a meeting with someone. Something is being organised. I don't know who and I don't know what about. But I don't think there are any more warm bodies to be sent to the UK.'

'So, what is it?'

'I don't know, but he's requested a meeting in two days 'time at the Safe House in North Kensington. You know the one, along the canal?'

'Of course, I do. Two days? That is Saturday.'

'Yes. At eight in the evening.'

'With who?'

'I don't know mate. I know nothing else. Listen, James, they know information has been fed to them. I'm a bit twitchy here. Do as you have to do, of course. But just be aware, they are looking for you. And me….'

'Understood. Be careful. And thank you.'

They both hung up. More to cram into Mitchell's head. He had debriefs with the two lads tomorrow. He had to keep unpicking the mess and piecing together the puzzle. He knew the shopping list for Knocker was going to be big, including a car. Or two, going by Phillips 'report. And now this. Changing tact? That would imply they have admitted their current operational model is not working, which was obvious. But it's not over. Not yet. They are definitely on to the fact they are being targeted, so now will be actively looking for who that person is. Mitchell was happy he had enforced no-comms on the lads. He felt like he was keeping them safe. He no longer felt safe himself. Or more accurately, he never felt safe in his job, but he felt even less safe now.

He needed to plan. Fast. He focussed on the Safe House, where the meeting was to be held. It was a diplomatic safe haven. Anyone from any country, doing any job, legal or illegal, official or off-the-grid, can go and be unchallenged. They can rest, hold meetings and recuperate. Everyone is equal in these Safe Houses. And everyone has the right to anonymity and to go about their business. A British Agent can't go in there and say to someone 'You are Mossad and you're about to assassinate an Imam on UK soil. 'It just doesn't work like that. Every country has Safe Houses like this. Mitchell knew it was impossible to get a mole in there or any listening devices. If he wanted to hear, or better still, see who was meeting up in the safe house, it needed to come from outside the building.

He also had a very small window to get this right. Could he ask the lads to assist? Would they? Or would they leave the spy game to the spies? Mitchell guessed they wouldn't mind, and it would be easier to ask them than to try and cut through the red tape of his own official channels. If he could place a camera himself, he could get one of the lads to collect it.

Mitchell went to Regents Park Barracks and rang Knocker's bell. He'd called ahead but didn't give any details. But Knocker was fully up to speed on the operation, so was expecting something interesting.

'Alright fella, come on in. 'He said as he opened the door.

They made their way to the store area and Knocker parked himself round the far side. There were two mugs of Tea on the counter. Mitchell was a coffee person but didn't bring that up. He appreciated the gesture.

'So, I've already pre-empted the boy's shopping lists. ' Knocker said. 'I've got Jim a new car. And transferred all his kit. I've got some more cash, ammo, some new threads and a fresh body armour each, thus far.'

'Thanks, Knocker. I'm guessing Mills will ask for a new car as well. Phillips said he was smashed into a wall. Why he drove it away, is anyone's guess. I've not had their debrief yet, though. Which is why I'm here.'

'Go on. Nothing can surprise me about this job now.'

'Well, I think we've got a chance of finding out who the lead Agent is. It's a bit of a sensitive subject, but I want to try and get video imagery of him at the Safe House in Kensington.'

'Sensitive as in you're not allowed to, because spying inside a Diplomatic Safe House is the biggest faux pas going?'

'Something like that.'

'What do you need from me?'

'A video camera. With a wide lens. We have a certain type back at ours, but I can't walk into our Q-branch and just sign one out. So....'

'I know the exact type you use, mate. I may have acquired one myself a couple of years ago.'

Knocker went to the back of his store and came back with the exact camera Mitchell was after. Mitchell wasn't a betting man, but if he was, he'd have placed a good wager on the fact this exact camera was the one that went missing after a Surveillance job. It wasn't a couple of years ago, it was less than one year ago. But never mind that now, Mitchell had what he needed.

'Thanks. 'I'll need it for a few days.

'No problem, 'said Knocker, 'You know how to use it?'

'I certainly do.'

'Including the positioning IR feature?'

'Including the IR feature.'

'Well then, it's yours. Best you check the batteries in it before you use it, though.'

'Thanks, Knocker. 'Smiled Mitchell. They were both playing the coy game over the camera. They both knew it was originally the Security Services, but Mitchell couldn't prove it and he needed it off Knocker for his new little mission.

'I need some more kit. Well, specifically, I think Jim will need some more kit.'

Knocker smiled and took out an imaginary notepad and pen, ready to take down the new shopping list.

The second round of live letterboxes was in a similar format as the first. Pretending to be a taxi driver was a good way of meeting a perceived random person on the street and having a private conversation. However, this time round, Mitchell's paranoia was through the roof. Instead of pulling over on the road, like the lads were hailing a cab - as they did last time, Mitchell didn't want to stop the taxi. He didn't want to take the chance of any CCTV in London spying on him. He was convinced by now, all cameras were on him, and they were being run by the Russians. He knew, of course, this wasn't the case. But he imposed strict rules upon himself and thus far, they've kept him alive.

So, this time, He gave the lads a road to be on and Mitchell would be driving his black cab down that road at a certain time. London traffic permitting.

Jim was first, as he had all the kit to collect, and Mitchell didn't want it in his presence for any longer than necessary.

On Shaftesbury Avenue, mid-morning on Friday, Jim slowly walked the street. Watching, profiling like he always did. He was watching for anyone that might be watching him, and he was also watching for a Black Cab, with its TAXI light off and a certain registration plate. The plan was, as soon as Mitchell saw Jim approach, he'd turn his light on, indicating that he was ready for a fare. Then Jim could get in, without drawing suspicion. This happens in the middle of the street all the time, so there was no need to be pulling over.

Jim Saw the light on a Black Cab turn on. He checked the Reg and then confirmed everything by eyeballing the driver. With a flat cap and Ray-Ban sunglasses, Mitchell looked more like a caricature of a cabbie than a real taxi driver. Still, it was him. As Jim made his way over, A man in a suit raced to get in the taxi. He had already half-opened the sliding door when Jim put his arm in front of him, blocking his way.

'Sorry fella, this one is mine.'

'I don't think so. I was here first. Now get out my way.'

The man tried to push past Jim's arm. There were only seconds to go before Mitchell had to follow the flow of traffic and move on. Jim took the only appropriate action he could. He moved his right hand from in front of the man, and as he tried again to get in the taxi, Jim grabbed him by the collar of his shirt. He started to twist his wrist. The man was wearing a tie and it started to instantly cut off his air supply. Jim pulled him back and whispered in his ear, 'If I say the taxi is mine, it's fucking-well mine. 'And threw the man back.

The man gasped and cried out 'Assault! I'm calling the police! 'All potential witnesses must have been looking away that day, as no one came to the gents' assistance.

Jim sat in the back of the cab and smiled in the mirror at Mitchell.

'Jesus Jim, I thought that was him then.'

'Him?'

'Well, a Russian. I thought I was in for it.'

'No mate, just a prat in a suit. Anyway, how are you? You look tired.'

'And you look fucked, if you don't mind me saying?'

'I do feel pretty special.'

Mitchell and Jim discussed the last job in detail. They discussed the target himself and that it was reported he was safe, soon after the Jaguar left the main route it was on. They discussed the use of thunderflashes and grenades and the car chase that took place. They discussed the fight and how it all ended. Before they moved on, Jim asked the one thing that was still bothering him.

'Why was the construction site empty, Mitchell?'

'Well, would you believe it, there was a Health and Safety issue. The Local Authority had closed the site due to non-compliance with the main contractor. They had only walked everyone off-site an hour before you went crashing through the gates. And it all got resolved shortly after. Phillips 'team had to then explain to the contractor why they still couldn't get on site. They blamed the Local Authority, so the contractor went through the roof at them. It was all quite amusing for a short period of time.'

'Sounds hilarious. 'Jim didn't mean to sound so unimpressed, but he just wanted an answer, not the whole back story. He was past that point now. He looked down at his feet. There was a large sports bag.

'Is this for me?'

'It is. So, I've taken a guess as to what you might need. Rounds, cash etc. And there is some equipment there for a task I need you to do.'

Mitchell explained what was needed from Jim. As he did so, Jim looked through the bag for the bits of kit he may require As they got closer to Jim's drop-off point, Mitchell concluded by saying,

'I hope this is going to give us the information I need to close this Mission.'

'But you've not said what that information is?'

'You know I'm not just going to say. Just in case I'm wrong.'

'I know, I know….'

'It would be nice to conclude this Mission. Right, this is you…'

'It would indeed. Thanks, Mitchell. I've got all I need then, see you next time.'

Jim took the bag and got out of the taxi. He had a set of car keys in his hand. He pressed the fob and parked on the side of the road two cars down, was his new wheels. This time it was a Ford. Jim looked over his shoulder and walked to the car. He quickly popped the boot and held it down, to stop it from opening all the way up. He saw his kit in the back. He threw the bag in, closed the boot and got in the driver's side. With one final look about and an adjustment of the mirrors, he was off.

Mills got in the taxi on the North side of the River Thames, near Tower Bridge. The process was the same as with Jim - walk up to the taxi in the street, as opposed to waiting for Mitchell to park up. Mills got in the taxi and started with some banter.

'I hope you're not on the higher tariff.'

'Mills, 'answered Mitchell, 'You can have this fare on me.'

'Very decent of you. So, what do you want to know?'

Again, the last job was discussed in great detail. Mitchell was interested to hear there were two of them and impressed at how Mills dealt with them.

'Why didn't you leave the car? 'He asked, 'Jim did.'

'Just felt better to keep it close. I'm quite attached to it, to be honest. Jim having it rough as well?'

'Well, you both are working hard to resolve this. We can swap your car at your convenience.'

'No problem. What's next? Same as normal, another dead letterbox in two days?'

'As it goes, no. Not this time. I've got Jim on a task for me, and I was hoping you can help him out?'

'Go on.'

'He's collecting something for me, and he will be in the canal late at night. He needs cover getting out the canal and sorting himself out.'

'Sure, what's he collecting, an old shopping trolley?'

'Every chance he might bump into one! No, it's only a punt, to be honest. But I'm hoping to get some information.'

'OK, well, I guess your wish is my command. I mean, it'll be nice to see Jim.'

'Thanks.'

The two finished their conversation as they went over the bridge to the South. Mills guided Mitchell to an area he now knew well. Somewhere where he could get a coffee and stroll home. He got out of the taxi and gave the cursory tap on the roof as you do when you're saying goodbye to a friend.

Mills started to walk towards a coffee shop when his pocket started to buzz. He gave a look behind him, to make sure Mitchell was long gone. He instinctively moved closer to a shop doorway, so he was out of sight from the main road, just in case. He took out of his pocket a small mobile phone. Not a smartphone, a cheap one you can buy from a market trader. The screen showed 'Withheld Number'. Mills answered. 'I wasn't expecting you to be calling me. 'He said.

CHAPTER 23

Mitchell didn't sleep Friday night. He had too much to do. He tested and retested the camera. He made sure the IR worked so he could place the camera at the correct angle, to get the best hope of any footage. He put the camera in a waterproof sealable bag and tested the footage. It was grainy at best, but it was going to have to do. Mitchell had decided to keep the details of this task to himself. He was going to place the camera under the bridge. Not because he didn't trust anyone, but because at this stage of the game, he just wanted absolute certainty that the camera was going to be placed where he wanted it, to get any information possible. The bridge he was going to use was a footbridge over the canal. It wasn't one that went over the towpath. So, there was no chance of someone walking by and seeing it or kicking it. The only true risk was if a canal boat clipped it as it went through the tunnel. If that happened, or if the camera falls into the canal and he was the one placing it, then that's on him. If he asked Jim to place the camera and it fell into the canal, then they would be no further forward, and Mitchell knew Jim would take something like that personally. It was better this way.

Not one for unnecessary risks, Mitchell had asked Phillips ' team for protection in the area. So, the plan was quite simple. Phillips 'team would be scattered about, minding their own business, as you do at half-past three in the morning. And then Mitchell would drive up and park as close to the bridge as he could. He would then personally get into the canal and place the camera himself, using IR goggles to point the lens at the window of the Safe House. He'd hold the camera in place with fast-drying cement and as soon as he was happy, Mitchell could get out the canal and go back to his car.

CHAPTER 24

Vladislav was elated with the prospect of meeting the contact. His conversations leading to this point had been very productive. He knew he was on his back foot after losing five agents to his mission. A mission that was being hung around his neck as a failure. However, he had one last go at being truly victorious. And it would not cost him time or agents or resources. It would cost him money. But money was something The Kremlin had plenty of. And in the light of not having any sort of victory in this campaign since it started other than Compton, the idea of taking out Great Britain's throat was an exciting thought.

Vladislav was hoping that as well as the lure of money, this person he is due to meet later that day, would be a true believer. It's always better when they want the kill, and it's not just for financial gain.

Mitchell sat in his chair. Thinking. He was tired, but he was focused. He needed to play one last hand to ensure he got the footage he was after. He was merely hours away from capturing the orchestrator of all this carnage on video camera. He needed to make a call. He just needed to be very delicate with it.

Every now and then, he smelt himself. Even after a long shower, he still smelt of canal water. He got up. Moving around woke him up and he could smell himself less that way. He picked up a landline phone. He dialled the Whitehall operator and asked to be put through to a certain extension. When he got to that operator, he asked to be put through to a different line again. He was masking his call trail the best he could. The phone rang. Eventually, it was answered.

'Hello? 'Came a very English-sounding voice.

'Hello, I'm calling from Crow. 'Said Mitchell. Modern intelligence stemmed from the formation of the RAF, and the Codenames they gave each unit at the time of formation were all the names of birds. The RAF gave themselves Albatross, the king of the skies. And it filtered down from there. By the time they got to MI5, only small nuisance birds existed. Or so the rumour has it…

'How can I help?'

'You have a guest visiting later today. In fact, they may already be with you. They will be having a meeting later tonight and I was wondering if you could give them a certain room to have that meeting?'

'You know full well I cannot do this.'

'I know. OK, I understand. I promise you, no one is looking at you personally or is near your building and no one is compromising the integrity of what you are doing. Your full protection is in place. I was just hoping you could facilitate this request?'

'What room?'

'Second floor. Canal-side?'

There was a long pause and then the voice spoke.

'I don't know or care who visits this building. You know this. That is not my concern. But if I offer a room to an experienced person, they will smell a rat. The best I can do is, if asked, I can suggest where they could hold a meeting. That is it.'

'That will have to do. Thank you.'

The phone went dead before Mitchell finished speaking. Everything now was in place. Or as near to being in place as it could be. Paper-thin strands of intelligence tying together to create a chain that leads to the perpetrator. This had better work.

Jim had spent his Saturday going over the kit Mitchell, or probably more specifically Knocker had provided. There was a mini-rebreather system. That was the bit of kit that caught his eye. He knew it was there, Mitchell told him about the job, but he'd not got it out of the bag until Saturday morning. It was much snazzier than the ones he's used in the past. It was smaller with a good commercial mouthpiece. Not like the huge lump of plastic the Military version makes you put in your trap. There was also the chemical-crystals as well, for absorbing Carbon Dioxide, so he put it all together and had a quick breath through the system to see what it felt like. He sorted out the clothes he would be wearing and was hoping Mills had the brief and was bringing a spare set for him, for when he got out the canal. The rest of the day, Jim relaxed. He ate, snoozed, wanked and snoozed some more.

Mills tried not to overthink the call he had the day before. After a few days on this mission, he had got himself that phone. He had checked in at irregular slots throughout his entire career. There was always some information that needed to be passed on.

This time around, Mills got the phone and touched base out of habit, more than anything. He wasn't obliged to in any way, but it made him feel useful and when he got the callback, he was glad he did. 'A guy wants to meet with you, so he does.' And so, that evening, Mills will meet this guy. Whoever he was. There will clearly be some mutual benefit in it. Otherwise, he would have not got the call. After that meeting, he can go and complete his task for Mitchell.

'And after that, 'Mills said out loud to himself as he made himself some lunch in his flat, 'I might treat myself to a pint.'

CHAPTER 25

Vladislav got to the area of the Safe House early. No reason, other than he was just keen. He could finally see how his legacy would play out. How his name would be immortalised. How he could return to Russia victorious and respected.

The Safe House was an old Edwardian-style building. It was in keeping with its surroundings. He walked up to the door and pressed the buzzer. On request by a male voice, he gave over Russia's diplomatic immunity code and less than ten seconds later, he was buzzed in. Inside it was clean and well presented. But that was it. No documentation or any indication at all that it was nothing more than an empty building in the middle of London. The hallway was about twenty meters long and at the far end was another door. Vladislav went through the same process and the door buzzed open. Inside, the building opened up to a labyrinth of hallways and doors. Most of the doors were shut, a few were open. The scale of the building was deceiving. It was like it had the Tardis effect. Vladislav walked the corridors and every now and then he would see someone sitting in a room, minding their own business. Reading the paper, drinking coffee and in one case, someone even had a pistol out on a table. But nothing hostile. No one was talking to anyone else.

A man approached Vladislav. He spoke in perfect Russian.

'Welcome. As I understand it, you've not been here before?'

'No, But I have used a similar facility on the other side of London.'

'Perfect, then I guess I don't need to explain any etiquette to you. Please help yourself to whatever you need and just inform me when you leave.'

'Thank you. There is one thing. I am having a meeting soon. Where would you suggest I hold this?'

'Perhaps try the second floor, to the south of the building away from the bedrooms. You'll find somewhere private there I would say.'

'Thank you,'

Vladislav made his way up a flight of stairs and instinctively found himself heading south. Towards the canal-side of the building. He walked past closed doors which he assumed were bedrooms with Agents in them. Catching one last decent nights ' sleep before they go on a mission. Or resting up between flights in and out of the country. He missed that life. Though at the time it was not all that glamorous, it was certainly better than how he'd been living and working in recent times. He found a room with its door open. He walked in. It was a plain room with magnolia walls and a window on the far side. There was a desk and a chair. It was big enough to hold a dining table in the middle, but with just the desk to one side, it felt bigger than it probably was. Which was fine. He went to find the coffee machine. He had ten minutes to his meeting. He would have coffee on the table as a gesture when this man came in. That was good enough hospitality as far as Vladislav was concerned.

Mills was very intrigued by the meeting he had been ordered to attend. More often than not, he was being asked for information. And the level of sensitivity of that information was directly proportional to the threat levels and paramilitary activities at that time. But Mills was told this meeting could change everything. And there was a lot in it for Mills, as well. All very cryptic, but Mills trusted his unit.

He walked up to the door of the Safe House and pressed the buzzer. When a voice answered, he gave the word he was told to use. He had no idea it was a Diplomatic Immunity Code.

He was buzzed in and slowly walked the hallway to the second door. Same process. This time, when he got through the second door, he was met immediately. He was met by the same person who met Vladislav. He spoke in perfect English.

'Good evening.'

'Evening.'

'I'm aware this is your first time here. Let me take a moment to outline some housekeeping.'

'OK.'

'Where you are is a Diplomatic Safe House. It doesn't exist. And while inside it, you don't exist. No one knows you and you know no one. Even if you see someone you recognise, you ignore them. No business, political or other is done here. Are you with me so far?'

'I think so.'

'Good. Everyone in this building carries equal weight, and you cannot use the fact you have seen faces here to your advantage. You cannot go back to, for example, your respective intelligence agency and tell them you have seen *So 'n so* from whatever country. Do that, and it will get fed back in and you will not only blacklist yourself, but you will cause Diplomatic unrest and you may be the person losing out. Still with me?'

'I think so.'

'OK, feel free to find a room to rest. You can eat from the restaurant and help yourself to refreshments. If you need a room for the night, I can arrange that. If you need medical attention, I can also probably assist. If you need to get to your Embassy, we can arrange transport. That's about it.'

'I am supposed to be meeting someone.'

'Ah, of course. I'm not sure who you are meeting, but you may find someone on the second floor, far-side of the building.'

'Thank you.'

Mills unbuttoned his coat because he was warm. In doing so, he flashed his pistol.

'Best to keep that out of eyesight for now. You're not the only one here carrying. But you're not a face anyone recognises. That elevates interest anyway if you understand me. The last thing you need is attention you don't need.'

'Understood. 'Mills buttoned up his jacket and pointed towards the stairwell at the end of the hall in an inquisitive manner.

'Be my guest. 'Said the gent.

Mills walked the hall and had a sideways look into the open doors. Most of the people he saw looked like middle-aged businessmen. Minding their own business. Most were Caucasian, there was one middle eastern looking guy who Mills convinced himself he recognised. And one Oriental guy, who had a scar on his face, going over his left eye. The eye was dead and was just a blurred white mess. The guy looked like he had jumped straight out of the cinema screen of the latest James Bond movie.

Mills walked upstairs and down a corridor of closed doors. The end door was open. The light was on.

'Here we go Mills, 'He whispered to himself, 'Lets see what is going on.'

Mills walked into the room without knocking. He saw in front of him, an older guy, who looked weathered, but his eyes were bright. 'Switched on', as they say. He stood with a gait and was reasonably dressed. He didn't seem to be armed and when he spoke, he had what sounded like a German accent, though accents all bled into one with Mills. He seemed startled to see Mills, even though it was 8 pm on the dot, but soon offered him coffee.

Vladislav was making a coffee from the pot he had brought in when he felt someone standing in the door. He turned to see a man. A man he thought he recognised. He wasn't sure, but it might be the man from the CCTV. 'Could this be? 'Vladislav's thought process raced at a hundred miles an hour and the idea that he could have been double-crossed and this guy was here to kill him did spring to mind. But then, it felt like poetry that he of all people was here to do some work for Vladislav himself. He also realised that his own true identity is not known, and the last thing he needed to do was give it away at this late stage.

'Good evening. I am glad you arrived. Please, please help yourself to coffee.'

The coffee was on the table at the far wall, Mills had to walk across the room to get to it. Vladislav circled wide to give him the room he needed. At one point in the centre of the room and though set back, square-on to the window, Mills turned to talk to the German, as he felt uncomfortable having his back to him.

'Do you want a top-up?'

'Nein, I am good thank you.'

Mills carried on to the table, after his quick check to make sure he was not about to be executed. He made a coffee and then stood two paces away from the table.

'How can I help?' He asked.

'After making enquiries, you have come recommended. We are looking to make a significant, what shall we say, impact, on the British Sovereign.'

'The Royal Family?'

'Correct. You are Irish Republican Army, yes?'

'After a fashion.'

'I am sorry, I do not understand.'

'Yes. Yes, I am. I just exercise my duties in a different way. But I am a true identifier. That's what you wanted, correct?'

'Yes, yes indeed. This is good. And you err…. Protect them? Are you police?'

'Don't worry about me. All you need to know is that yes, soon I will be protecting them.'

'Soon?'

'I have some work to finish, and I will be back protecting the

Royal Family.'

'Work you say?'

'Not yours to worry about. You are German?'

'Yes, forgive me if my English is not so good.'

'Your English is better than my German. So, you're fine. But why is Germany planning an attack on the Royal Family?'

'We are all, how do you say, a front, yes? I am a middleman. I do my job and that is it.'

'And your job is to recruit someone to do your employer's dirty work?'

'You romanticise the point. I have a vast amount of money to pay you. If you accept, your life will be different forever. House, car, woman. You cannot have what I can offer you with a government wage.'

'And my organisation also benefits, as I understand it?'

'A contribution will be made to your cause, yes. But think of the good you can do!'

'You don't need to sell it to me. I just need to picture it in my head.'

'Picture Six Million pounds in a Swiss bank account?'

Mills paused for thought. If this meeting had come to him from any other avenue, he'd think someone was taking the Royal piss.

'So, what is the deal?' he asked.

'There is no rush. Soon you will be back on the Royal

Protection Team, yes? You said so yourself?'

'At some point.'

'And you will be protecting Prince William and his family?'

'It's not a guarantee, but I could manoeuvre things to make that happen.'

'Then it is simple. You need what? Two days to think it over? Call your people and they will call my people, 'Vladislav was being very nonchalant about this part of the conversation. As if it was old hat to him. He was even waving his hand around in a very European looking way. To Mills, it seemed more of a French or Italian thing than German. 'And then we have a deal. Your money will be put to one side and sit there until you complete your duties.'

'And if it's a, no?'

'Your people said it would be unlikely you would say no. They said yes for you.'

'Yeah. So yes, of course. I don't need two days to think about it. But it won't happen soon. There is a process to follow. And like I said, I need to be reassigned first.'

'Yes, of course, your current mission. What did you say it was again?'

'I didn't. And I won't.'

'Of course. Forgive me. I am just humbled to meet a man so embedded as you are. It is quite something.'

'It is what it is. And flattery will get you nowhere.'

'I don't understand?'

'Forget it. OK, are we done? I will call my people. We have a deal. I'm the one taking all the risk here. This will be the biggest upset in British history. I don't want to be the scapegoat for this.'

'Your money and immunity are already guaranteed. We just need you to pull the trigger.

'Twice.'

'Yar.'

Vladislav walked forward two steps and offered a hand to shake. He walked crooked like he had a hip issue or some sort of spinal injury. Mills stepped forward and shook his hand. They were square in the middle of the room.

Mills was the first to leave the room. He put his coffee mug, still full from not touching a drop, down on the table and gave the weird German a nod as he walked past him and out the door.

Vladislav stood where he was. Elation took over him. He was finally getting what he wanted. For a financial cost that was already dismissed by Putin, he now had an agent on the inside of the Royal Family's own protection team. And soon-enough this agent will assassinate Prince William and his first son. The second and third in line to the throne. If ever there was going to be a statement, this was it. And Vladislav could watch it all unfold in front of the TV. He would then be accepted home with open arms, as a hero. This was good. Seeing this man face to face, knowing he was accountable for at least three, possibly more of his comrade's deaths, was not so good. At first, he felt obliged to kill him on the spot. But if his comrades were any good, they would be alive now and the job would already have been done and Vladislav would not have to go to these lengths.

'This is the way of life 'He thought to himself as he picked up the Irishman's coffee and drank it all down in one go. 'This is the way of life.'

Mills had time to walk and think before his rendezvous with Jim. In all the years he'd been feeding information back to his unit in Ireland, nothing like this had ever come up. He'd been asked to spy, give information, quieten down a situation and influence many operations. But never a hit. But what a hit it was. It was easy for Mills to separate his work and his duty. His work was in the British Military. And he liked being good at what he did. That's why he is where he is. Because he's good, the best, and he revelled in it. But that didn't mean he was some rogue. He never faltered on his job. He just *added* to his tasks, if needed, to support his unit back home. If his unit needed information on what Army Battalion was going to be in Northern Ireland, then it was Mills 'duty to find out and feed that information over. It was that simple. It was that easy. But now? Now he had a chance to be an active player and do something immense. And get serious cash as well. He wanted to know what his unit was getting out of the deal. Money as well, he guessed.

He still didn't really know what Jim's task was. All he knew was Jim was in the canal and Mills was to help him get dry and dressed after. Doing this at 10 pm seemed a bit silly, as the streets and therefore canal towpath was still busy enough. But Mitchell knows what he is doing, that is for sure. So, Mills didn't overthink things. He walked to his car and opened the back nearside door. On the back seat was a rucksack. It had clothes and a towel and the other bits that Mitchell had handed over to help Jim out of the water. He put it over one shoulder and slowly started to walk the streets in a general loop to the area he will soon be meeting Jim.

Jim had spent the last couple of hours checking his equipment and reading the map and looking at the canal. He was seriously pissed off because he didn't have internet in the flat and couldn't do some Google Maps of the area. But so be it. Mitchell had said the camera was being deployed in the early hours of Saturday morning. But because of battery life and the risk of it being spotted or damaged, it needed to be collected Saturday night. It seemed a bit high-risk to Jim, going out for a dip at 10 pm, but your job is your job. Mitchell asked, Jim couldn't really say no. So, his plan was to get into the canal, a tactical bound away from the bridge, drift there, collect the camera and drift to the rendezvous point to meet Mills. Who should have some warm kit for him to get changed into. Jim worked it out, he would be in the water for an hour. In plain clothes, that's a long time. Long enough to start going down with hypothermia. Sometimes, Jim hated the fuck out of his job. Bring back dogfights with Russian agents, all is forgiven.

CHAPTER 26

The sun was going down. Jim checked his watch. It was time to leave. He collected his equipment and headed out. He was going on foot all the way there, as the canal was close to his flat. Throwing his car into the mix, being parked at one point and surfacing at another would just add hassle he didn't need.

The rebreather was in his satchel. Where grenades and ammunition should be. Seeing as this mission was pretty heated, and they were off the grid for a very obvious reason, he felt a bit uneasy about being so light on weapons and ammo. As he walked to his start point, he was in full surveillance mode. Every single person was a potential threat. He was constantly watching and profiling and covering his arcs.

At his starting point, he left the road and walked under a bridge that ran over the towpath. Above was the main road. By the state of it, the bridge was clearly used by homeless people and junkies. There were empty beer cans and a bag of rubbish. There were a couple of those silver canisters that have gas in them that all the kids are on these days. There was some crap graffiti on the underside of the bridge and a couple of nesting pigeons were tucked up in the rafters. Lovely, thought Jim. He was wearing cotton cargo pants, instead of jeans as they were lighter and held less water. He had a long-sleeved t-shirt and a light jacket. He was going into the canal fully dressed. He couldn't exactly get changed into his swim pants or a wetsuit.

Slowly, quietly, he unpacked his rebreather. It had a strap that went over his neck and a second that went around his torso. It sat just beneath his ribs. The breathing tube came out one side and the mouthpiece was sealed on to that, so the whole thing was one unit. No chance of bits falling off. He took out some goggles and a nose clip. He wrapped up his satchel and put it into a pocket of his jacket and then zipped the jacket up. He gave one final look down both directions of the towpath and gave a cursory look up to the sleeping pigeons. With that, he put in the mouthpiece, nose clip and goggles. He crept to the edge of the canal and lowered himself in. Stood bolt upright, the water came up to his belly button. He took a moment to adjust to the change in temperature, and then fully submerged. The first breath using rebreather equipment is always a 'compose yourself' moment. You need to breathe harder than normal. Harder than using a scuba tank. So, you need a minute or so to breathe, compose yourself, watch for escaping air and watch the surface for someone who has seen you enter and has come over for a snoop about.

All was well. Jim was half lying, half sitting on the canal floor. Thick sediment was around his feet. He needed to stay off the bottom to stop all that muck from being kicked up. Even in a canal and at night, that change in water density will cause a shadow on the surface. And to someone looking for it, that would be a tell-tale sign. In almost pitch black and with the cold water already stabbing away at him, Jim started to pull himself along the wall towards the bridge. If this was the sea or a harbour, the current would pull him along. He would quite literally drift to his target. But tonight, he had to slowly, very slowly tease his way forward, making sure he gave off no sign at the surface. He was going slower than walking pace. It was going to take him twenty minutes to get to the bridge around the corner.

Seeing that Mills' walk to the rendezvous site wasn't far, he ended up doing quite a big loop so he could stay out of the general area for as long as possible. He did wonder if Phillips' team was about. But he guessed not. This wasn't the same job as the last two, or four if you included Jim's. So, they were on their own. Which was fine. It would be nice to know what was going on, that was all. Being kept in the dark at this stage of the game felt a little bit childish to Mills.

He got to the area he needed to be. He crossed onto the towpath and sure enough, there was a bush set back in a small patch of grass and shrubs. That was the base. Mills had a look over his shoulder. There were people out on the street and a single jogger with her Labrador with a reflective collar had just jogged past on the towpath, but right now, all was quiet. He got low and climbed into the bush. He nestled in. It was actually quite roomy and secluded. Big enough for the two of them. On the far side was a brick wall, separating the road from the canal. So, he put the bag down and perched, leaning against the wall. He checked his watch.

Jim got to the target bridge. He surfaced just his face at first, to look left and right and see where the camera was. He could see it concreted into the corner where the bridge met the canal wall. He raised his left hand and grabbed it. It took a few good tugs to break away the concrete and get the camera in his hand. He was cold. He was starting to shake. Not moving wasn't helping. So, he put the camera down his t-shirt, so he felt it next to his body and re-submerged. He was better off moving. He still had thirty minutes to the rendezvous.

It was nearly time. Mills got out the towel and the clothes. He put the clothes in a pile separate from the towel, so he could grab that first. There were also plastic shopping bags to put wet clothes in. He set everything up and exited the bush. He looked left and right down the canal. All was quiet. The street behind was not. He looked, but the wall was high enough that no passing stranger could glance over and see what was going on. He checked the time again and crouched by the canal. Credit where it's due, he didn't see so much of a ripple in the water before Jim's head appeared. Jim was spot-on at the location. The pair found themselves staring at each other for a split second before Jim put an arm up for assistance. Mills grabbed the arm and pulled Jim up, before pulling him over and out the canal. The two, bent at the waist, moved quickly to the bush. It was only a couple of paces. Jim still had the rebreather in his mouth. Mills led them into the bush and indicated where Jim could sit.

Jim sat and took his goggles off first, which Mills thought was strange. But then he saw the pressure marks around Jim's eyes and guessed they must have been really tight. Jim took out the mouthpiece and turned a switch on the rebreather before he took off his nose clip. He took off the equipment and then looked at Mills. Jim was shaking uncontrollably. This was why Mills was here. Without talking, Mills leaned forward and took his jacket off him. He then pushed Jim's head down and pulled the soaking wet t-shirt off his back. The camera fell to the floor. Both saw it. Neither mentioned it. Mills then got the towel and started to dry Jim's torso. He rubbed really hard to get some warmth back into his arms and body. Jim started to control his breathing. Mills got a dry t-shirt and helped Jim put it on. Jim then stripped waist-down and dried himself while Mills wrung out the wet clothes and put them in bags. Jim finished getting dressed and sat rubbing his legs to get some more blood flowing to warm himself up.

'Cheers,' he said.

'Fucking any time. You must be freezing.'

'Jesus yes. You can never get used to it, can you?'

'No, here. 'Mills offered a hip flask to Jim.

Jim took a swig. The whiskey was hot and comforting. He gasped after the first swig, and then took a second before handing it back. Mills too took a couple of swigs. Longer ones than Jim.

'You alright?'

'Yeah, just need a couple of minutes to get some feeling back in my hands and feet.'

'Of course.'

'I tell you what, I'll be glad when this one is over. I should be on the run-down to going outside.'

'I know. What are your plans for when you finally get there?'

'Have a lay-in!'

Both had a silent giggle at the joke.

'Where are you now then? 'asked Mills, 'Where is home?'

'A village in Hertfordshire. We have a place just on the outside of the village. It's a barn conversion, near nothing except the local pub.'

'Nice place to have a lay-in!'

'It is as well, mate. It's all Mel really, it's her home village. And she's the brains earning the big bucks. Couldn't afford it on a Bootneck's wage.'

'Mel?'

'Melissa'

'When you say we? Is that you and your family then?'

'No, just the wife and me.'

'Don't want kids? I mean, while you're still serving?'

'Well, that's a bit of a thing at the moment.'

'Sorry, I shouldn't have asked. Too personal. That is my thing, you see. Don't want kids right now. Not ruling them out. But I need to find a missus first to have them with!'

'Ah, you're fine. No, what it is, she wants kids. We both do. But it's me. I'm a Jaffa, aren't I?'

'Really?'

'Yep. Shooting blanks all day long.'

'Oh right. Yeah, that must be a strain.'

'A bit.'

'What does she do then? If you say she's on the big bucks?'

'Prosecution lawyer. Been involved in some high-profile cases recently. Properly good at what she does.'

'Happy days mate.'

'What about you, still flying solo, at your age?'

'Yeah, kinda. You know what it's like. Loved hard when I was younger but married to the job.'

'Aye, it's the story of a lot of us, isn't it?

'Yeah. Hey, do you remember Afghan?'

'Farrah?'

'Yeah.'

'I remember it alright. Wish I didn't, sometimes.'

'It was the most fucked-up tour, wasn't it?'

'I still don't believe it was real.'

'It was mate. We were both there.'

'Yeah. At least it was warm....'Jim was clearly trying not to talk about the last time they worked together.

Mills took the hint and brought the conversation round to the current job.

'What were you doing tonight then?'

'Picking this up.'Jim had the camera by his side, still in its waterproof bag. 'Mitchell asked me to collect it.'

'What was it watching?'

'Fuck knows. I wasn't told anything. Including why he could place it, but I had to collect it.'

'Minimising his exposure, no doubt.'

'Yeah. And I guess he wanted to have it pointing at exactly what he needed it to be pointing at and only he knows what that was.'

'Where?'

'Down there, along the canal. Under the small footbridge.'

Mills started to put things together in his head. This was not good. Not good at all. Had he been exposed? Impossible. This job was to do with the mission, was it not? Was Mitchell not looking for a Russian? Was the German, with a bad German accent, really a Russian? Was he the Russian? The more Mills played out the options in his head, the worse it felt for him. He now had his orders from his unit at home. And that the deal had been made by forces higher than him. Was he being stitched up? Was this a desperate act on the part of the Russian? Was this a really, really bad coincidence? There was only one way to find out. And that was to see the video footage. He hedged his bets and tried his luck.

'When are you handing that over to Mitchell, then?'

'Tomorrow. live letterbox.'

'Yeah... I've got one as well. First thing, as it goes. When is yours?'

'Midday. In Green Park, of all places. I think he got spooked by the taxi thing too much and wants to play the safety in numbers game.'

'Spooked?'

'He thought I was Russian.'

'So that makes sense, he wants to meet me in Trafalgar square. Look, if you want that to get to him first thing, I can hand it over?'

'It's an idea, I suppose. But you know what Mitchell is like. He will get twitchy at his plan being altered.'

'True. Well, it was just an offer. How are you feeling now?'

'Warmed up. I guess we had best make a move before someone comes along and spots us.'

'Don't think they will want to meet us, two fellas, hiding in a bush.'

'They might try to join us!'

'Jesus. OK, we got everything?'

The pair checked all around them. Making sure everything was packed away and they could make a swift getaway. They paused and waited for a couple of minutes. Completely silent, listening to the traffic on the road and making sure no footsteps were coming along the towpath. They gave each other a knowing look and left the cover of the bush around the side where they entered and got on to the towpath. Jim went right, after having a cursory look to the left. Mills went left. In the direction of the bridge.

CHAPTER 27

Mills walked towards the footbridge. It wasn't far and as he got close, reality dawned. That camera must have been looking at the Safe House. Mills recognised its location. Even though he entered from the front, it's not hard to map it out in your head. That was it, slightly set back from the canal. And the camera must have been looking at it. And, more specifically, through a window. Where was Mills only a couple of hours earlier? That building, in a room with a window. 'Second floor, far-side.' One of only two scenarios now existed in Mills 'mind. Either after all these years, his links to Ireland had been worked out, or more likely who he met was the Russian. It was all dropping into place, his fears from earlier were becoming reality. He needed that video.

Jim walked along the towpath at a decent pace to warm himself up. The camera was in his satchel, squeezed in next to his rebreather. Mills had taken the wet clothes and towel. Jim heard activity on the road. It was close to eleven o'clock, the roads were busy. A single man walked towards him on the towpath.

The man moved directly into Jim's line, so there was no way of passing. They either stopped or walked into each other.

'Got the time, mate?'

'No.'

'What's in the bag?'

'Pardon?'

The man pulled a knife. A small one, a flick knife maybe. He was nothing more than an opportunist thief. 'Not another knife.' Jim was sick to death of knives and had no time for playing games. There was no more conversation. Jim smashed his left foot into the inside of the guy's right knee, buckling him over. Jim then grabbed him with both hands, on the shoulders of his jacket, and using all his body weight, twisted and threw the guy against the wall next to the towpath. The guy went down instantly. He didn't move. Jim stepped over him and walked on. About ten paces down the path, he paused. As much as he had zero time for robbers, knives and being mugged by a robber with a knife, the last thing he needed was a dead civilian on his hands. He walked back to the body. It was not moving. He crouched down and felt for a pulse. It was there. He moved the guy into some sort of recovery position and made sure his airway was clear. That was it. That was all the help he was getting and frankly, more than he deserved. Before getting back to walking home, Jim picked up the knife and tossed it into the canal.

Mills picked up the pace and made his way back to his car. His mind was racing. He needed that video camera. All was on the cusp of being ruined. Never mind the money, he was about to be exposed for everything. He'd be linked to the Russian, which in reality he wasn't, then he'd be pulled in by the Brigadier and the whole world would be unstitched. He got to his car and walked to the boot. Before opening it, he had a quick look over his shoulder. He opened the boot and held it low. Inside was all his kit. A bag of ammunition and grenades. A second bag with spare clothes. Rope. A rifle. Another pistol. Bolt croppers. And a crossbow. Mills dropped the bag off his shoulder into the boot and picked up the crossbow. It had a holster on the side where six bolts were kept. He tucked it the best he could under his jacket and got himself as quickly as he could back onto the canal. He walked past the bridge and the Safe House looking over the canal. He walked past the bush. He was blindly following Jim's route, as he had no idea where he was or heading to. He came to a man on the towpath. Unconscious. He thought at first, he was a junkie that had just done himself an injustice. Then, in the light of a streetlamp out on the road, he saw a huge bump and bruise on the guy's head. It could only have been Jim. Mills carried on.

Jim had crossed over another bridge to the far side of the canal. He wasn't too far from home. He knew this area well now. He was in a good place with things. He was warmed up and had completed his mission. And if what Mitchell said was true, all this shite might soon be behind him.

Mills was closing in and saw Jim on the far side of the canal. Mills got off the canal towpath by using a break in the wall and got himself onto the street. It was lined with parked cars and though there were street lamps, the cars gave enough cover from view. He picked up his pace and got ahead of Jim. He wanted to be square-on when he took the shot.

Jim was getting close to where he was going to leave the canal and join the road. There was a break in the wall along the towpath and there were a few steps up to the street level. He turned and being in a now-jovial mood, he shot up the steps in two bounds.

Mills was square-on. He was leading Jim with the crossbow sights. As soon as Jim was lined up, Mills would put a bolt through his torso. Jim turned left, away from the canal and quickly climbed some stairs. Mills was about to lose him. He pulled the trigger. A bolt flew.

The bolt hit Jim in the left leg. It went in the back of his thigh and came out the front. It got stuck in his leg with equal amounts showing front and back, on the outside of his thigh. It missed his femur by an inch. Any further over and his whole leg would have been shattered.

The pain hit Jim's head like a lightning strike. The pain in his leg came a second later. His whole body crumbled, and he screamed in agony and rage. As he fell back down the stairs, the bolt made contact with the floor and caused even more pain. Rage turned to fear. He had just been ambushed. Fight or flight instincts kicked in. He had to move. He had to get out of there. He couldn't get back up the stairs. Forwards or backwards along his route on the canal were his only options. Training made him go back the way he came. Along the proven path. He dragged himself up onto his strong leg. He looked down and saw blood flowing from his left leg. He may have a damaged artery. He hopped and limped the few paces back to the walled part of the canal. Every time his left leg took pressure, he had to work hard to stop another scream of pain. He turned to the wall. It was about five feet high, and the other side was the road. It was the only cover he was going to get. On top of the wall were small plastic spikes, to stop pigeons from landing. He had no choice. With all his might, he jumped using his right leg and pushed his hands onto the top of the wall to get himself over. He dragged himself up but the pain in his hands was unreal, he collapsed onto the wall. The spikes went into his chest. The pain was even worse than with his hands, as there was no meat to absorb the pressure. The spikes went straight into his sternum and ribs. He dragged himself over, scraping over the spikes as he did. When the bolt touched the wall, he had to muffle another cry of pain. He had to twist as he finally got over the wall to make sure he didn't land left-side down. As he landed, he heard the sound of a second bolt hitting the wall. A sharp whistle followed by a shattering impact.

Jim pulled himself up into a crouched position. If he was walking, getting home from here wouldn't take too long. But the same route, with a crossbow bolt in his thigh, was going to be a struggle. What made it worse, was he couldn't afford to be seen. His quickest option was along the canal, but that was clearly out of the question. The second option was along the main road he was now on, but he was going to be spotted by a driver or pedestrians. The only remaining option was to go home the long way. He quite literally had to shuffle in a zigzag down the back roads and footpaths to get to his flat. He had to choose the quietest route, which also gave him the best cover from his attacker. The real concern now was bleeding out.

He had a thought - maybe he could blag his case a little bit. He took a small flashlight from his jacket pocket. He shined it over the wall in the general direction of where he thought the bolt came from. He knew he was never going to see whoever took the shot, but they didn't know he hadn't got a mid-range weapon on him. The truth was all he had was his pistol. It wouldn't make an accurate shot over that distance, but anything was worth a go right now. If shining the torch bought him a head-start to get out of there, it's what he needed.

Mills saw the light beam coming over towards him. He saw the play coming from Jim. It confirmed two things: One, Jim didn't know it was Mills taking the shot. If he did, he wouldn't be trying to give the impression he could return fire. And two, it meant Jim was still OK enough to think like this. I.e., he wasn't dead or close enough to being dead for Mills 'liking. Mills had ducked down to peer over the wall, but when the light beam didn't point at him directly, he moved on to the next phase. He was furious that he missed a second time. He stood up and made a point of covering the crossbow the best he could under his coat. He now needed to get over that side of the canal and finish Jim off. He took off on foot back down to canal level and over a bridge.

Mills cautiously made his way to the far side of the canal and found a pathway through the wall onto the road. He walked up to where Jim had jumped and landed street-side. There was blood on the floor. Jim was gone, but there was a trail of his blood that led across the main road and down a small side street. Mills followed the trail of blood. Now and then, a car would pass him, and he had to stop and turn away from the headlights to hide his crossbow. It slowed down the stalk of his prey. But his prey was injured. No rush. At road junctions or pathways, Mills had to look carefully for the blood. Jim was changing direction often. Mills continued to pursue until he saw Jim in the not too far distance. Mills ducked out of sight and watched. Jim hobbled into an estate. Flats. It must be where he was living. Mills took a wide arc around the front of the block. There were too many lights still on in the homes for him to feel comfortable walking up as he was. He continued to watch from afar, and stood on a side street, watching the estate when he finally got hold of Jim again. He was on the first floor, making his way to a front door. Mills smiled as he watched Jim enter his flat.'Got you. '

Mills paused for thought. He couldn't just walk in right now and execute Jim. He had a crossbow on him and there was too much activity in the estate to get away with this. Jim was alone with no comms to the outside world, and he was wounded. Badly. He wasn't going anywhere. Mills quickly ducked away down a small side road and made his way back to his car.

CHAPTER 28

By the time Jim got to his flat, he was in a bad way. He had lost a considerable amount of blood. His skin was cold and waxy. He had sweated through his clothes, and they were now dry again and stained with salt. His t-shirt was ripped and red from where he had scrapped over the spiked wall. His heart was racing. His mouth was dry. He felt light-headed and basic skills like getting his keys out of his pocket were a chore. He got himself inside and headed to the living room. He pulled the front door over to close it but didn't even realise he didn't have the strength to close it properly and it rested on the catch.

He needed to focus. He needed to administer serious trauma control to his own body. He couldn't think where to start. He couldn't think. He felt like he was floating. He stumbled over to his table. He went for his stash that he asked Kingston to get for him. Kingston had supplied Jim, on Jim's request with some morphine pens, the type that gets issued to Military guys on tour or you might find with a paramedic crew. Some opiate pain killers, Cocaine, adrenaline and a few other bits he could use if needed. Tonight, it was needed.

He took off his jacket and t-shirt. His torso hurt as the clotted blood stuck to his t-shirt pulled on flesh.

He took out a morphine pen and stabbed it into his left arm. It took a few seconds for the pain to start to subside. But it didn't subside much. Any movement and his leg would still buckle, and the pain would bring him to screaming. He put another morphine pen into his arm. He felt more nauseous than relieved of pain. He tried to focus. He looked at his small digital clock on the table. It seemed to take an hour for each second to pass. Then Jim blinked and nearly an hour had gone by. He reached down and picked up a fold of cocaine. He took it all. Quickly he was focussed. Buzzing. In pain, but lucid. He needed to act.

He started to assess his leg wound. He couldn't do anything with his trousers on. So, he cut them off with a Stanley knife. Shoes and socks came off. He was there, naked trying to work out what the fuck to do with the crossbow bolt in his leg. He needed more coke. And he took some opiates as well. He tried to wash them down with beer, but it made him feel sick. He couldn't drink anything. Even a sip of water made him feel sick. He needed fluids. He needed to get the bolt out and he needed to patch the wound. He needed a plan. 'Think Jim, think.'

He opened the fridge and took out the pouches of blood he had harvested from the last Russian. He got out a giving-set and inserted the needle into a vein in his forearm and taped it down in preparation. He opened the window. It was guillotine-style, so he pushed the sliding part all the way up, so the window was as open as it would go. He found some cord and pulled over, with all his might, a kettlebell. He carefully tied the cord to the back of the crossbow bolt. He used a mountaineer's knot that pulled tighter the more tension it was under. So, there was no way it would come off the end of the bolt. The other end of the cord went around the handle of the kettlebell. Jim looked at the clock. He still couldn't work out if time was flying or standing still. He checked his preparation on the table. Blood, drugs and trauma control kit. He took some more opiates for good luck. He climbed onto the windowsill, which because he was in an older block, was just wide enough to balance his torso on. He leaned down and pulled up the kettlebell and rested it on his hip. He was wedged into the window area, on his right side, right foot pressed against the inside of the window space, his left leg was lifted so his heel was against the frame, so there was no way of his leg or all of him going out the open window. The kettlebell was on top of his left hip. Its weight pressing hard on his pelvis. Jim held the handle of it in his left hand. He gave one final look at his supplies for confirmation. He gripped the kettlebell's handle hard. He took some short sharp breaths, psyching himself up. He screwed his eyes closed and threw the kettlebell out the window. He didn't feel the cord go tight. He didn't feel the crossbow bolt move. He just felt pain. Like he'd been shot with it again, but this time from the front to the back. His whole body was pulled back a couple of inches and then he lurched forwards and he fell to the floor. Bloodshot from his reopened wound like how a rainbow is pictured by kids, a big arc from origin to destination. He screamed in pain and rage. He pulled himself up to table height. Another morphine-pen. This one went into his good thigh. More coke. It didn't take any more pain away, but it helped to keep him focussed and not pass out from the morphine. He got out the trauma kit and patched the front and back of his leg. He was still feeling nauseous. It had occurred to him that the spikes on the wall were covered in pigeon shit, and he probably had an infection in his cut chest. Not much he could do about that now. His focus was staying alive. He got a tourniquet from the trauma kit. Not for his leg, but he grabbed the pouch of blood and attached it with the tourniquet to his arm. He connected the feeding line and started feeding blood into his system. It felt good to get fluid inside him and he even started to sweat again. He didn't feel much pain, but he felt weak and sick. He felt dizzy. He felt light. He collapsed on the floor.

Mills was on his way back to Jim's flat. He had his silenced pistol on him. Time had passed and he hoped Jim was asleep and all Mills would have to do was shoot him in his sleep and retrieve the video camera. He got to Jim's estate and found the stairwell that led to the first floor. He was about to take out his pistol and shoot the lock when he saw the door was on the latch. With gloved hands, he gently pushed it open.

Jim woke up with a start. He woke up in pain. He dragged himself up off the floor to table height and dropped his face into the cocaine and breathed in hard through his nose. It felt like someone had just turned on the Blackpool illuminations in his head. He was with it. In fucking agony, but he was with it. Just. He took some more opiates with water. The first actual fluid he had taken on in hours. He instantly started to sweat again. Sweat and blood covered his body. He stood, taking most of his weight on his right leg, and inspected his left leg. The patches and bandages on the wound were red-through. His blood resupply had run out. He was about to take the pouch off his arm when he heard a noise. Mills stood in front of him.

Mills crept forward. He heard some movement in the room in front of him. He got to the doorway and saw something from a horror movie. Jim was standing there naked, covered in blood and sweat, with infected wounds on his chest, soaked-through bandage on his left leg, a face covered in cocaine and a giving-set strapped to his right arm. There was blood everywhere. Jim was high as a kite. Mills guessed Jim was not going to be in a good state. In fact, he was kind of hoping he was already dead. But this, this was something else.

'Alright fella, 'Jim greeted Mills, he was actually smiling. 'What are you doing here? 'Jim was slurring. Mills clocked the drugs. No wonder he was happy.

'Jim, what the fuck is going on?'

'I got shot.'

'Shot? With a gun?'

'No, with a big, fucking thing…'

Jim was very animated. He couldn't say what it was, he couldn't think. He started to show Mills what he was shot with. Like a game of charades. He tried showing the bolt and the crossbow action. Eventually, Mills got bored of it and seeing as he knew the answer, gave it.

'Crossbow?'

'Yeah! Big fucking crossbow.'

'By who?'

'I dunno. The Russian twat?'

'Where is it? The crossbow bolt?'

Jim just lifted his left arm by way of pointing out the window. Mills didn't ask how.

'You umm... OK?'

Jim tried to hold his gaze.

'It really fucking hurt, Mills.'

'I bet'

'I think I'm in a bad way.'

'You are.'

'Why are you here? 'Jim could hardly focus. He didn't know how long cocaine lasted, but he was starting to hurt again. He took some more painkillers. Different ones. He didn't know what ones. He didn't care, he just wanted the pain to go away.

'Umm... Phillips came to my door. He opened my envelope. There was a dead man on the canal near where we did that job a few hours ago and he guessed it was one of us.'

'He wasn't dead? 'Slurred Jim.

'Well, he was, mate. Anyway, Phillips flipped a coin and came to my flat. But it wasn't me. And instead of Phillips coming here and worrying you, I mean if you knew you had killed a civilian, you might be in a bad way. So, I offered to come and talk it through with you. You know, seeing as we're on the same page. You know what Phillips is like, Copper first.'

'Makes sense. 'Nothing made sense to Jim. But he couldn't think straight enough to challenge anything.

'Why have you got all this shit?'

'Just in case.'

'In case you had a junkie party?'

'In case some cunt cross me with a shotbow.'

'You can't be taking cocaine.'

'Why?'

'You're not with it.'

'You put whiskey on your cornflakes, shipmate. 'retaliated Jim, swaying as he pointed an accusing finger at Mills.

'Booze is legal.'

'Oh, cos all we are doing here is well above board?'

'You feel guilty about it all?'

'No. Just saying.'

'What's with the blood?'

'Just in case.'

'From where?'

Jim just stood there. Looking at Mills.

'From a Russian?'

'Yarp.'

'You took blood from a man you just killed, just in case you needed to resupply your own at some point?'

'.... Yes, 'Jim had to think of the answer after such a long-winded question. He didn't want to be tricked.

'What is wrong with saline?'

'Oh, yeah. That would have worked as well.'

'Fuck sake. Do you want to get dressed?'

'Do you want to get dressed?'

'Jim.'

'Mills.'

'Jim. Get dressed.'

'I want a drink of water.'

'Go and get a fucking drink, then.'

Jim gave Mills a look and then turned to the kitchen. He hobbled over. When Jim was in the kitchen, Mills reached for the video camera that was on the table. He picked it up. He was about to pocket it when the side panel swung open, it hadn't been shut properly after being opened. The SD card was missing. Mills put it back before Jim returned.

'So, look Phillips wants to talk to you about the body.'

'I didn't kill him.'

'But still…'

'Mills, I'm kinda fucked right now. I need my beauty sleep.'

'OK, I'll tell him you will talk later today. Do umm… you want me to give Mitchell that video camera? I'm seeing him soon.'

'No, it's ok. It's my job.'

'But you just said you need your beauty sleep.'

'I can set my alarm.'

Mills was starting to lose patience. He needed that SD card. And if Jim was not going to hand it over, Mills was just going to have to kill him and look for it. Jim turned to face the table, Mills had no idea what he was looking for. More drugs, probably. But it didn't matter. He started to draw his pistol when he heard a noise in the doorway.

Snake's leg was still in a cast from the knee down. It was a fibreglass one, so he could walk on it without crutches. It was filthy and stank. Snake wanted revenge for being thrown off the balcony. But first, he had to wait until he was back to some sort of physical ability. He'd been up all night planning his revenge. He had a revolver. He was going to shoot the guy in the leg to teach him a lesson and then throw him over the balcony. Snake wanted to make a statement of his own. He guessed early hours on a Sunday was the best time to catch the guy out. He walked through the estate with a limp. His mending leg still was not taking all his weight. He walked alongside the block he was after. Up one flight of stairs and he would gain entry through a window. If Snake could do anything, he could break into a flat. Once inside, he would shoot the guy awake while he slept and drag him to the balcony and throw him over. Job done.

As he passed underneath the guys flat, Snake was missed by an inch, from a falling kettlebell. Closely followed by an arrow of some sorts, tied to the kettlebell. It scared the shit out of Snake. But then he heard the scream of pain. Whatever was going on, the guy was not in a good way. No better time to strike. He limped as fast as he could up the stairs and to the guy's front door, which was open. Revolver in hand, on the side like he'd seen in the gangster movies, he crept inside.

He stood in the doorway of the living room, confronted with the guy who threw him off the balcony who looked like he was being tortured by a second guy. Who, by the looks of it, was just holstering a pistol.

'Oh, hello! 'Called out Jim, still slurring.

'What the fuck is going on here?'

'Who the fuck are you? 'Demanded Mills, who had re-drawn his weapon as soon as he saw Snake. The pair were in a Mexican stand-off.

'I'm Snake.'

'Snake?'

'Snake, 'said Jim, 'It's a lovely name. Did I ever tell you that?'

'Fuck off.'

Jim pulled a face.

'Who is Snake? 'Mills asked Jim.

'Snake is a wanker that I threw off the balcony.'

'He broke my fucking leg. 'Snapped Snake, 'Who are you? ' He asked Mills.

Mills didn't grace him with a decent answer. He just lowered his pistol and put a round into Snake's good leg. In the shin. Snake crumbled and shouted in pain. His revolver fell out of his hand and landed a foot away from where he fell.

'That's who the fuck I am.'

Jim giggled and pointed like a school child.

Kingston had been sitting in his car all night. Saturday was always his busiest night. But in the early hours, all was quiet. His eyes were red, and he was ready to turn in. His patch was quiet. Head one last transaction to do, then he was done. He was taking payment owed to him for pills from a local prostitute at his car window when Jim hobbled back to his flat. If Kingston had seen Jim, then he might have gone up straight away. But he saw Mills first and that was why Kingston started to take interest in what was going on. Since Jim had moved in, no one had been to visit.

No friends, No police, no pissed-off wife. No one. Until now. Early hours on a Sunday morning. And he walked straight in. Did he have a key? A few minutes later, Kingston saw Snake walk up to the flat door and invite himself in. Snake. Of all people? After the balcony incident, that didn't sit right. And Kingston wasn't sure, but he thought Snake had a gun. If he did, then something was going down. He decided the best thing to do was to invite himself to the party also. The last thing Kingston needed was a dead punter.

Kingston arrived at the living room door, with his pistol drawn. He didn't know what to expect, but it wasn't what he saw.

Mills focussed his weapon on the new stranger. Kingston returned the gesture.

'Who the fuck are you? 'Demanded Mills.

'Who the fuck are you?'

'What the fuck is going on? 'Wept Snake from the floor.

Jim started to laugh hysterically.

'This is like that film.'

'What? 'cried Snake.

'That film. You know. The film.'

'Fucking no. What film?'

'Reservoir dogs! 'Jim was clearly impressed with himself for seeing the scene the way it was.

'What the fuck is going on, man?'

'I've had a bad day.'

'Hang on, you two know each other? 'Asked Mills.

'Yeah.'

Mills turned to Kingston.

'You sold him that shit?'

'Free world. Who are you? The Police?'

Jim started laughing.

'He's not the Police. Nee-naw nee-naw. No, he's not the police and yes, he sold me this stuff, at a very good price I was told. And he wanted to sell me stuff, but he's a nobber so I threw him overboard. 'Jim said, quite impressed with himself.

Kingston and Mills looked at each other.

'We cool?'

'Yeah.'

'So, what is goin 'on?'

'Nothing. Without sounding rude, you and that piece of shit there, are not needed.'

'Needed?'

'You don't need to be here.'

Kingston turned to Jim, then looked away at the sight of the naked guy, in the state that he was, still smiling at himself for the film comment.

'Any chance you could get dressed?'

'I've already tried. 'piped up Mills.

Jim's head was fuzzy. But it was starting to clear. He wasn't OK with how things were. He turned to Mills.

'You got any money?'

'You what?'

'Cash?'

Mills gave Kingston a sideways look.

'Yeah. Why?'

'Give him a grand for me.'

'No.'

'Don't be a dick, I'll give it back.'

'I don't care about that, but I'm not giving my cash to a dealer.'

'I don't need more gear.'

'No, you don't.'

'Just give him the money.'

Mills reluctantly pulled folds of notes from his pockets and bunched them together. He handed them to Kingston.

'There's about eight hundred there.'

'What's this for? Dealing with him? 'Asked Kingston, pointing to Snake.

'No, he's a gift. Just before you walked in, he was saying how shit you are as a drug dealer.'

'Was he now?'

'Yeah, 'Mills joined in, 'He said you couldn't sell an aspirin to Keith Richards.'

'OK, well it looks like Snake and I are going to have a chat.'

'What the fuck! 'Snake protested.

'Can you get rid of him?'

'Yeah. 'Kingston made a call on his phone. He clearly had people waiting to back him up if he needed it because no sooner had he hung up, than two big guys came through the door, picked up a protesting Snake and took him away.

'What is the cash for, then? 'Insisted Mills.

'Don't worry. 'Jim waved off the question, 'You can disappear mate, as well.'

'I don't fucking think so. Leave you here with a drug-dealing, pistol carrying gangster?'

'It's fine.'

'No.'

'He said it's fine.'

Mills had his back up again. He didn't care about the Kingston thing. But he needed the SD card.

'Who the fuck are you to tell me it's fine?'

Mills and Kingston squared off. It took a naked Jim to put

himself between them to break the deadlock.

'Mate mate mate, it's fine. We got our shit to do. I got the timing. It's all OK. Go on, fuck off.'

Mills remembered Jim's live letterbox with Mitchell, Green Park at midday. That will have to be when he gets the SD card. Clearly, there was a level of protection here that Mills didn't realise was going on.

Mills started to walk out the flat, past Kingston. Maybe for cover, because of the situation, maybe he forgot the situation, but he left by saying to Jim:

'Just call me if you need to. 'And with that, he left. Jim knew he couldn't call Mills. But was too far detached from that thought process to fully work out what he meant.

When alone, Kingston asked Jim about the cash.

'You need more gear?'

'Do I look like I need more gear?'

'Then what?'

'You may have noticed, I'm in a bit of a bad way. I could do with being left alone for a few hours.'

'Left alone? You mean no more visitors?'

'Exactly.'

'Including the Irishman?'

'What Irishman?'

'Your mate that just left.'

'He's not Irish.'

'He is, my friend.'

'He's not.'

'How long have you known him?'

'Years.'

'How well?'

'Enough.'

'Not well enough.'

'He's not fucking Irish.'

'Right, let me ask you this, have you ever heard the saying No Irish, No Blacks, No Dogs?'

'Yeah. A seventies thing?'

'Yes. No outsiders were welcome in pubs. Irish road workers and Windrush Blacks.'

'And dogs.'

'And fucking dogs.'

'I don't get it.'

'Your friend is Irish. He is an outsider. It takes one to know one. You, you're not from London. That is clear. But you fit because you are English. Culturally, you just blend. You are part of this country. I am not. I am Jamaican. I was born here, but I'll never be part of here. Neither will your mate. I am telling you, he's Irish. Not that it is a problem of course until you insisted he wasn't?'

Jim said nothing. He couldn't think about it right now. Did he need to think about it right now?

'I'll let myself out then?'

'Ta.'

Kingston left. Jim heard the door lock snap shut. Jim looked down at his body. He was a mess. The effects of the drugs were starting to fade. He was tired. He hurt. He took one last painkiller from the table and washed it down with a mouthful of water. His eyes were starting to shut. He sat on his fold-away bed he had kept in the living room. He picked up his alarm clock. He started to count back in his head. 'Meet Mitchell at 12. Leave at 11, up at 10. 'His vision was blurry. He fell back onto the bed and was asleep before his head hit the pillow. The alarm clock fell out of his hand. He had not set the alarm before he passed out.

CHAPTER 29

Mitchell was on edge all Saturday and Saturday night. What if the camera was found? What if it fell in the water? What if he was followed and Jim was swimming into an ambush? What if Jim couldn't find it?

Mitchell now wished he had said to meet earlier in the day, but at the time he just wanted to put as much space and time between him, the canal and Jim. Off the physical grid as much as possible. By the time he was due to meet Jim, he was so tired, his eyes hurt, and his mind was foggy. Green Park was as safe a location as any. Hidden in plain sight, as it were. Mitchell had enough of the taxi game and for his own sanity and nerves, wanted a more conventional live letterbox. He waited for Jim to show up at the rendezvous, with a coffee and a copy of the Economist magazine.

Mills was in his car, circling the area like a Vulture looking for a carcass to pick at. Green Park was small enough to observe from the road, but not small enough to be able to sit back and watch everything from one location. And his fear was ending up face to face with Jim out in the open and having to do something rash that will compromise him. Mills still had this under control. He just needed the SD card from Jim and kill him. That would end this dog shit operation, get him back on the Royal Protection Team and then he can carry out his orders. It could all be over within a matter of weeks. And Mills could be living like a King himself on a beach somewhere no one has heard of. The thought of that alone was motivation enough.

Mills clocked Mitchell, sitting on a bench near the centre of the park. 'How cliche, Mitchell. 'Mills thought to himself as he slowly circled the area. It was two minutes to midday. Jim will be close. Pulling into a disabled parking space on the side of the road, Mills could move his rear-view mirror to see Mitchell sitting there. Mills now had angles of the whole area. He could see face on if Jim was approaching from one direction, and had a mirror view of the other direction and a good eye on the rendezvous point itself. All he had to do now was sit, watch and wait.

Time dragged on for Mitchell. Like swimming through tar. He had to refrain from constantly checking his watch, but rather he counted seconds to best guess the time. He counted to sixty seconds four times since he last did have a look at his watch, and going by his timing, it was now two minutes past twelve. 'Must be on the underground. Mitchell waited.

Mills waited. No Jim. Had he given false information? Why would he? Did he know and not let on? Unlikely. Especially after seeing him only a few hours earlier. Patience Mills, patience.

Mitchell was growing increasingly nervous. He needed the video camera, or more specifically the SD card. He needed to see who the Agent was. There was every chance he was known to the Intelligence Service and if that was the case, all this could be ended very quickly. But with the rush of the operation in the canal, there were too many factors that could have gone wrong, and Mitchell was increasingly paranoid that he had been found out himself. He looked at his watch again. Six minutes past twelve. No Jim. Was he OK? Was Mitchell himself in danger, was he being watched right now?

Mills watched intently as Mitchell fidgeted on the bench. Jim will be here any second. The hustle and bustle of London never stops. Cars, people walking in the park, busses and coaches. It was a convoy of coaches parking up that blocked Mills 'view. Three of them. And as if they knew what they were up to, intentionally getting in Mills 'line of sight, dozens of tourists flooded out onto the pavement. Mills could not get any angle between the busses to see Mitchell. Furious, Mills had to get out on foot to see what was going on. He got out of the car and slammed the door closed. He didn't lock it. He walked over the street and stood amongst the tourists. He looked towards the rendezvous point. No Jim. No Mitchell. Fuck. Mills scanned the immediate area. He saw Mitchell walking off, away from the area. They must have had the live letterbox at that exact time. It would make sense that if Jim was running late, Mitchell would just want to take the camera and go. The only option now was Mitchell. Mills can still stop his meeting from being uncovered. This was still salvageable. Just. If nothing more, he could not go back to his unit in Ireland and say he's lost the opportunity and the money promised. He made his way back to his car. He got in and pulled out in front of a bus which had to brake hard to stop hitting him. The last thing the bus driver needed was to hit someone pulling out of a disabled bay. Mills followed the flow of traffic and eyeballed the park for Mitchell.

Mitchell was walking to the edge of the park and looking like he was intending to cross the road. Mills manoeuvred himself in place. If he could do anything, he could get a car through traffic. He stopped just as Mitchell was about to cross the road. Instead of sounding the horn, which would have been too overt, he knocked on the inside of his windscreen which gave off just enough noise to get Mitchell's attention. Mitchell gave Mills a genuine look of concern and then without any more prompting, walked around the front and got in the car.

'Mills! I wasn't expecting to see you.'

'No, I'm sure.' Said Mills as he pulled away. He hadn't even looked at Mitchell since he got in the car. Mills was focused on the traffic and avoiding any sort of eye contact or real conversation.

'What is going on? I mean, why are you here?'

'Not an easy one to explain.'

'Go on?'

Mills could hear the concern in Mitchell's voice. Still in traffic, still not looking at Mitchell, Mills reached under his thigh and pulled up a cloth. It was soaked in Chlorophyll. He slammed it into Mitchell's face. He pressed Mitchell's head back against the rest and held it in place despite Mitchell's desperate effort to get free.

CHAPTER 30

Mills took Mitchell to a location he had already scoped out and prepared for this exact situation. Though he did think it would be Jim he was extorting the SD card from, who would have been a tougher egg to crack. Mills had spent the few hours after being in Jim's flat getting together what he needed. After not retrieving the SD card due to the freak show he witnessed, his options were getting fewer and fewer by the minute. He had wanted to intercept a wounded Jim before he got to Mitchell and beat the SD card out of him. Now Mitchell had it and things were escalating.

Mills had scoped out a disused warehouse, boarded off to the outside world. It was on wasteland south of the river. Mills got to the wasteland and parked the car inside the warehouse. In front of him, was a large table, some rope and an assortment of tools that were there to be used as torture devices. He dragged Mitchell out of the car. Mitchell was starting to come round and the shock of him being dumped onto the table shook him into focus. But it was too late, rope ties had already been placed on each leg of the table and Mills got one wrist secured before Mitchell understood what was happening and could put up a fight.

'What the fuck is going on?'

'Morning Snowflake. Did you sleep well? 'Said Mills in a psychotic voice, as he grabbed Mitchell's ankle and pulled that to the corner of the table and secured it.

'Mills? Mills, I'm fucking scared, what are you up to? ' Mitchell struggled and protested. Mills paused, he got in Mitchell's face and eyeballed him.

'You should be scared. 'He said in a Kerry accent, 'Things are about to get pretty desperate for you, my boy.'

Despite Mitchells best efforts, he could not stop the strength of Mills and soon he was tied face up on the table, in the middle of the warehouse. He tried to scream. Mills laughed and cut him off.

'You honestly believe I'd do this where you could be heard?'

'What are you doing, Mills?'

'Well, to be true with you, right now it should be Jim on that table, not you.'

'But why Mills? Why? What is going on?'

'I tried to get the camera from him, you see. Keep this between him and me.'

'The camera?'

'Aye. Tell me. How did you know?'

'Know what?'

'Don't play fucking coy with me! Tell me now. How did you know I'd be in that building?'

'I didn't Mills. I was after the Russian. He was having a meeting there. I wanted to see who he was, so I could end this.'

Mills paused. Enraged. The German was the Russian? *The Russian?* Confirmation of that point alone was enough. Had

Mills been played? Had he been set up? His unit would never do that to him. The Russian wanted an assassination on the Royal Family. Mills and Jim had been too good at their jobs and now it has come to this.

'Give me the SD card.'

'Is it you who met the Russian? Why Mills? Tell me why? I need to know?'

'Give me the SD card.'

'I don't have it.'

'Bullshit. I saw you at Green Park. I saw you sitting there, and I saw you walking away after your meeting.'

'Jim never turned up, Mills. Please. Why are you doing this? What was the meeting about? Why were you meeting him? Do you know him?'

'Stop talking. You clearly don't understand what is happening here, do you?'

'No. Tell me?'

Mills leaned in again.

'This is the end of the road for you, my boy. Last chance, give me the SD card.'

'I swear Mills, I don't have it. Jim never showed up.'

Mills was furious. The irony is that Jim, despite saying out loud he had a meeting and was going to make it, clearly has fucked something up. His leg? Infection? Slept in? Drugs? Whatever it is, Mills had gambled incorrectly on this one. And it was about to cost him, and Mitchell, massively. His only option now was to get back to Jim's flat. But first, he had to deal with Mitchell.

'So, tell me what you know, Mitchell. Tell me how you knew the Russian was going to be there?'

'I got a call from an agent in Moscow. The one that gave me the initial lead on the radio transmissions.'

'And what did this agent say?'

'Only that the Russian wanted a meeting.'

'With who?'

'I don't know.'

'Bullshit!'

'I don't know Mills. And I don't know why it was you that met him?'

'And you never will.'

Mills tore open Mitchell's shirt. He placed an iron on Mitchell's bare skin. The iron was plugged into an extension lead that led to a socket in the wall. Mitchell started to beg for Mills to stop. He tried to move his torso to shake the iron off, but he was pulled tight over the table and could not get the leverage he needed. Mills walked over to the socket and kicked the switch on with his boot.

The cold plate of the iron soon started to feel warm against Mitchell's skin. And then it got hot. Mitchell screamed with fear. His whole body was tense and trying to pull a wrist or an ankle free. The heat intensified and soon, Mitchell could smell burning flesh. His body started to sweat. He could feel the heat go past his skin and heat up his sternum. His heart beat faster and faster.

Mitchell banged his head back repeatedly off the table and screamed in pain.

Mills got in his car. He had enough room to do one big turn inside the warehouse. As he circled around, he smiled at Mitchell as he lay on the table struggling and screaming.

'Time for Jim 'he said to himself as he pulled out of the warehouse. He didn't even stop to close the doors. He didn't care. No one could hear Mitchell. He didn't care if they could. It was too late now. It was only a matter of minutes before the iron would kill him.

It took just over seven.

Jim came to at the sound of his door opening. His focus was crystal clear. He reached for his pistol and aimed it at the front door. Even from this angle, he could hit someone in the chest. It took a split second for him to acknowledge it was Phillips. Jim slowly sat up on his bed as Phillips walked in with his hands up.

'Fuck me, Jim, what happened to you?'

'I had a bad fucking night of it.'

'You're not the only one. We need to go.'

'What happened?'

'Not here. Completely believe Mitchell's paranoia now. We need to get you somewhere safe so we can talk.'

'OK. 'Jim tried to stand up, but his left leg gave out. He sat back down on the bed.

'Can you get me some jeans and a top from the bedroom

please?'

'Of course.'

When Phillips left the room, Jim quickly took one more opiate pain killer and necked the last of a glass of water that was on the table. He inspected his wounds. There was no point changing his dressings now, not if they had to go. He looked at the clock. 'Shit.'

'I missed my meeting with Mitchell. What a cunt.'

Phillips walked back in with some clothes.

'Well, that's part of the answer, I suppose. We need to go. You're in a shit state, I'll drive you.'

At that point, Kingston appeared in the doorway. A pistol in his hand. Phillips reacted by pulling a pistol of his own.

'No. No. No.' said Jim giving a dismissive wave to the stand-off. 'I can't go through this shit again.'

'You said no visitors. I didn't see him arrive. That's on me. But I can sort him out for you.'

'It's fine. He's on my side.'

'Then you are a fucking cop. I knew it.'

'Eh?'

'I know who that is.'

'And I know who you are, Kingston. I arrested you years ago.'

'My point exactly.'

'Gents. As I understand it, we are way beyond all of that and this is not why we are here. Correct?'

'Correct. 'Said Phillips.

'But you are a cop, so spill.'

'I'm not. I wasn't when you asked before, and I'm not now.'

'We have to go. 'Insisted Phillips.

'OK'

Jim reached round in his satchel and pulled out some money. To Phillips 'best guess, it was over two thousand pounds. Jim also reached under the table and found some gum stuck to the underneath. He pulled it off and prized it open. In the middle, was an SD card. He put it in his pocket. He had a quick look around the flat. He handed the money to Kingston.

'What's this for?'

'I need everything in this flat gone.'

'Everything?'

'Everything. The paper off the walls. Burn it all. Can you do that for me?'

'I don't see why not.'

'Thanks. Then leave the flat. Someone will be around in a couple of days to change the locks. Let them.'

'And then?'

'And then I couldn't give a fuck.'

'OK.'

'Ta, 'Said Jim, then looked at Phillips, 'Let's go.'

Phillips and Kingston eyeballed each other as Phillips and Jim left the flat. Kingston got on the phone.

Sat in his car, on a side street, Mills watched everything. He watched Phillips walk up to the door, let himself in. He saw the drug dealer go into the flat shortly after that. And then after a few minutes, Phillips and Jim left. The drug dealer was still in the flat. 'Where the fuck is that SD card?'

Mills was raging. It was all falling apart in front of him. He was now fucked. He didn't know who had the card. The only truth was if they didn't know it was him in the meeting the night before, they soon will. This as far as Mills was concerned, was all Jim's fault.

'Fuck him. 'He said, as he pulled away in his car, 'He's going to destroy my life, I'll destroy his.'

Driving down the London streets, he got his phone out and dialled the number. When it was answered, Mills gave his request.

'I need you to find an address for me, fast.'

CHAPTER 31

The drive to Regents Park Barracks was a silent one. Jim had questions, but Phillips insisted on not talking about anything until they met with the Brigadier. So, Jim sat there, trying to clear his head. Annoyed at himself for missing the letterbox with Mitchell. He was still hurting. He felt feverish and hoped it wasn't the pigeon shit from the wall in his cut chest. Jim sat there and waited. Watching out his window as the film reel of London went by.

At Regents Park Barracks, the pair of them went into the first meeting room they got to, just inside the door. There was no walking down corridors or stairs. There were no safe doors and no brief about being listened to. Inside the meeting room, there was the Brigadier. Stood in chinos and a shirt with brown leather shoes. He looked exactly as you'd expect an off-duty officer in the British Army to look. No one sat down.

'Jim, I'm sorry to have to bring you in like this.'

'Sir. What is going on?'

'You look like shit. Do you need a drink of water or a seat?'

'No thank you. Can you please tell me what is happening?'

The Brigadier and Phillips briefly looked at each other, before the Brigadier continued.

'Mitchell is dead.'

'Shit. What happened?'

'Well, what we have pieced together is Mitchell was trying to find out who the Russian was.'

'Yeah, with the IR video camera?'

'Correct.'

'I have the SD card here.' Jim got the chewing gum out of his pocket and unfolded it and handed it to Phillips.

'OK, thank you. That might help. I think the Russian worked it out and went after him. And it was my guess he was coming for you two as well.'

'Me and Mills? Where is Mills?'

'We don't know.' Said Phillips, 'We opened his envelope as well and I sent one of my team to find him. But he wasn't at his flat. He could be out, I suppose?'

'As well?'

'Pardon?'

'You said you opened his envelope as well?'

'Yes, of course. To find his address?'

'You didn't give it to Mills before?'

'No? Jim, I don't understand?'

Jim took a deep breath in. Things were not adding up. Think Jim, think.

'What happened to Mitchell?'

'Killed. 'Answered the Brigadier, 'Or more like tortured to death.'

'How?'

'The Russian tied him to a table and put an iron on his chest. Boiled his heart.'

Jim stood there, eyes wide. For the first time today, he was completely focused.

'He put an iron on his heart?'

'Yes. 'confirmed the Brigadier, 'It was like something out of…'

'Ireland. 'Jim finished his sentence.

'Yes. Jim?'

'I need a car. I have to go. Now.'

The Brigadier saw the desperation in his eyes. Jim was on to the truth, and he knew it. He handed his keys over.

'Blue BMW out the front. Take it.'

'Thank you, Boss. Watch the SD video. I pray to fuck I am wrong.'

And with that, Jim left. Phillips opened the laptop on the table and inserted the card.

CHAPTER 32

Mills had got a call back not twenty minutes after he had called his unit. They had found the address he was after. It was easy. Mills wasn't even out of the city yet, so he could navigate himself easily onto the M1 motorway and head in the direction he needed.

Jim's home with his wife was a beautiful barn conversion. Exposed beams kept the traditional feel, but large glass folding doors on a tasteful extension gave the barn an open and bright look. The barn was on land that a Farmer had sold on and there were no boundaries to indicate where their garden stopped, and public land started. Their back garden eventually met a small road that the Farmer still used. If you didn't know it was there, you'd completely miss it. To the front, there was a driveway that stretched down towards the main road, which led to the local pub in one direction and rolling country in the other.

Mills had parked his car on the driveway, at an angle, so another car could not get past. He marched up to the house. Not bothered if he was seen. He wasn't. The front door was a classic looking door made of Oak and with a big iron handle. Mills turned it. The door was unlocked. He let himself in.

Jim drove as fast as he reasonably could through the streets of London. He wasn't wearing his seatbelt and for the first few minutes, the car was beeping at him telling him to put it on. He didn't. But he did find the blue-lights button next to the dashboard. So, he turned that on. The BMW's grill started to flash blue, as did the reverse lights. Finally, people started to move out his way and he could pick up the pace. He wanted to be wrong about this. He wanted to be so wrong.

Phillips and the Brigadier were fast-forwarding through the video. There was no time on the screen, so they had to forward all the way through the day until they got to the evening. The video swapped from colour to a grey IR image. It was clear enough. All the details were still in place. All the way down to see the lines in brickwork. They watched intently as there was a flash of a man in the window the camera was looking at. They tried to rewind frame by frame, but it didn't give a clear shot of his face. A few moments later, he walked past again. This time they paused the video and saw an image of a middle-aged man. Neither of them knew who it was. Both knew Mitchell probably would have, but neither said it. Phillips pressed play. Seconds later, another figure appeared and for a split second, turned to look in the direction he came. They paused the video again. It was Mills.

Mills crept through the house. He had his pistol on him, but it wasn't drawn. He had zip ties and a pair of handcuffs in his jacket pockets. If Jim was going to fuck his life up, he was going to fuck up Jim's. Mills heard movement. He crept towards the back of the house. In the kitchen, Jim's wife Melissa was loading the fridge after going to the shops. She felt something was wrong and turned to see a man standing behind her. Mills grabbed the back of her head with one hand and covered her mouth with the other. He manhandled her over to the island table in the middle of the kitchen. She kicked and punched Mills. She broke free from his grip and screamed as loud as she could.

'Now now, Sweetheart. We both know no one can hear you.'

'Who are you?'

'That really does not matter.'

'What do you want?'

'To balance out the injustice of irony.'

Mills went for her again. She moved and grabbed a large kitchen knife and held it out in front of her.

'Oh, come on, you know you shouldn't play with knives.'

'My husband will be back in a minute.'

'My dear, we both know that isn't true, don't we? 'Said Mills with a smile.

He had walked closer to her and when Melissa dropped eye contact for a moment, thinking about how he would know that about Jim, Mills reached for the knife with his left hand, brushed it to one side and stepped in to give her a punch to the face with his right. The knife flew to the side of the kitchen. She nearly fell to the floor, but Mills grabbed her by the hair and dragged her back to the table. He took out a zip tie and secured her right wrist to a table leg. She was fighting and kicking. She was face down on the table and being held there by a man of fearsome strength. Mills got another zip tie around her second wrist. Before he went to tie her legs to the table, he got his face close to hers and breathed into her ear.

'You can blame hubby-dearest for this.'

As Mills went to the back of the table, he took out some more zip ties. He held down one leg and tied her ankle to the leg of the table. Melissa gave a big kick with her free leg and kicked Mills backwards. Zip ties and the pair of handcuffs scattered on the floor. Mills decided enough was enough. He stood himself up and walked over to her.

CHAPTER 33

Jim drove as fast as he could out of London. When he got to the M1, he pushed the car to over 120mph to gain lost ground. He hated the fact he had no comms to his wife. He needed to know she was OK. She was not safe, he knew it. He needed to warn her. He needed to do something. The only thing he could do now was get to her. He pressed the pedal some more and the car lifted to 125mph. He came off the motorway and pushed through traffic as fast as he could. The traffic died down the further into the countryside he got. He still had blue lights flashing and he was on the car horn as much as he needed to be. He stopped for no one. Jim knew the quickest way to his house and took the quiet road that led along the side of the village. He cornered hard into the farmer's road. Jim dropped gears to give his engine some torque and came off the road onto the field. The field that became his garden. Jim drove head-on to the glass doors. With seconds to go, he took his pistol out from its holster and scooped his right arm with the pistol in hand, behind the seat belt and pulled it across his body. He braced with his left hand against the steering wheel. At the very last moment, he closed his eyes and kept his foot on the pedal and drove through the doors.

CHAPTER 34

Mills had ripped Melissa's skirt and underwear off. Red marks were on her body from where the cotton had dug in before it ripped. Mills smiled. Then, he heard something. He heard a car outside. A car that was being driven hard. Mills turned to look out of the glass doors.

'Oh, my dear, you were right. And it could not have been any more poetic.'

Mills stood to one side of the kitchen, in the doorway just out of view of the glass doors.

The car came crashing through. The only thing that stopped it was the brick pillar that was built to support the extension. Jim opened his door, pistol in hand ready to find Mills. Mills found him first. Mills came over and put a boot into the car door, shocking Jim and pressing him to the car frame. Mills opened the car door and slammed it shut again. Jim dropped his pistol and started to fall to the floor. Mills opened the car door with the intent of slamming it closed again. But Jim pushed himself off the car and tackled Mills. The two spun and Mills got free from Jim's grip. The pair stood up and exchanged hard punches to each other's faces. Cheekbones were swollen and gums were cut on teeth. Mills then drove his right shin, in a sort-of Thai boxing manoeuvre into Jim's left thigh. Jim screamed in agony and collapsed to the floor. Blood seeped through his jeans. Mills started to put the boot into Jim's face and torso. Jim had to grab Mills 'leg and use it as leverage to get back up to his knees so he could start re-engaging in the fight. He punched Mills 'kneecap square-on. It was enough to bring Mills down slightly and Jim could jump up and reach for his throat. The pair scrambled again. Mills had the reach advantage and punched straight into Jim's sternum. It broke Jim's grip on his throat. Jim staggered back. Mills came up close and Jim let go a head-butt into Mills ' nose. Mills screamed in rage and came back with a series of punches. He kicked at Jim's leg again. Jim lost balance and Mills grabbed him. He used all his strength to throw Jim against the wall. Jim hit it like a ragdoll and slumped to the floor. Jim was motionless for a moment. Melissa cried in the background. Mills walked up to Jim, checking to see if he was done for. Jim looked up and then reached up with his right hand and locked his grip into the waistline of Mills 'jeans. Jim got his thumb under the grip of his fingers and twisted his wrist as tight as he could. At this stage, Jim was working on instinct. He had nothing else he could give right now. Mills tried to pull away. Jim was a dead weight on him.

'Fucking fine. You can watch, then. 'Snapped Mills.

He grabbed Jim's wrist and dragged Jim like he was a dead body over to the radiator. He scooped down to pick up the handcuffs on the way. He got to the radiator; it was of Victorian style. Mills pulled Jim's left hand close. He snapped the cuffs onto Jim and the radiator pipework that ran into the floor. Jim was not with it at all and could not stop Mills.

Mills caught his breath, turned and looked at Melissa, smiled and then took his time to walk back over to her. He stood behind her, eyeing up his prize. 'If Jim wants to fuck my life up, I will fuck his up.'

Jim's focus became razor-sharp the moment he heard his

wife scream. Primitive instincts brought his awareness back in line. His eyesight was crystal clear. And what he saw filled him with dread and guilt and rage.

Jim tried to get over to her, but the cuffs didn't let him move. He pulled at them, the metal cut into his wrist. Jim pulled and pulled back and forth with his whole body against the radiator. He tried to get a foot on it and pull his wrist out of the cuffs. He shouted at Mills, insulting him, calling him a coward, telling him to come over and carry-on fighting. Mills ignored every word. He didn't even look over his shoulder. He was fixed on what he was doing to Jim's wife.

Jim went beyond desperation and for a moment, had clarity, he needed to think. Shouting and pulling against the radiator was amounting to nothing. Inaction. And the only way to change what is happening around you is by making a decision and taking action. Any action is better than inaction. He reached for a zip tie. He had to lay flat on the floor to get one. He pulled himself up and using his teeth and spare hand, wrapped the zip tie around his left upper arm. He pulled it as tight as he could with his teeth. He leaned down again and reached for the knife that was on the floor. His fingers just made it. He had to pull it towards him by fingertip before he could grab the handle. He sat himself up. He placed his left forearm on the ground and raised the knife as high as he could. He looked at his wrist for a split second, then he heard Melissa scream. The knife came down.

Mills was extorting his victory over Jim through his wife. And enjoying it. He was only aware that Jim was silent when he himself had stopped and the only sound in the air was that of Jim's wife crying and his own heavy breathing. He paused his breath. He turned to look where Jim was.

There was a flash of blood and then Mills saw stars. Jim had come up behind Mills and using all his body strength, had led with his left arm in a big circle to get as much weight behind him as possible and swung the knife round with his right. As Mills turned, the knife made contact with his cheek. Not what Jim wanted. He wanted to bury the knife in Mills 'head. But good enough for now. He was off Melissa. Mills stumbled and fell to the floor. He was lying on his back with a huge open wound to his face that went all the way to the bone. Jim walked over to Mills. He stood at his feet and looked at him. Mills slowly opened his eyes and saw Jim stood there, left hand missing and the knife in his right. Jim stepped over Mills, so he was straddling his body. He squatted down and sat on Mills 'torso, pinning his arms with his legs and his body weight on Mills ' stomach. Jim held the knife up for Mills to see. And, without breaking eye contact, not once, started to carve up Mills 'face. Strip by strip Jim gently, almost with care, took the flesh off Mills. He cut his cheeks and held up the knife with the flesh on it for Mills to see as he screamed. Jim simply flicked the knife to one side and the flesh flew off onto the floor. Jim then went for lips, ears and nose. Mills screamed in agony. Choking on his own blood as it filled his mouth, coughing it up into Jim's face. Jim moved his hand along the knife, so he held the blade by the tip and went for eyebrows and even flayed the skin off his forehead. There was nothing that resembled a human being at the end of it, never mind Mills himself. But Jim wasn't finished. He was now in his dark place. The place you must go to survive the worst. Love and hate are the same emotion. Absolute extreme. To love unconditionally and to hate uncontrollably requires the same level of commitment. It's beyond a conscious thought process. Jim stood up and stepped down Mills 'body. He bent down and placed the knife at the crotch of Mills 'jeans. Jim pressed and pulled the knife up. It cut his jeans and cut through Mills 'scrotum. Another scream. Jim held the knife out to the side and dropped it. It landed in the wood flooring, the point into the floor, and handled up to the ceiling. Jim bent down again and reached into Mills 'jeans. He felt round in the blood until he got hold of what he wanted. Jim stood up. And as he did, one of Mills 'testicles came with him. It was connected still, but as Jim stood fully upright, it pulled and ripped away. Mills screamed. Jim eyeballed Mills. He made sure he had eye contact with him. Jim slowly and deliberately put Mills 'testicle in his mouth and bit down. The last thing Mills saw before he passed out was Jim smiling and eating his bollocks.

Jim snapped out of it when he heard Melissa crying. Guilt overwhelmed him. He picked up the knife again and went over to her. He cut the zip ties and when he cut her legs free, tried to make her decent. He helped her off the table and the pair collapsed on the floor, crying and both saying sorry to the other. Jim had lost too much blood. It got dark and he didn't have the strength to say sitting up. The last thing he saw was his wife. The last thing he heard was the police sirens on their way.

CHAPTER 35

Jim sat on the bench in Regents Park, waiting for the Brigadier. It did seem a bit daft they were meeting in the park only a stone's throw from the Barracks. But if that's what the Brigadier thought best, so be it.

Jim had been in an induced coma for ten days. A lot had happened in that time. He knew that much. The Brigadier walked up, holding two coffees. Jim went to stand up to meet the Brigadier, but the gesture was waved off by the Brigadier. As he did so, some coffee split out of the disposable mug and hit the back of his hand. He didn't pay any attention.

'Where do you want your coffee, Jim?'

'Oh, can it go just there, please?'

The Brigadier placed the coffee down next to Jim.

'Thanks.'

'You're welcome.'

The pair sat for a moment, knowing they had to talk, but neither knowing where to start. The Brigadier broke first.

'How's the hand?'

Jim looked down at his left hand. His fingertips showed through the cast he was wearing. They were pale and waxy.

'I tell you something Boss, The Navy Surgeon at Haslar is a fucking miracle worker. He's got my hand back on. Most of the smaller blood vessels can't be reconnected, so he says it'll always be this colour. But he got it bolted on and some tendons reconnected. So in time, I'll be able to move my fingers again and stuff like that. I'll lose all strength in it, but for the sake of not looking like some dickhead who chopped his own hand off, losing strength is a hit I can take.'

'Yeah, he told me that you couldn't have made a better cut. Exactly the right place - between the bones, as it were. Anything else and you might not be so lucky.'

Jim looked at the Brigadier.

'Not that lucky is a word to use right now.'

'It's fine. But you know the Surgeon?'

'I wasn't going to not check up on you. But as it goes, yes. He and I go back many years. He was the Surgeon lead on HMS Argus during various campaigns. He has worked on and saved quite a few of my Troopers over the years.'

'Fair enough. So, what is the story? What has been the fallout while I've been asleep?'

'I don't know where to start, Jim.'

'Let's start with Millbrook.'

'Yeah. Daniel Millbrook was born Seamus Donoghue. His birth parents were from Kerry. Teenagers. And so, made to give him up. He grew up in the care of Nuns. Being disconnected as he was, he saw the romance in the cause of the IRA. So, when he was a boy, he became a runner for them. He was then adopted by a couple who couldn't conceive. They moved to Manchester and all his official Irish links disappeared. They even changed his name completely. This made him feel even more disconnected and an outsider. He made connections back to Ireland in his early teens and vowed to be a soldier for the cause. His grooming or introduction to the IRA was complete when he was tasked to join the British Army and spy on tactics and gather any relevant intelligence.'

'That's nothing new, we all know that the Irish try to infiltrate training bases every single year.'

'Yes, but he flew through vetting. He was a good little English boy now.'

'With Irish parents?'

'Jim, I've got Irish in my bloodline. As do you, no doubt.'

'Right, then what?'

'Then Millbrook became a Paratrooper and passed Selection to join SAS. He was a great soldier; you must know that.'

'My opinion is pretty jaded right now.'

'Yeah, quite. But this is it. He had zero emotional links to either side of the fence. His service to the Queen and Country was exemplary. And then, when he did serve in Northern Ireland, things over there were quiet. No Casualties on either side. And this was because he was feeding into his Irish unit where the Army was. Telling them where to avoid, when to move weapons so they were never found. He was protecting the IRA from the British. And when he left, it all kicked off. Remember a few years back when the Welsh Guards took massive casualties over there because the Catholics hit the Protestants hard? And the Guards tried to calm it all down?

'Of course.'

'Well, the six months leading up to that, Millbrook was over there. Setting up the IRA's chess set for them, so when Millbrook left the country, their game was in place to do some real damage.'

'Right, so what was his link to the Russian?'

'There wasn't one. The Russian called the Kremlin after you and Millbrook stopped and killed the second set of assassins. Assassins are expensive. The Russian was losing money and face in the light of you doing your job. So, he went for another tact. He wanted to pay someone to hit the British hard. So, he reached out to the one establishment that knew how to fuck with us.'

'The IRA.'

'Yep. The Russian got consent to pay a vast amount for the execution of Prince William and Prince George.'

'And Millbrook was going back to the Royal Protection Team.'

'Correct. The meeting that Mitchell videoed was setting all that up.'

'And Millbrook thought Mitchell had the camera or card at least and went to extort it out of him?'

'Yes. I'm surprised he didn't get it out of you.'

Jim gave the Brigadier a disapproving look.

'I mean, seeing as he'd already tried to kill you with a crossbow. When he was in your flat that morning?'

'We were not alone then. I guess he didn't have the right

opportunity. So, what about this Russian? Is it carrying on?'

'It would appear not. Phillips did a very good job of leaking back to Ireland that Millbrook was dead. That put the cat amongst the pigeons, and it got fed back to Russia. Another failure, as it were. So, the last I heard through Vauxhall Cross was that the Agent here had been summoned back to the Kremlin. I've been given assurances that he never made it there.'

'Good. Through Vauxhall Cross?'

'Mitchell had a link in Moscow. When it all kicked off over there, he left the country. Accusations of moles and snitches were going around. He came home and debriefed me personally on the intelligence exchanges he and Mitchell were having.'

'This espionage game is fucking epic.'

'Yes. Which brings me on to you.'

'Boss?'

'I need to make sure you are looked after. What you've done is one of the biggest acts of selflessness this country has witnessed. Beyond duty.'

'Flattery will get you nowhere, Boss.'

'Ha, of course. Well, this is where I am with everything. Commendation-wise, you are to receive the George Cross for valour outside a war zone. You are to be awarded the CBE for your efforts. I have another five hundred thousand pounds of Government bonds for you, seeing as Millbrook won't need his. I've got a sign-off from the MOD for you to receive a General's Pension, as well. And I'm assuming you've got insurance to cover your hand?'

'Of course. It's worth three hundred thousand to me. The irony is, in the small print of the insurance paperwork, it says they won't pay out on injuries that are self-inflicted.'

'I can sort that out.'

'You sure?'

'Of course. So, you've got one-point three million pounds as your retirement fund. That's the best I can do for you. And the insurance company will pay out on your home?'

'Yes, but we are going to move.'

'Understandable. How is your wife?'

'In a bad place.'

'I bet. She was at your side every day while you were induced.'

'I know. Thing is, it's early days, but she's pregnant.'

'Well, congratulations. That is good news. Move house. Start a family. New beginnings.'

'You don't get it. That night on the canal. When I got the camera. Me and Millbrook were talking. He must have realised things right then. He was asking me questions. Normal shit you'd talk about with someone you've served with on and off over the years.'

'Right.'

'I told him that night that I couldn't have kids.'

The Brigadier paused. He suddenly saw it.

'And your wife?'

'How do I tell her she can't keep it? I mean, the emotions she is going through right now. I've only been awake a couple of days. She's not stopped crying. She wants a child more than anything. Tell her to ditch this one and we do IVF? It doesn't really work like that.'

'Jim I can't even begin to imagine. I had no idea.'

'Fucking neither did I until two days ago.'

'And what are you thinking?'

'I'm thinking Mel has put up with my job for too many years. She works hard and is a humble and good person. She doesn't deserve any of this. But she does deserve to be a mother. So, we are having a baby together. And it'll be mine.'

The Brigadier smiled.

'That is good to hear Jim. I do have one more bit of information I'd like to share with you.'

What is that?'

'The news went back to Ireland that Millbrook was dead.'

'Yeah?'

'He's not.'

The blood fell from Jim's face.

'Jim, what you did to him was fucking immense. Not unjustified. But Jesus, they'd put you in Broadmoor for that. When Phillips and his team got to your house, they took you and your wife off to the police station, correct?'

'Yeah.'

'Phillips was the only one left behind. He patched Millbrook to hold in enough blood to stop heart failure. Under my direction, Millbrook was taken to Haslar hospital. He was two rooms down from you while you were under.'

'Fucking Hell, Boss!'

'Jim, listen. The surgeon who looked after you, Surgeon Commander Jenkins, also looked after Millbrook.'

'Looked after?'

'Is still looking after.'

'Boss, what the fuck?'

'Jenkins is one of my closest mates, Jim. We went to Cambridge together before I joined the Army, and he joined the Navy. Millbrook should be dead. Never mind the loss of blood. Infection of his open wounds should have killed him by now. All his nerve endings are open on his face. We literally cannot mend him, because if he ever took his case to a human rights court, it would cripple everyone.'

'Then let the cunt die!'

'Jim. 'Reassured the Brigadier, 'We will. Jenkins is administering just enough antibiotics to stop his body from going into septic shock and dying. But not too much so that he gets comfortable. He is fed on a drip. He has no pain relief. We are literally keeping him alive. Just. And he is therefore being kept in as much pain as possible.'

'Why?'

'As a favour to you.'

'How long?'

'Jenkins retires in six weeks. He has promised me the very last medical act he will undertake will be the withdrawal of antibiotics to Millbrook. Millbrook will then be left for as long as it takes for his body to shut down. And then cremated.'

'Thank you.'

'It's over Jim. As of today, you are a civilian. Your Military Testimonial will be posted to you. No airs and graces. You know better than that.'

'I do.'

'Is there anything else you need from me right now?'

'No. Thank you.'

'Go and live the life you have earned.'

And with that, the Brigadier stood up and walked away. He didn't look back.

Stood across the park, Melissa bought a coffee from a kiosk. She watched at an angle so not in their line of sight, as the Brigadier met with Jim. She knew Jim would be telling him about the baby. They had agreed to that. She watched as the Brigadier stood up and walked away. She watched as her husband slowly got to his feet. And then stood upright. Broad shoulders and tree-trunk thighs. He looked taller than his actual height. He always did when he stood like that. She walked across the green in front of her, so she was standing square on to him. She started to walk towards him.

Jim watched the Brigadier leave. He sat on the bench for a while, assimilating the information. There was a lot of it. But he was weathered enough to know you can't dwell on the past. You can't change it. You can only learn from it and use it to move forward. The question was how. 'Options Jim, options. 'Jim breathed in and realised that technically as of now, his Military nickname was no more? He slowly stood up. His left leg was stiff. He stood bolt upright with his heels together. He saw his wife across the park. He smiled. Then after twenty-two years of Military service, he took a step forward to start a new chapter in his life. As a civilian.

THE END

ACKNOWLEDGEMENT

Special thanks to:

Mark Mangan
www.bitly.com/marksarthole

For helping to bring this book to life.

ABOUT THE AUTHOR

George Reardon is a former Sergeant in the Royal Marines. He served with 45 Commando as well as under the umbrella of UKSF. He served operationally in Iraq and Afghanistan and worked across the globe, from Central America through to Indonesia. He now lives in England with his family.

Other writing projects include movie screenplays. Gravelbelly is his debut novel and the first in its series.

Printed in Great Britain
by Amazon

53823945R00165